MAKE YOUR SAVE

ASTON ARCHERS
BOOK THREE

CALI MELLE

Edited by Rumi Khan
Proofread by Amy Pritt
Cover Art by Essasketch
Cover Design by Cali Melle

PLAYLIST

WILLOW - TAYLOR SWIFT
I AM NOT WHO I WAS - CHANCE PENA
MY HOME - MYLES SMITH
LITTLE BIT BETTER - CALEB HEARN, ROSIE
BAD DREAMS - TEDDY SWINS
2HANDS - TATE MCRAE
GUILTY AS SIN? - TAYLOR SWIFT
EVERYWHERE, EVERYTHING - NOAH KAHAN, GRACIE ABRAMS
SWEET HEAT LIGHTNING - GREGORY ALAN ISAKOV
ORDINARY - ALEX WARREN

PROLOGUE
ROWAN

One year ago

I hate coming back home.

It's not that I don't like my hometown, it's more what comes along with it. It can never be a peaceful visit. Instead, it's always filled with drama of some sort. My two siblings typically end up in an argument and then my father disappears and my mother ends up getting upset.

My sister, Raven left as soon as she turned eighteen and I was right behind her two years later. The two of us went on to play hockey professionally and Raven is now an assistant coach for the Bridgewater Bears. Our parents tried to get Beau to play hockey at a young age, but he was never really into it. He has always had his own agenda with everything he does and Beau Taylor lives life by the seat of his pants.

He's four years younger than me, five and a half years younger than Raven, and he's always been a wild card. He put our parents through hell in high school and after he was diagnosed with bipolar disorder, it brought a level of understanding to our family, but it didn't excuse his behavior.

"I love this new vase you made," my mother says, setting the piece of pottery down on the center of the table. "Have you heard from your brother at all?"

I glance at my mom as I finish drying a dish and set it down on the counter beneath the cabinet it's supposed to go in. Something resembling dread rolls in the pit of my stomach. "No. I texted him when I was boarding my plane but he didn't respond." Which also wasn't uncommon from him. "I figured he was just coming tomorrow morning."

Beau and I aren't exactly close and we never really were. It's not easy to have a relationship with someone who doesn't fucking like you. He's always had a chip on his shoulder toward Raven and me, making his dislike of us known. When we were growing up, he always blamed us for everything and played the victim, refusing to take responsibility for the fucked-up things he's done.

I tried to help my brother, but he just kept pushing back. At some point, you get tired of bailing out someone who would never extend the same favor to you.

It's been a few years since all three Taylor kids were home for Christmas and I can't help but feel jealous of Rae for being the one who gets the free pass to not show. Last year, she was sick. This year, she's blaming it on work.

She's not the only one who works for a professional hockey team. I know her excuses are bullshit, but I don't call her out on it.

"Beau said he was going to come by tonight. He was finally going to bring Hadley over."

How he ended up with Hadley Reed is still a mystery to me. She and Beau started dating about six months ago and it seems like she's been helping to keep him on the straight and narrow.

"When was the last time you talked to him?"

My mother opens her phone, tapping on the screen as her brow furrows. "I talked to him at 10:30 this morning," she says, her eyes lifting back to me as she locks the screen and sets it down on the counter. "He said they would be over after dinner, but it's almost nine now. I would have imagined they'd be here sooner."

I watch her as she picks up her phone, unlocking the screen once again before she scrolls through her phone. She taps on it, lifting it up to her ear as she tries to call him. I can hear it through the speaker pressed to the side of her face as it immediately goes to voicemail. "Did you try calling him earlier?"

"I did." She tips her chin, worry invading her blue eyes. "His phone was still on then, but it seems like he's turned it off." I know she's concerned and it's hard not to be, although none of this is uncommon for my brother. Beau has disappeared for months at a time while off his meds and lost in a bottle of alcohol. "He's been doing so well, Rowan."

"I know, Mom," I tell her, my voice soft as my heart breaks for my mother. It's easier for me to have a hard exterior toward my brother. I'm not the one who gave birth to him and raised him. I was merely a bystander in Beau's shit show of a life. "I'll drive by his house and see what's going on."

Her expression is unreadable, but I don't miss the appreciation in her eyes. "Thank you, hon," she says quietly, her lips pursing as she reaches for me, her hand squeezing mine. "Take my car."

"I'll be back in a little bit," I tell her, tipping my chin as a mix of emotions sweeps through me. Sadness for my mother and a myriad of things toward Beau. For once, just one fucking time, could he make this woman's life a little easier?

I head out into the garage, climbing into the sedan before pressing the button to lift the garage door open. As I ease out into the driveway, I pull out my phone, opening up my messages as I tap on my sister's name.

ROWAN

Be glad you didn't come home again.

RAVEN

What did Beau do now?

You know what, I don't even want to know.

ROWAN

Just do me a favor and remind me to be busy next year.

RAVEN

Deal.

Tucking my phone back in my pocket, I head in the direction of my brother's apartment, trying to ignore the nagging dread rolling in my stomach. This isn't like the last time. Beau's phone died and time must have slipped away from him. He hadn't decided to go off his meds again and joyride across the country while drinking himself into a stupor and maxing out credit cards.

I push the memories away, focusing on the road for the next thirteen minutes while chewing on the inside of my cheek until it's raw. I faintly taste blood as I pull up along the curb out front, an exaggerated sigh escaping me as I put the car in park and kill the engine. My footsteps are heavy yet rushed as I stride to the front door.

It's supposed to be shut and locked, but it's ajar and I slip inside, not stopping until I reach the elevator. He lives on the fourth floor and the car is beginning its descent down to the lobby. As the doors slide open, I step in and head up to Beau's floor, my heart pounding erratically in my chest. It feels like the longest ride of my life.

I head out into the hallway and there's a loud bang echoing throughout the building. I glance around the common area, my gaze flickering between the three apartment doors, as if I'm waiting to hear the sound again, trying to figure out where it was coming from. It doesn't take rocket science to figure out it came from the middle one. 402. My brother's apartment.

The door flies open and a flurry of auburn hair comes whipping out as she slams it shut behind her. She doesn't see me at first, tears streaking down the sides of her face as she tucks her chin in against her chest. I'm silent as I watch Hadley, assessing the moment as her chest heaves. She sucks in a deep breath, exhaling slowly as she wipes the tears away from her cheeks.

Her chin lifts, her eyes widening as she sees me standing a few feet in front of her. "Rowan?"

"Is everything okay?"

Her nostrils flare, her bottom lip quivering before a harsh laugh escapes her. "It depends on who you ask." She wipes at her nose, shaking her head as she pushes away from the door. "Your brother seems to be doing just fine."

My eyebrows tug downward, a crease forming between them as I corkscrew my lips. I'm so goddamn confused, I don't even know what piece of this puzzle to touch first. "He's okay?"

"Oh, he's great," she says, waving her hand as pain washes over her expression. "He's getting ready to head to the airport."

Confusion only grows within me as the door behind her opens. Hadley jumps toward me, her body practically colliding into me as she moves away at lightning speed. My hands instinctively wrap around her biceps, my gaze meeting my brother's over the top of Hadley's head.

Beau narrows his eyes as a cruel smirk forms on his lips. "Well, this is cute. Look at you cleaning up after me." His behavior isn't shocking and it's a sure indicator that he has in fact fallen off the wagon. "One man's trash is another man's treasure."

"Watch it, Beau," I warn him, a bite in my tone as I push Hadley behind me, making sure she's safe. "You may be my brother, but I won't hesitate to put you on your ass if you keep saying stupid shit."

"Ooh," he half sneers, lifting his hands as he makes them look like he's trembling. "I'm shaking in my boots." He rolls his eyes, pulling his door shut behind him as he looks around me at Hadley. "He's the better pick anyways." Beau moves past the two of us, his shoulder knocking into mine as he walks directly to the elevator.

"Where are you going?" I ask, my feet moving as I step up behind him. I hate that this is the relationship I have with my brother. I've always hated it. I want to knock him on his fucking ass, but I control myself, drawing my anger inward. "Are you off your meds again?"

He lets out a heavy breath. "Jesus Christ, you sound just like everyone else." He spins on his heel, his gaze like a laser point on me. He doesn't answer my question, and that's the confirmation I need. "I can live my life however the hell I want, Rowan."

"I don't give a fuck how you live your life, Beau. I'm here for Mom, not for you, and definitely not for me," I tell him, my tone clipped as I step into his space without hesitation. "You told her you were coming after dinner and then your phone was off and she was worried."

"And she just had to send her star son to come check on the degenerate." He lets out another harsh laugh, the sound like sandpaper against my eardrums. "I'm fine, Rowan. I'll call Mom on my way to the airport so she can hear it from me." He sets his jaw, shoving his foot between the elevator doors. "Is that good enough for you?"

My nostrils flare as I stare back at Beau. "Perfect."

Beau doesn't give either of us a second glance or another word as he steps into the car, the doors shutting behind him. The silence hangs heavily in the air and I let out a frustrated breath as I'm acutely aware of Hadley standing behind me.

"I know he's your brother, but he's an asshole."

I slowly turn around, a ghost of a smile dancing across my lips. "I use the term brother loosely for him." My eyes scan her face, seeing the conflict written all over her expression and I want to wash it all away. "Where is he going?"

"He said there's nothing here for him in this town. Someone named Darcy said he can come stay with her in Boston. He basically thanked me for my time and told me ours was up."

Boston? Darcy?

I have no fucking clue who she is or what could possibly be there to make him throw everything away like this. Unfortunately, this is Beau. This is what Beau does.

And no one can stop him from doing what he wants.

"I don't know how I could have been so stupid." She shakes her head, her gaze dropping down to her feet. "He knows how to be charming and I fell for the charade like a fucking idiot."

I can't help myself as I step toward her. My forefinger slides under her chin, tipping her head back to look up at me. "Hey, no, stop," I tell her, my voice soft as I lift my other hand to brush away her tears. "This is what Beau does. He uses people and then when they've served their purpose, he discards them like trash."

Anger runs through my veins. This isn't the first time Beau has broken someone's heart and it's not the first time I've had to explain to them that it's not them.

"He has issues—a lot of fucking issues—and not a single one is your fault or has anything to do with you." I swallow roughly, the painful reminder lodging itself in my throat. "Not everyone is a problem you can fix. You can't help someone who doesn't want to help themselves."

Hadley stares up at me, hope shimmering behind the pain in her hazel eyes. "Thank you for saying that, Rowan," she practically whispers, a soft smile cresting her lips. "Deep down inside, I think I always thought I could somehow help him overcome his struggles . . . but now I can see I never could." She pauses, letting out an exhale. "It's just reassuring to hear it from someone else."

"Do you want my advice?"

She pulls in her bottom lip, biting down as she jerks her chin. "Sure."

"You leave all of this in your past. You forget about

Beau, you heal, and you move on." My tongue darts out to wet my lips, her gaze dropping down to my mouth before bouncing back to my eyes. "And you do not look back."

"You're right," she agrees, confidence washing over her expression as she pushes her shoulders back, straightening her spine. "He was never the one for me and we should have just stayed friends. He was just a lesson for me to learn."

I can't help the guilt that floods me. My brother should come with a warning label for anyone who crosses his path. I hope one day he can find happiness and something to settle his soul, but it's not something he was ever going to find in Hadley Reed. She's too good for someone like him.

"Come on," I say softly, my hand dropping away from her as I motion toward the elevator. "I'll walk you out."

She's quiet and I give her this moment of silence as we ride down to the lobby. She collects herself, zipping up her coat as we walk through the foyer to the front door. Her eyes instantly find me, a smile on her lips as I hold open the door for her.

"Thanks again, Rowan," she says, dipping her head forward as we stop in front of the building. "I know you didn't want to come check on him, but I'm glad I ran into you."

My tongue tangles as I stare down at her. Fuck, she's beautiful, and my brother's an idiot—a goddamn fucking fool. He was never deserving of someone kind and patient like her. "Me too."

"Merry Christmas," she tells me, spinning on her heel as she begins to walk away. She gets ten feet away before I start walking after her.

"Hey, Hadley?" I call out, the cool breeze carrying her name with it.

She slowly turns around, her nose already red and her cheeks rosy. She tilts her head to the side, her lips parting as she stares at me. "Yeah?"

"If you ever find yourself in Aston, let me know," I tell her, tucking my hands into my pockets.

A gentle smile drifts across her lips. "Okay."

"Good night, Hadley Reed."

Her eyes shine brightly under the moon, hues of brown and green swirling together. "Good night, Rowan Taylor."

CHAPTER ONE

HADLEY

"I think I might be in love with you, Hadley."

Laughter spills from my lips as I pull open my locker and grab my purse and coat. Sliding my arms into the sleeves, I turn around to look at Cole, one of my co-workers. "That's a bold statement, Cole. You're going to have to give me a little more than that."

He chuckles, walking over to the fridge as he pulls out his lunch box. I already know what's inside because Cole Andrews is as predictable as they come. Every day, his boyfriend packs his lunch for him, and every day, it is the same exact meal. A picturesque salad inside of a glass container, another glass container with mixed fruit, and some kind of a salty snack.

"Did you not see that they sent next week's schedule? I don't know whose dick you sucked, but you got them to change our shifts at the last minute."

Rolling my lips between my teeth, I bite back my smile, my nostrils flaring as I shake my head at him. "I can promise there were no dicks sucked."

He clicks his tongue. "What a damn shame."

I've been here in Aston for three months now on a traveling nurse contract. This particular assignment is only for thirteen weeks, so I only have a little over a week left. Cole works at the Aston Medical Center full-time and when I started my assignment here, we hit it off immediately.

When I first moved here, it was supposed to be temporary. After the mental fuck Beau put me through, I needed a break and I jumped on the opportunity to be a travel nurse. I needed a breath of fresh air, a new start if you will.

This is my fifth contract now and the first that I've grown attached to where I'm living. It's a place I could see myself calling home. It's a shame there isn't a full-time position available at the hospital, because I wouldn't think twice to jump on that opportunity to extend my time here a little longer.

"Do you need anything while I'm out?" I ask Cole as I slide my purse up and over my shoulder. Neither of us are supposed to be working the night shift tonight, but two of our co-workers convinced us to switch with them so they could go to a concert.

Having to eat lunch at one o'clock in the morning is really weird.

Cole raises his eyebrows at me. "Please tell me you're not eating gas station food."

I snort, shaking my head as I roll my eyes at him. Cole is extremely health-conscious and I think the thought alone might make his brain hemorrhage. "Not today," I tell him with a laugh. "I forgot my food at home, so I was going to run there and grab it."

"I think I have everything I need here," he says with a smile as he motions to his various containers now spread out on the table in front of him. "Damien never misses."

"If you guys ever want to adopt a child, please let me know." I bat my eyelashes at him, tilting my head to the side with a sweet grin as I press my hands beneath my chin. "I need someone to pack my lunches like that for me."

Cole chuckles again, tilting his head to the side for a beat. "Let me call Damien and ask him if he wants to adopt a grown child."

I lift my hand to my lips and blow him a kiss as I move toward the exit of the break room. "I knew I could count on you."

Cole blows a kiss back, turning his attention down to his phone as he taps on the screen and then moves it to his ear. It's almost one o'clock in the morning, but Damien tends to stay up to talk to Cole before he falls asleep.

The two of them are so sweet and adorable, sometimes it's sickening.

I walk down the hallway, heading in the direction of the employee exit when I see the cleaning crew are currently working on sanitizing the floors down that stretch. I stop, waving to one of them as they lift their hand to me and I turn back in the direction I came from, moving to the front of the building.

Late at night like this, it's usually quiet here. The front desk is typically occupied by Janet, who usually has her nose buried in a book, although she's not there when I walk past. Labor and delivery is where there's a little more hustle and bustle, but tonight they floated Cole and me to the postpartum care unit, so it's been pretty laid-back.

I slip through the lobby and past the sliding glass doors that lead into a small corridor before the main entrance. A weird feeling slides over my shoulder, almost like my phone vibrated, which is weird at this hour. Shifting my purse, I attempt to reach inside to pull out the device, but instead I knock my bag onto the floor.

My footsteps halt, annoyance washing over me as I watch two lip balms roll on the floor, along with the rest of my belongings strewn across the ground.

"Damn it," I mutter, dropping down to my knees as I begin to collect my things. I move my bag closer, holding it open as I start to toss things back into it, not caring where they fall inside. I find my phone and there isn't even anything on it. It was a phantom notification.

A soft whimper, followed by an exhale, sounds from behind me, catching me off guard and half scaring me. I quickly glance over my shoulder, tucking my phone into my back pocket, seeing that I am, in fact, completely alone. "What the hell?" I laugh to myself, shaking my head as I start to climb to my feet. "I'm around babies so much, I hear them everywhere I—"

My sentence is interrupted by the sound of a cry. Soft and barely audible, but it's there. I'm not hearing things. I know the sound of a real baby and that was not my imagination. I glance around, my gaze surveying the corridor, coming to a stop when I see the safe haven station. The small bassinet shifts and that's when I realize it isn't empty.

Our safe haven station is an area that the hospital has set up for mothers to safely give their babies up anonymously. It protects them from being charged with child abandonment while allowing them somewhere safe to leave their child. There's a bassinet to leave the infant inside and there's a bell that's normally triggered by the door opening and again when the baby is placed inside.

My feet move without a second thought or hesitation as I secure my bag over my shoulder again. I look back at the front desk, seeing Janet is still nowhere to be seen. My heart pounds in my chest as adrenaline spills into my veins. I don't know how she didn't hear the bell, unless it's not working properly.

As I reach the bassinet, it shifts again, the infant inside growing restless. I look down, my chest constricting as I see the sweet little one with a pastel pink hat on, breaking out of the white blanket it's swaddled in. There's no hesitation as I reach into the bassinet, lifting the baby into my arms to console. It's a stupid move on my part, considering infection control and a number of health concerns, but I can't bear the sight of the distress setting in.

Two pieces of paper and an envelope fall onto the tiny mattress as I tuck the baby against my body. "Shh," I murmur, wrapping my arm to hold the infant close as I use my other hand to retrieve the papers. My eyes scan the first piece of paper, seeing it's a birth certificate. My forehead creases as I briefly scan it, seeing the baby's name listed as Lucille Maeve Taylor.

A little girl.

Adrenaline has completely taken over my entire body and I feel like I'm moving through a dream right now. An alternate reality where I have no idea what the hell is really happening here. When I flip to the envelope, confusion washes over me as I see a name written in cursive across it.

Rowan Taylor.

What the hell?

My attention immediately moves to the last piece of paper, my stomach feeling like it's going to fall out when I realize it isn't a piece of paper. It's a photograph . . .

Of Rowan.

My mind cannot process or keep up with the information unfolding in front of me. Scratched on the other side of the photograph in the same cursive handwriting are three short sentences.

Rowan Taylor is her father. He can give her a better life than I ever could.

I'm sorry.

Holy shit. I'm momentarily frozen. My feet won't move. I don't know if my heart is beating. I can't get my lungs to cooperate. I stare down at the baby who's now asleep in my arms and then look at the things in my other hand. The picture of Rowan.

My ex's brother.

This might be his baby and I'm not sure he even knows about it. Considering the fact that the baby was dropped here at the safe haven, I'd be willing to bet he knows nothing of her existence. If I take the baby inside, she'll immediately be placed in custody of child protective services. She'll be thrown into the system and Rowan will have to fight to get her.

If she is actually his child . . .

I glance back at the front desk.

Janet is still MIA. I don't think or breathe. Some type of panic kicks in, rendering any logical thought useless. My feet begin to move and I don't know what the hell I'm doing. Reaching into my back pocket, I retrieve my phone, scroll through my contacts, and immediately tap on Rowan's name.

At this point, I'm already outside without even realizing I walked in the opposite direction of where I should have gone with the baby. Rowan answers on the third ring and there isn't a single ounce of guilt inside of me for waking him at this hour.

It's been almost two months since I ran into him here when he was at the hospital for his friend.

"Hadley?" Sleep is heavy in his tone, but it is laced with concern.

"Rowan. I'm sorry to wake you up. I don't even know what the hell I'm doing." I pause, realizing I'm standing in the middle of the parking lot, holding someone else's baby. "Holy shit," I breathe as the situation hits me like a ton of bricks.

"Hadley." His voice is louder now, clearer and fully awake. I have his undivided attention. "What's going on? Are you okay?"

"Yes. No. I don't know." The words tumble from me in a rush, the panic setting in as it weighs heavily on my shoulders. I keep walking in the opposite direction of the hospital like a goddamn fool. "I'm on the corner of Miller and Somerset. I need you to come here."

The sound of rustling comes through the speaker. "I'm on my way."

I sit down on the bench by the bus stop, ending the call without another word as I hold the baby close to my body. I stare down at the sweet baby girl, my eyes scanning her delicate features. Her button nose crinkles, a smile cresting her lips before her expression relaxes again.

The severity of this situation settles in my chest like a block of concrete.

I just walked out of the hospital with a baby that isn't mine.

What the hell did I do?

CHAPTER TWO

ROWAN

Tripping over my own feet, I shove them into my slides, grabbing my keys as I pull open the door to my garage in a rush. I haven't seen or heard from Hadley since I ran into her at the hospital when Riley was there. When I told her to let me know if she was ever in Aston, this isn't what I had imagined. I didn't imagine getting woken up by a phone call in the middle of night.

Hearing the sheer panic in her voice left me feeling unsettled. A chill slithers down my spine, tangling around my spinal cord. My movements are rushed, but they aren't quite fast enough as I wait for the damn garage door to open.

As I start to drive, I don't even know if I closed the door, but at the moment, I don't care. I don't know what happened, but she called me. She needs me and after I found her the night that my brother ended things with her, I feel like I can't leave her hanging. I have to help her.

It's a short ride into the heart of Aston and I know the intersecting streets she gave me. It's right down the street from the hospital which has me even more worried and confused.

The entire drive is a blur. I move on autopilot, somehow getting there in one piece as I race down the streets in the middle of the night. There isn't any traffic and barely any cars on the road. It's a quarter after one when I slip onto the street, my eyes laser-focused as I slow down, looking for her as I drive.

Relief floods me as I see what looks like her sitting beneath a streetlamp, tucked away from the elements on the bench at the bus stop. Her head turns to the side when she sees my headlights as I come to a stop along the curb. Leaning across the center console, I push open the door as she reaches it before I even have the chance to get out and open it for her.

Hadley slips inside, her body turned away from me at first. She looks awkward with her arms in front of her body, bending in a strange fashion to pull the door shut.

"You came." She lets out a breath of relief, her voice barely audible.

"You needed me," I tell her, my voice catching in my throat. "Are you hurt? Are you okay?"

She slowly turns, her body adjusting in her seat as she turns to face the front of the truck. "I'm okay," she admits, glancing at me as she starts to angle her torso to me. My eyebrows scrunch as my gaze drops down to her arms positioned near her chest.

"Hadley . . ." My voice trails off for a moment, my heart pounding erratically in my chest as I see what she's holding. It's a baby. A whole-ass tiny human. "What's going on?" My eyes widen slightly as I realize that it might be hers. "I didn't know you had a baby."

Her nostrils flare, her slender throat bobbing as she swallows roughly, blinking back the moisture that coats her eyes. "I don't," she chokes out the words, shaking her head at me as she holds out a small stack of papers. "But you do."

My heart flatlines in my chest, my airway instantly constricting. "No," I argue, my head moving back and forth. "That's not possible. I—I don't have—" I pause, the words dying on my tongue. There's no fucking way. Not a goddamn chance. I may not be a saint, but I'm always careful. "I don't know what the fuck is going on here, but you have to take it back to the hospital."

"Rowan, I can't," she whispers, her eyes searching mine. Devastation along with perturbation engulfs her expression. "If I take her back, they're going to think I tried to steal a baby."

"Okay, I'm sure if you explain whatever the hell happened, they will under—"

She pushes the papers closer to me. "Please, just look at these, Rowan," she pleads, her face on the edge of crumbling. I'm reluctant to take them, but I do it anyway. I'm trapped in a state of shock and denial and honestly . . . I don't know what the fuck is even going on in my mind right now.

It's like everything moves in slow motion. Hadley watches me, cradling the small infant in her arms as I look at the things she handed me. First is a picture of me, but it's not one someone would have gotten from the media. My mind starts reeling and I remember where it was taken. It was a party that I went to with Carson for his cousin's thirtieth birthday.

I flip over the picture, reading the note scrawled in perfect cursive writing.

Rowan Taylor is her father. He can give her a better life than I ever could.

I'm sorry.

There's no fucking way. This has to be a joke or some kind of a ploy for money or something. I drop the photo onto my lap, my eyes scanning the birth certificate. Lucille Maeve Taylor. Almost three weeks old. She gave this little girl my last name without me even knowing of her existence.

Hell, there's no proof she's my child. Any name can be written on a birth certificate.

I look at the mother's name and it instantly jogs my memory. *Selena Mackey.* My stomach sinks as I play over that entire night, remembering the brunette I ended up talking to. We barely exchanged names, played a few drinking games together, and then I ended up fucking her in their laundry room because we didn't have a chance to make it to a bedroom.

Fuck.

I glance at Hadley, the emotion welling in her eyes palpable as I swallow past the lump lodged in my throat. My eyes drop back down to the baby, nausea rolling in the pit of my stomach. She can't be mine. The details of that night are hazy at best, but I've never made a mistake like that before. I've always been careful to make sure shit like this didn't happen.

Letting the birth certificate float onto my lap, I look back at the envelope with my name written across it. I slip my finger along the seal, tearing it open before pulling out a perfectly folded white piece of paper. There isn't a single crinkle in it and my breath catches in my throat as I slowly unfold it, unsure of what I'm about to find inside.

Rowan,

    I don't know where I should start, but I suppose saying sorry is probably a good place. I should have called you when I first found out I was pregnant. Springing this on you isn't right, but I also know me keeping the baby is equally not right.

    When you and I met, my life was a mess—it still is. I had just gotten out of a shitty situation, but I was using pills and alcohol to numb the pain. When the morning sickness started, I thought it was just my body unable to handle the things I was doing to it.

    And then I found out I was pregnant.

    I hadn't planned on telling you about

any of this because this isn't something I ever wanted. My sister took me to the clinic for an abortion, but I couldn't go through with it. I never wanted a baby but the thought of living with that on my conscience was too much to bear.

My entire pregnancy was spent teetering on the edge of whether or not I should keep her. Whether or not I could ever be a fit enough parent to raise another person.

When Lucy was born, I knew I couldn't. I knew this is not for me and she deserves a shot at a real life. A chance with a loving parent who can give her everything and you can do that for her. You can provide for her in ways I will never be able to.

I don't want your money. I don't want anything from you.

I just want her to have a chance at a good life.

I'm sorry.

Selena

I'm barely breathing as I read over the second to last sentence three separate times. My heart barely moves inside my chest, although I can hear the sound of my blood racing through my veins, whooshing past my eardrums. My palms sweat and the muscles in my jaw hurt from clenching my teeth.

Slowly releasing my jaw, I suck in a breath, turning my head to look at Hadley. "This is some kind of a joke, right?"

Hadley's lips part, discontent encapsulating her facial features. "I don't know," she admits, her voice gentle. "I was going out for my break and found the baby with those things. I didn't read the letter."

"This has to be a joke." I look at the baby and then look out the window, looking for someone—anyone—to be watching us with a camera or something. I can't find anyone. The street is empty. It's just Hadley and me and the baby here. My eyes fly back to Hadley's. "What the fuck am I supposed to do?"

"I don't know."

"Is she even actually mine?

She pulls her bottom lip between her teeth. "I don't know."

"Fuck," I mutter, my eyes squeezing shut as I suck in a breath. My chest expands, and I hold it before releasing it in a rush as I look at her again. What the hell am I supposed to do with a baby? I don't even know if she's my child. "How did this even happen?"

Her forehead creases as her eyebrows lower. "I mean, if you slept with her mother—"

"No, I know how babies are made," I tell her, snorting at the irony of her response, given our current situation where we're sitting in my car. "The baby. How did you end up with her?"

"Oh," she starts, rolling her lips between her teeth as she looks out the window toward the hospital. "I found her in the safe haven. It's a safe area for mothers to leave their babies if they cannot care for them. No one pressed the button on the wall, so I'm not sure how long she was there. I was the first to find her and after I read the note on the back of the photo, I panicked."

I stare at her for a moment, my body rigid as I process everything she's telling me. "You weren't supposed to do that, were you?"

Her lips turn downward, tears brimming along the waterline of her eyes. "No, I wasn't. I panicked and walked out with her before anyone saw either of us. If anyone else found her, she would have been put into the system and then foster care, and then if she is yours, you would have had to battle to gain custody of her."

"Hadley," I say her name softly and slowly as I reach over, my hand squeezing her shoulder. "It's okay. You reacted and I'm not mad at you. This is just a lot to process." I look down at the baby as my own panic begins to set in. I go over every option in my brain of what to do next and honestly, I'm about to pull a fucking Hadley move right now.

Grabbing my phone, I scroll through my contacts, knowing exactly who I need to call. Lifting the phone to my ear, I listen as it begins to ring and it's finally answered just before it goes to voicemail.

"Why the fuck are you calling my fiancée in the middle of the night?"

"I need your help," I tell Lincoln, not bothering to answer his question. I called Nova because she's done this before. I can't call Nash and Riley. They have their own infant they're busy losing sleep over. "Can I come over?"

The sound of a hushed voice and rustling sounds in the background and I hear Lincoln mumbling something before he speaks to me again. "The door will be unlocked."

"Thanks."

I end the call, setting my phone down as I glance back at Hadley. My eyes search hers for a moment, getting lost in the emotional depths of her eyes before I lean forward. She inhales sharply and the faint scent of vanilla invades my senses as I grab her seat belt, pulling it across her body as I'm careful not to bump the baby.

"What are you doing?" she questions me, her eyes on me as I sit back in my seat and reach for the gear shifter to put the car in drive. "I have to get back to work."

"Not tonight, you're not. Call them and tell them you're sick or something," I tell her, half laughing because this is fucking ridiculous. "We're going to see my friend and his fiancée who can hopefully help us."

"It's illegal to drive with a baby in a car without a proper car seat."

I cock an eyebrow at her. "Okay, outlaw. You walked out of a hospital with a baby that isn't yours." She blinks as I point out the obvious to her. "Is that legal?"

"Well, no," she admits, letting out a nervous breath. "I guess nothing we're doing tonight is."

"I'll drive slow," I promise, bobbing my head as I pull the car away from the curb, my knuckles turning white as I tighten my grip on the steering wheel. Hadley doesn't speak another word as we ride in silence to Lincoln and Nova's house. I'm struggling to get a grip on reality, struggling to process how I went from sleeping comfortably in bed to driving in the middle of the night with Hadley holding a sleeping baby in my passenger seat.

A baby that I may be the father of.

She's so quiet, I can't help but wonder if something is wrong with her or if this is normal for some babies. My mind is absolutely blown by how quickly my life has been turned upside down.

All I can do is hope Lincoln and Nova can come up with some kind of a solution . . .

Otherwise, I fear Hadley and I may be royally fucked.

CHAPTER THREE

HADLEY

I don't think there's a specific word in the dictionary that would come close to describing how awkward I feel in this moment.

Standing beneath the porch light, I glance at Rowan with the baby in my arms as he turns the doorknob on the front door of his friend's house. He's quiet as he pushes it open, holding it for me as I step in ahead of him. The house is warm and smells faintly of vanilla and coffee. It's comforting and welcoming and for a moment, I'm glad for the silence that encapsulates us.

Rowan looks down at me, a terse look on his face before someone steps into the foyer at the end of the hall. She's a beautiful woman, her eyes bright, yet her face tired as she stares at us for a moment. She's wearing a pair of lavender silk pajamas and her blonde hair is piled on top of her head in a messy bun.

"Hey," she says softly, walking closer to the two of us. She stops in front of Rowan, pulling him in for a hug. "What's going on? Lincoln said you needed our help with something and it was urgent." She releases him, turning to face me with a smile on her face. "Hi, I'm Nova."

"Hadley," I tell her quietly, forcing a smile onto my face.

Her gaze immediately drops down to the baby in my arms. "Oh," she says softly, her eyes filled with concern as she looks up at me. "Who is this?"

"Her name is Lucy," Rowan informs her, his voice gruff as he stays behind her, eyes bouncing from the baby and back to me. "Hadley found her abandoned at the hospital with some things insinuating I'm her father."

"I'm guessing this is what you needed help with." She glances at him, before looking back at me. "May I?" Nova asks, holding her hands out to take the baby.

Instinctively, I glance up at Rowan and he gives me a swift dip of his chin before I smile at her, moving the baby from my arms into hers. She holds her perfectly, tucking her against her body. "Oh my goodness. She's so tiny and so precious."

Footsteps lumber down the stairs and I glance up, catching sight of a man walking down toward us. His hair is a tousled mess on top of his head, his eyes landing on Nova as he tucks his hands into the front pockets of his Bauer hoodie.

"Ro," he says with his chin lifting, glancing at me as he tilts his head to the side as he holds his hand out for me to shake it. "I'm Lincoln, Nova's fiancé. Rowan and I play together."

I slide my hand into his, giving him a gentle shake. "Nice to meet you. I'm Hadley."

Lincoln narrows his eyes on me for a moment before directing his gaze to his fiancée. Nova looks up at him, the softest smile glazing over her lips. "What's this about?"

"Apparently Rowan might be a father." She smiles down at the little girl. "Isn't she just so sweet?"

"She is," he agrees, although there's a hardness to his tone. His stare slices back to me and I hold my breath, waiting for him to bare his teeth at me. "I'm going to go ahead and cut to the chase. What is your motive here? Are you trying to trap Rowan in something?"

"Lincoln," Nova warns him, her voice low and stern. Her eyes cut to his face as his stare hardens on me. "Stop being an abrasive asshole when you don't even have all the details."

The color drained from Rowan's face a while ago, and his eyes are vacant and lost. "It's not hers," he says slowly, his chest rising as he inhales deeply. "Hadley's an old friend and she used to date my brother."

No one speaks and the silence is deafening. Something shifts in the air around us and my chest begins to constrict, that paralyzing feeling creeping over me as it feels like the walls are closing in on me. My insides quiver and I hold my breath for a moment, attempting to steady my heartbeat.

What a first fucking impression I'm having on who are clearly two of the closest people to Rowan Taylor.

"Do you guys want coffee? I sure could use one,"

Nova chimes in, finally breaking through the silence as she glances around at the three of us. No one answers and she dips her chin, forcing a tense smile across her lips. "Let's all go in the kitchen and we can talk about what is actually going on here."

The baby begins to stir in her arms, her little fist instantly going to her mouth as she lets out a cry and begins to suck on it.

"Grab the diaper bag from Rowan," Nova instructs Lincoln, motioning toward the bag. "I'll change her diaper and give her a bottle, assuming there are things in there."

"Whoever dropped her off left enough things for a few days."

Lincoln grumbles something under his breath, taking the bag from Rowan, and he's the first to spin on his heel as he heads into the kitchen at the end of the hall. Rowan looks at me for a moment, his lips parting almost as if he's going to say something, but instead, he shuts them and rubs his eyes.

Nova follows behind her fiancé, shushing the baby and leaving Rowan and me to bring up the rear. He falls in step beside me, his voice reserved for only my ears.

"Sorry. I'm not throwing you to the wolves, even if Lincoln makes it seem that way." He pauses, his eyes finding me as we reach the end of the hall. "He can be a pit bull, but I promise he's a good guy beneath the tough exterior."

"I know how this probably looks to them," I tell him, shrugging my shoulders before straightening my spine. "I'm a big girl. I can take care of myself." I glance down at the watch on my wrist as it vibrates, seeing it's a message from Cole. "Shit, I need to call work."

"Go ahead, I'll wait with you."

I give him the softest smile as I pull out my phone and dial the number for my manager. She answers on the second ring and I give her a bullshit excuse, telling her that I ended up getting sick while I was on break. It's a blatant lie, but she seems to accept it without any questions. I resist the superstitious urge to knock on wood, because the last thing I need is for karma to bite me in the ass and actually make me sick.

I quickly type out a message to Cole, telling him the same excuse so my story adds up. He sends a message back, questioning me on what the hell is going on, but I put my phone on Do Not Disturb as I glance back at Rowan.

He's watching me, his expression unreadable before he finally motions toward the kitchen. "Ready?"

I swallow roughly over the lump lodged in my throat, half feeling like I'm moving through a dream as I jerk my chin at him. He moves before me, stepping through the threshold, undoubtedly leading me directly into the wolves' den. Lincoln is busying himself by the counter, setting out four coffee mugs before picking up the carafe to fill them with steaming liquid.

Nova sits down at the island, holding the baby still as she motions for the two of us to sit across from her. "Let's start from the beginning so we can clear up any confusion."

"Okay," Rowan starts, looking at me as if he doesn't know where to start exactly. Lincoln joins the three of us, setting mugs down in front of Rowan and me, and then Nova as he presses his lips to the top of her head. Rowan lets out a breath and I know he needs me to step in.

"At the hospital, we have an area set up in the foyer that is our safe haven area. It's for mothers to safely leave their babies if they realize they cannot or do not want to raise them." I watch Nova's eyebrows pull together, sadness washing over her expression. "I know, it's sad, but it's the safest option for a baby that's abandoned." I save her the heartbreaking alternatives I've heard of when it comes to babies being abandoned.

"When I was leaving for my break, I found her in the bassinet, but whoever dropped her didn't press the button to alert staff members." I pause for a moment, realizing how fucked up this is about to sound when I admit that I walked out with her, but I have to give them the truth. I have to be straightforward with my potential mistake. "I found her birth certificate, a photo of Rowan with a note about him being the father, and then there was an envelope addressed to him." I let out a deep breath, my shoulders sagging with it. "I walked out with her and called Rowan."

Nova swallows, adjusting the bottle in the baby's mouth. "You walked out of the hospital with a baby that may or may not be Rowan's," he says, his voice flat and tense. "That might be the most irresponsible fucking thing I've ever heard."

Nova stares at me. "What would the alternative have been?"

"She would have immediately been thrown into the

system and then a foster home and hopefully adoption. If Rowan would have found out about her after that, he would've had to go to court to get custody of her. Not only would he have to prove that she's his, he would have to prove he didn't abandon the mother while she was pregnant."

"Well then, I can see why you did what you did," Nova tells me softly, her eyes warm as they search mine. "You weighed your options and made the decision you thought was best."

"It didn't feel right to not tell him."

Lincoln doesn't appear to be on the same page as Nova. "You made a life-changing decision for him without him even knowing. You should have taken her into the hospital and let it be sorted the way it should be."

Rowan interjects, his eyes hard as he stares at his friend. "No, she did the right thing. If she would have taken her inside, I may have never known about the baby."

"Please tell me you're at least going to get a paternity test," Lincoln grinds out, his nostrils flaring.

"I'm not a fucking idiot," Rowan snaps at him before running a frustrated hand through his hair. He turns to me now. "But speaking of that, what are my options for a test?"

"My friend's boyfriend works at the local lab," I explain, already having this semi planned out in my head. Cole's boyfriend may be able to help us, but that means I'm going to have to let them know what's going on. "I wanted to check with you first before asking him, but I can see if he can help. Usually results take a few days."

"Is your friend trustworthy?"

I stare at Rowan for a moment, mulling over the thought inside my brain. Considering how precarious this situation is, I need to really think things through before I tell Cole what is going on. If I'm careful enough, I can give him a different version of the story and he'll never have to know the truth.

"Yes," I tell him, attempting to sound convincing. There's no one I trust fully, but this is the most viable option we have at this moment. "I'll do whatever I have to do or say to get this to happen."

Rowan's nostrils flare, his dark blue eyes burning holes through mine. "I don't want you to get in trouble for any of this, Hadley." His expression softens as he continues to stare at me. "You didn't do anything wrong, okay?"

"Tell that to the police," Lincoln mumbles under his breath, the words piercing my heart. I'm so conflicted and so torn. Did I fuck everything up or was what I did truly the best option?

"Fuck off, Matthews," Rowan barks at him, shaking his head. "You're supposed to be helping me, not making this fucking worse."

"Both of you, shut up," Nova snaps at them, her head whipping back and forth between her fiancé and Rowan. "Hadley did what she thought was the right thing. This is where we are now and there is nothing we can do to change the chain of events." Her tongue darts out to wet her lips as she focuses on Rowan. "The real question is, what are you going to do if the baby isn't yours?"

Rowan's face goes even paler than it was before. He lets out a shallow breath and I don't miss the way his body falls rigid. "I didn't think that far." The pulse in his throat is visible, pounding faster.

"Every hospital has a safe haven," I interject, attempting to save Rowan from the way he's beginning to spiral inside his head. "I will take her to another one if that's what it comes down to." I already know in my heart that I could never do that, but I don't know how the hell I could legally keep her myself.

Nova looks between the two of us and I'm not sure she's fully convinced. "Okay. Just as long as we have a plan for each possible outcome." She glances at Lincoln, lifting her brow at him. "We're going to help them with whatever they need and stop being so judgy, right?"

Lincoln's expression softens as he stares back at her. "Yes." He looks at Rowan, his face serious. "Whatever you need, I'm here for you." He directs his gaze to me and I'm momentarily shocked. "I'm sorry, Hadley. It wasn't fair for me to pass judgement on you and the situation before having all the details."

A man who apologizes? Nova really hit the jackpot.

"I appreciate your apology," I tell him, feeling a bit awkward with the attention solely on me. "I know it didn't look good with the way we showed up. I promise I am not trying to trap Rowan in anything. If he wants this entire thing to go away, I will accept full responsibility for the baby and my actions."

Lincoln stares at me for a moment before he seems

to be pleased with the things I've told him. The corners of his mouth turn upward, just the slightest, although they're too tense to resemble a smile. He inclines his head forward and lets out a sigh. "So, what's the plan next?" He glances at the time on the stove. "It's almost two in the morning and we have a morning skate and a game tomorrow."

"Fuck, I'm sorry," Rowan tells him, shaking his head as his shoulders sag. "I didn't even think about tomorrow. I literally panicked and you guys were the first ones I thought to call. I know Nash and Riley have an infant they're dealing with, so I didn't want to bother them."

"Ro, stop, you called the right people." Nova smiles at him, pushing back her chair as she rises to her feet. She walks over to me, handing me the baby to burp her before she goes to rinse out the bottle. "I have all of Poe's stuff in the basement. I was saving things in case we have a baby, but you can use them until you know what's going on."

Lincoln also rises to his feet, along with Rowan, and the three of them disappear into the basement as I hold the baby, gently patting her back until she lets out a few belches. After she's apparently comfortable and all the gas bubbles are dissolved, I shift her back into my arms as the men begin to bring things up into the kitchen and out to Rowan's car.

They manage to load a bassinet, a changing pad, and some other miscellaneous things in the trunk. Nova is the last to come up, setting a proper carry type car seat on the counter. Lincoln grabs the base, going out to the car to secure it in the back seat with Rowan as I strap the baby in.

"I know you know what you're doing with babies since you're a nurse, but Rowan has no fucking clue," Nova says softly, handing me a blanket to tuck around the baby. "He's going to need as much help as he can get."

Rowan and I haven't discussed any specifics, but the last thing I planned on doing was leaving him to figure this all out on his own.

"I plan on doing whatever I can do to help him."

Nova stares at me for a moment, her expression free of any negativity. "I don't disagree with what you did and honestly, I probably would have done the same thing. However, we don't know what kind of a mess this could potentially turn into and I just want to make sure Rowan has as much support as possible."

"You have my word, Nova," I promise her without a single ounce of hesitation. "I won't leave him to do this alone."

"No one wants to do it alone," she says quietly, a tender smile drifting across her lips. "Trust me, I know from experience."

The boys walk back in, Rowan stopping beside me as he glances down at the baby. His eyes are glazed over, almost as if he's operating on fumes right now. "Are you ready to go?"

Guilt pricks at my spine as I know I'm the reason he's disconnected and numb. His world has been turned upside down and he's still struggling to process everything that's going on around him.

Nothing could have prepared him for a mindfuck quite like this one.

"If you are."

He glances down at the baby, his jaw tightening as he grabs the carrier, lifting it from the counter. "As ready as I'm going to be."

We say our goodbyes to Nova and Lincoln and they wait by the front door as Rowan and I get the baby secured in the back seat. He's silent as I climb into the front, but he finally looks at me as he's about to pull the car away from the curb.

"Will you come home with me?"

I turn to look at him, my breath catching in my throat. "Sure."

"I just . . . I don't know what the hell I'm doing and I'd feel better if you were there with me."

I stare at him for a moment, emotion washing over me, but I quickly push it away. "Of course. Whatever you need."

Rowan runs his tongue over his teeth. "Thanks." He tips his chin, although his voice is distant and barely audible. He directs his attention back to the road, pulling the truck away from the curb as we head in the direction of his house.

Guilt washes over me as we ride silently through the night. All of this is my fault and I'm afraid when the dust settles, he might never forgive me for this.

CHAPTER FOUR

ROWAN

"What do we do now?"

Hadley looks my way, her eyes meeting my stare in an instant. "I'm not sure. I'm around babies all the time, but this is the first time I've ever brought one home."

Home.

How fucking weird. This used to be my home and mine alone . . . how quickly that has changed.

Pulling my phone from my pocket, I glance at the time, realizing we're now approaching three o'clock in the morning. I have to be up in a few short hours for our morning skate since we have a game tomorrow night. Well, I guess technically it's tonight now, considering we're in the early hours of the next day.

"We're supposed to take her out of the car seat, right?"

"That would be a good start." Hadley stifles a laugh, biting back a grin as she tips her chin at me. "Why don't you go get the bassinet and things from the car and I'll get her out and changed? Maybe we'll get lucky and she'll stay asleep, or at least go right back to sleep and then we can try and get some rest."

I stare at her for a moment, anxiety washing over me as it mixes with a million other feelings I can't possibly begin to dissect. The words tumble from my lips before I get a chance to even think about them. "You're not going home, are you?"

"No, Rowan," she says, shaking her head as she lifts Lucy from the car seat. Her soft hazel eyes meet mine and she pushes a stray hair away from her face. "I'm not going to just throw you to the wolves."

My lips crinkle as she uses the same phrase I used earlier. Nodding at her, I leave her in the living room with the baby as I head out into the garage. As soon as I step away from them, my mind is on a rampage, moving a million miles a second. I'm still in a state of disbelief, almost as if this can't possibly be my life.

I don't want kids. I've never wanted kids. When I fucked Selena, it obviously wasn't with the intention of getting her pregnant. Hell, I never even got her number, so clearly it was never supposed to go past that night.

But then again, I feel like a fucking asshole. I can't imagine what she must have been going through the last ten months. She clearly has her own issues and it's most likely best if she doesn't have to be responsible for a child, but what the fuck?

I have an entire fucking hockey career. There are weeks at a time when I'm not even here.

What the hell am I going to do with an infant that needs me?

Grabbing the bassinet, I leave it just inside the house before moving back to the trunk. Nova gave me some essential things to use for now, but not the necessities we need like formula and diapers. I don't even know what the hell else a baby needs, so I'm going to have to figure all of that out too.

Honestly, I'm not mad at Hadley. How could I possibly be angry with someone like her? Hadley is a gentle soul and she's one of the kindest people I've ever met. There isn't a single mean bone in her body. I've always admired her strength and her ability to find the good in the bad.

However, on the other hand, I wouldn't be in this situation if she wouldn't have told me about the baby. It's conflicting, almost too conflicting for my brain to sift through the bullshit.

I don't want a baby, but I don't like the thought of my daughter growing up with a different family either. I'm not comfortable with the thought of someone else raising her. Who's to know what kind of house she would end up living in? What kind of life would she have? Would she be fucked up just from the knowledge of her parents not wanting her?

I head back into the house, grabbing the bassinet as I head into the living room. It's some kind of a portable one that Nova said to use temporarily, but I will have to get her a crib at some point. I'm going to have to turn one of my guest rooms into a whole-ass nursery.

My head fucking hurts.

Hadley slowly lowers her into the bassinet after I have it set up and she moves over to the diaper bag, pulling various things from inside. Things that I don't even know what their purpose is. I'm standing close enough to smell the faint hint of her—vanilla and berries.

"I'm going to make a list of necessities and things we need to get," she explains as she stacks two cans of formula on the coffee table. "Everything her mom left should get us through the next day or two." Hadley stands upright, glancing at me as her eyes scan my face. "Why don't you go get some rest? I've got her for the night."

"I don't know if I can sleep right now," I admit, my voice barely audible as I'm cemented in place. "I just—" I pause, letting out a deep breath, realizing I'm standing closer to Hadley than I thought, staring into the depths of her eyes. There's almost a halo of gold around her pupils. "Are you okay with her if I go for a run?"

"Of course," she tells me softly, a tender smile on her lips. My mind memorizes the freckles spread across the bridge of her nose, dispersing across the tops of her cheeks. "I'm here for whatever you need, Rowan. Anything you need."

Relief floods me, although it doesn't come close to washing away the anxiety inside of me. My gaze travels down her body, taking in the appearance of her blue scrubs. Her car is still at the hospital and she doesn't have a single thing with her, yet she plans on staying here tonight anyway.

"I'll be right back," I tell her, not offering another explanation as I disappear from the living room, leaving her confused. I head up to the second floor and into my room before rifling through my drawers. I find her a pair of sweatpants and grab a t-shirt from my closet before stopping in the bathroom for a spare toothbrush and toothpaste.

Hadley's moving the other things we got from Nova into the living room when I walk back into the room. "What's all that?" she questions me as I set the small pile of clothing and stuff on the couch.

"I figured you might want to change out of your scrubs," I tell her, watching as she walks over to grab them. "There's a toothbrush too."

"Thanks, Rowan." She dips her head, reaching out to grab my forearm and give me a gentle squeeze. Her palm is soft and warm against my flesh, sending a spark of electricity up my arm. "Go clear your head so you can get some rest. I'm off tomorrow, so we can figure things out whenever you have time."

Her hand lingers and as soon as she lifts it away, I want her to put it back.

The muscle in my jaw tightens, my chest constricting as I attempt to suck in a breath. "Okay."

———

My sneakers pound on the concrete as I inhale through my nose, exhaling through my mouth. My brain feels a little quieter than it did when I started and I've been running for a solid twenty minutes now, essentially just doing laps around the neighborhood.

As much as I wanted to head out into my shed and take a few hits of that joint Carson gave me last week, this seemed like the healthier alternative. It would have taken the edge off, but what if it would have made me even worse anxiety-wise, considering the fact that there's a damn baby under my care now.

I need Hadley to talk to her friend about this paternity test. There are too many things hanging in the balance right now. If Lucy isn't my daughter, I honestly don't know if I am going to want Hadley to drop her off somewhere else. Mentally, that thought is harder to stomach than the thought of raising her— even if I have no idea how the fuck I'm going to do this.

There's an overwhelming amount of guilt hanging over me at the thought of willingly handing her over to be thrown into the foster system. We've all heard of those horror stories . . .

I'm finishing up my last lap, heading back to my house, when I start to slow down. My heart pounds quickly in my chest, my lungs screaming for oxygen as I jog for a bit. At this hour, this was probably dumb as fuck to do. I'm pushing my body when I should be resting it, especially before our game.

Coach Landry and Coach Watson are both going to be pissed if I don't perform well.

It's a good five minutes of cooling down before I'm stepping back onto my own property. The light is still on in the living room, along with the one shining on the porch. Hadley may have been the one to spring all of this on me, but at the end of the day, this isn't her fault. She's not the one who made a mistake and potentially got some random girl pregnant.

I have to be held accountable for what I potentially did.

Hadley and I have known each other for many years, but we were never close growing up. We didn't hang out with the same people due to our age difference. When Hadley was entering high school, I was on my way out. After that, the amount of times we ran into each other was few and far between.

Whatever this is between us is peculiar and she certainly doesn't owe me a single fucking thing . . . yet she didn't leave me alone to deal with this by myself.

She stayed.

I'm quiet as I let myself back into the house, entering through the garage and kicking my sneakers off by the back door. Running cleared my head enough to realize none of this can be dealt with tonight. Hadley's right. We both need to get some rest, especially because of the demanding day I have after I wake up.

The house is so silent, a part of me is worried as I make my way into the living room. I thought maybe Hadley would have turned the TV on or something, but as I walk into the room, it's just as silent as the rest of the house.

Panic erupts inside and I wonder if I spoke too soon. What if she decided not to stay? What if she took Lucy back to the hospital?

Every anxious thought dissipates as I step over to the couch, a gentle smile lifting my lips as I'm flooded with relief. Hadley's curled up on the couch, wearing my t-shirt and sweatpants, her lips parted slightly as she softly breathes. Her hand rests against the bassinet where Lucy's peacefully sleeping. Hadley's eyelashes rest against the tops of her cheekbones and I allow myself a private moment to drink her in.

Hadley Reed is drop-dead gorgeous. She's the type that turns heads every time she walks into the room, but not just because of her looks or her body. There's an air about her that demands everyone's attention.

It was impossible to not notice her when we were growing up, but that's all it ever was. A passing glance or a lingering stare. Settling down was never in the cards for me, and Hadley isn't the type of person you spend a fleeting moment with.

No, she's much more than a moment.

Grabbing a blanket from the other side of the couch, I drag it over Hadley's body, covering her up before walking over to my recliner. Exhaustion settles in my bones and as badly as I need to shower and change my clothes, I just don't have the energy. Resting my head against the back of the chair, I turn it to the side, my gaze landing on Hadley and the baby.

My eyelids grow heavier with every blink until slumber sweeps me into its depths with wandering thoughts of the two of them floating around in my dreams.

CHAPTER FIVE

HADLEY

Trying to get solid sleep with a baby waking up every few hours is literally a goddamn pipe dream.

And it's only been one night.

"Are you sure you're okay if I leave?"

I stare up at Rowan from where I'm sitting on the couch, my mind lagging from the lack of sleep as I take a few extra seconds to formulate a response. "Yeah, of course," I tell him, waving my hand dismissively before taking a sip of my coffee that's already grown lukewarm. "I've totally got this."

"We have our morning skate and then I'll be back for a few hours after that."

"Rowan, I need you to go about your day without worrying about Lucy and me," I tell him, attempting to sound stern, but all I sound is exhausted. "Go about your day as if the two of us aren't here."

He stares at me, his expression blank. "That's a little hard to do."

A sigh escapes me, my lungs deflating with it. "Yeah, that makes sense," I agree, shrugging with indifference. "I'm going to call my friend about the paternity test and hopefully we can get that sorted." I pause, glancing down at his clothes that I'm still wearing. "Am I able to use your shower then? I'm starting to feel a little crusty and was too tired to wash the day off before falling asleep."

"I am such an asshole," he sighs, closing his eyes as he drags a tired hand down his face. "Yes. Please, make yourself at home. Use whatever you need, eat whatever you want." He pauses, his eyes scanning the length of my body before he meets my face once more. "Did you want to run home and get clothes or something?"

I chew on the inside of my lip for a moment, glancing down at the baby and then at the clock before finally shaking my head at him. "I'll be fine. I'm going to call my friend about the paternity test and see if he can bring me some clothes."

Rowan is silent for a moment and I can't read his expression at all. It's completely justified, all things considered, I just don't know what I'm supposed to say or do.

"Call me if you need anything?"

I dip my chin, reaching for the baby as she starts to move around in the bassinet. Her little mouth opens wide, a soft cry coming from her as I begin to lift her into my arms. Rowan stays for a moment, his gaze studying my face before he finally moves.

The way he looks at me makes my heart skip a beat,

but I quickly shove the feeling away. If there's one person I cannot get involved with, it's him.

Rowan Taylor is known to never get involved with anyone, and I have plans. Plans to travel, plans to see the world, and a career I worked my ass off for.

Holding Lucy against my chest, I murmur softly to her, my body turning as I watch Rowan disappear into the kitchen before exiting through the back door.

It doesn't take me long to change Lucy's diaper before I settle back down on the couch with her again to give her a bottle. As she lays in my arms sucking down formula, I pull out my phone using my free hand, immediately going to my text thread with Cole, and open it up.

HADLEY

Call me when you can, I need your help with something.

He immediately calls me. I'm not surprised since he just got off work a few hours ago. Night shift is weird like that and I'm like Cole—it's hard to adjust bouncing back and forth between night shift and day shift.

"Hello?"

"Hey. What happened to you last night?" Cole questions me, not missing a beat. "Is everything okay?"

I'm silent for a moment. "I need your help, but I need you to promise me you won't ask any questions. I can't tell you what is going on right now, but I promise I will as soon as I can."

Now Cole is silent. "What the fuck is going on, Hadley?"

"Can you help me or not?"

He mutters something under his breath that sounds like a string of curses before his voice is clear. "Yes, of course." He pauses for a second. "Unless it involves digging a hole. I am not cut out for that shit."

I snort, my cheeks puffing out as I try to hold back my laugh. It's impossible and my entire face cracks as laughter spills from me. Tears spring to my eyes and I hastily wipe them away, refusing to let the exhaustion make me emotional. "Thank you for that. I needed that."

"What do you need from me?"

There is an endless list of things I need from him. For starters, my car would be helpful, but I already know I'm going to be asking more from him than I should. Not only am I involving Cole in this mess, but his boyfriend is undoubtedly going to be a key piece in this plan.

"I'm going to send you an address. Can Damien get a paternity test and run it without anyone knowing?"

Cole is quiet again. "What the hell kind of mess did you get yourself into, Hadley?" He lets out a breath. "Send me the address and let me talk to Damien. He's not going to be happy with me."

Honestly, I'm shocked that it didn't take more to get him on board. This is a huge risk for everyone involved right now and I wouldn't blame him if he told me no.

"I love you and I owe you."

"Hell yeah, you do." He snorts, a chuckle coming from him. "Do you need anything else? A human sacrifice? The head of a goat?"

I giggle, shaking my head as I pop the bottle from Lucy's mouth and hold her up to burp her. "You're two steps ahead of me."

"See you in a little bit," Cole says before ending the call.

I don't know how I'm going to repay him and Damien for helping me, but it's definitely going to have to be something big. Something grand. I have no one else close to me, no one else I can ask for help, yet Cole is ready to do anything he can, other than bury a body.

Thankfully, it's not that.

———

Cole sits in front of me, Damien directly beside him with his arm draped over the back of the couch. They're both staring at me, neither of them speaking as their gazes travel from Lucy and back to me. I watch them as Cole slowly turns his head to look at his boyfriend, the both of them sharing a knowing look before Damien bobs his head.

Cole looks back at me. "Hadley . . . we are on board with helping you, but I need a little more information to know what we're dealing with."

I hear something in the kitchen and I glance over my shoulder at the room, hearing what sounds like a door shutting, but there's no other sound. I look back at Cole, my lips parting as I try to figure out where the hell to begin.

"I'm just going to go ahead and ask," Damien chimes in. "Did you kidnap a baby?" He purses his lip.

"We know she's not yours and honestly, all of this is really strange."

"She's mine."

My heart stops in my chest at the sound of his voice. I look back, finding Rowan as he walks into the room. His hair is damp, most likely from the shower at the rink, and he's wearing black sweatpants and a gray hoodie. His dark blue eyes land on me at first before he looks past me to Cole and Damien.

"I found her on my doorstep in the middle of the night and I called Hadley for help."

Cole's eyebrows tug together. "And you are . . .?"

"This is Rowan Taylor," I interject, pushing my way back into the conversation to save Rowan from offering an explanation. That's a fact I wish I could erase completely. "He's an old friend and we ran into each other at the hospital a couple months ago."

"So, is the paternity test to confirm she's yours?" Damien asks Rowan as Rowan drops down onto the couch beside me.

Rowan doesn't answer at first as he stares at the baby asleep in my arms. He still hasn't even held her yet. "Yes."

Cole looks directly at me, his gaze laser-focused on me. "This is a huge risk, Hadley. I'm not going to let Damien do this for him if he's just some douchebag."

"He's not," I tell him, shaking my head as I vouch for Rowan. Rowan has never been anything but kind to me. He found me at one of my lowest moments in life and not once did I feel judgment from him. "He's a good one."

The muscle in Cole's jaw tightens as he looks back at his boyfriend. The two of them have a silent conversation before Damien reaches into his bag, pulling out a test kit. "I need to swab the inside of your cheek and the baby's. I can have the results by tomorrow afternoon, as long as I can do it in secret." He pauses, chewing on the inside of his cheek. "I won't be able to have the geneticist confirm, because of the nature of things, but if she's yours, it will be pretty evident."

"Okay."

Rowan doesn't say anything else and the process is quick as Damien swabs the inside of Rowan's cheek and then Lucy's. He excuses himself, walking into the kitchen as I get Lucy settled and walk with Cole and Damien to the front door.

"Are you sure this is going to be accurate?"

Damien jerks his chin and half shrugs. "They're pretty accurate, but usually we like to get a couple sets of eyes on it to confirm." He pauses, his lips pursing for a moment. "I'll do what I can to make sure the results are as conclusive as I can get them."

"That guy looks fucking lost," Cole adds, his voice low so Rowan can't hear him. He pulls me in for a hug, wrapping his arms around my body. "Give him a blow job or something to cheer him up."

Stifling a laugh, I push away from him, rolling my eyes. "Yeah, right. You go do it."

"I think not," Damien quips, wrapping his arm around Cole. "Come on, time to go before you get any ideas."

Cole laughs as Damien leads him onto the porch and

I'm quiet as I close the door behind them. Turning back around, I face the hall, a heaviness on my shoulders as I let out a deep breath. I will not be taking Cole's advice for cheering Rowan up. That's not what I'm here for. I'm here to help him with Lucy and nothing more.

Rowan's heating something up on the stove as I walk into the kitchen. He glances at me over his shoulder, his eyes resting on me for a moment before he turns back to face the stove. "Are you hungry?"

"Sure," I tell him, walking deeper into the kitchen before pausing beside him. He looks at me, his tired eyes meeting my gaze before he goes back to cooking. "Since Lucy is sleeping, do you mind if I go get my car and some things from home after we eat?"

His head whips to the side, his eyes wide as he searches mine. "You're going to come back, right?"

A crack forms in my heart from the fear that engulfs him. "I told you I wasn't going to leave you alone with this, Rowan."

His lips part as if he's going to say something, but he quickly shuts them. I watch his Adam's apple bob as he swallows hard. "Okay. I'm sorry, I just—I don't know."

"It's okay. One day at a time. Damien will have the results tomorrow and then I think having that concrete information will help you process," I tell him, attempting to psychoanalyze him, which he definitely didn't ask for. I pull out my phone, opening up the Uber app before requesting a pickup. I need to get to the hospital to get my car before I can go home.

My attention moves directly back to Rowan after I

secure a ride. "Tell me about your game days. Do you have a certain schedule or something? I think it's probably best if you try to keep life as normal as possible right now."

Rowan swallows again, jerking his chin. "Um, so we have a morning skate. Usually I shower, come home, and eat something. I go out to my shed for a bit and then take a nap. Carson has a chef that comes over and cooks our pregame meal, so I go there and eat and then head to the arena."

"Okay, this is good," I tell him, my head bobbing in a similar fashion. A little too eager, like we're both trying to convince ourselves everything is completely fine. "You eat while I run and get a few things and then Lucy and I will be out of your hair the rest of the day."

"Okay," he says slowly, his eyes searching my face again. "Okay."

I smile at him, reaching over as I pat him on the shoulder, attempting to offer some type of encouragement. My hand remains longer than it should and I can't help it. Seeing him like this, the way he's taking things in stride, it's honestly attractive as hell.

Knowing my hand is lingering for too long, I move it from his shoulder, my eyes searching his once more before I turn away from him.

"Hey, Had?" he calls out, the sound of his voice penetrating my eardrums as I reach for the front door.

I turn back to look at him. "Yeah?"

"Thank you," he says softly, appreciation radiating from his expression. "For everything."

Emotion wells in my throat and I know it's from the

goddamn exhaustion. I smile, swallowing back my feelings as I lower my chin at him. Rowan and I share another lasting stare before I force myself to move through the front door.

I have to keep moving. I have to make sure Lucy and Rowan are both good.

Because if I don't, who else will?

CHAPTER SIX
ROWAN

Everything in my field of vision is completely out of focus as I stare straight ahead, my gaze trained on absolutely nothing. I can hear the sounds of the voices around me, but I'm not focused on a single word being spoken. I can't let myself shift out of the safe space I've constructed inside my head.

If I drift back into reality, it will completely pull me out of the game and I can't have that happen. Not now, not when my team needs me.

The moment I walked into the building, I knew I was going to have to push thoughts of Hadley and Lucy from my brain. There's too much that's unknown in my life right now and there's no room for any of that on the ice. I have one job, one thing I need to focus on.

The least I can do is dedicate all my time and attention to my job and worry about the realities of life afterward.

We're in the second intermission. One period left. We're winning, but I won't dare to speak that out loud.

The second anyone talks about our lead is the second we end up giving up a goal. It has a way of adding an additional layer of pressure I don't need.

"You ready, bud?" Carson asks as he walks over and taps me on the shoulder. I glance up at him, inhaling deeply as I roll my tongue over my teeth.

"Fuck yeah, let's do it."

I rise on my skates, glancing around the room as the rest of the guys are getting ready to get their gloves on before we head down the tunnel. I catch Lincoln's gaze from across the room. He lifts an eyebrow at me, silently asking me if I'm good.

I don't need the reminder that no, I am in fact not good right now.

Inhaling, my nose scrunches and I slide my hand into my glove and the other in my blocker as I give him a firm nod. The guys begin to line up and we all make our way down the tunnel, each of us grabbing our sticks before hitting the ice.

A few of the guys skate around our zone while the rest either head onto the bench or gather around the front of it. I immediately make my way over to the net, knowing exactly where I'm supposed to be.

Being a goalie is a weird position in a way. You're playing a team sport and you are a part of the team, but it is a position that is its own singular entity. I'm not required to skate up and down the ice, playing offensively and defensively depending on the play. I have one position, one fucking job.

That doesn't take away from the work of the defensemen. They are there as the first line. They help to protect and guard the net. There's value in having a solid defensive player, but a goalie is that final line of defense. I am the one who is solely responsible for any pucks slipping into the net.

At the end of the day, if I let too many goals get past me, I am the one who is to blame for that loss.

Playing goalie comes with an insane amount of pressure and there are some days where it can be crippling. I've questioned this position many times as a child and just as many times in my professional career. I mean, let's be real, having frozen pucks coming at you at one hundred miles per hour is insane. The adrenaline rush of making a crazy save is unlike anything else I've ever experienced and I wouldn't trade it for the world.

It's a nice distraction when your life off the ice is up in fucking flames.

Setting my stick on top of the net, I dig my edges into the ice, scratching the surface around the crease. It helps to build a little bit of snow that can potentially slow pucks and it also helps to add a little more grip to the surface for me.

As I finish, the period is about to begin. I grab my stick and get into position, my gaze zeroed in on the center of the ice as everyone gets into their positions. All four wingers are lined up; the defensive pairs are where they're supposed to be and both centers are ready.

My heart pounds in my chest, my nostrils flaring, and I take a deep, steadying breath as time is suspended in the air. The ref holds his hand out and less than a second later, he drops the puck onto the ice.

Caleb wins the face-off, sliding it across the ice to Nash. I watch as play commences and they take off down into our offensive zone. The moment that happens, the pressure lifts, but I make sure to hold on to it, just enough to keep me on my toes.

In a game like this, you should never get too comfortable. When you're comfortable, you become complacent, and that's exactly when and where mistakes happen.

I've made my fair share of mistakes, but I try to limit them. There's no room for fuckups in a position or a career like this.

Or anywhere in my life, really.

———

"Taylor, you're quiet," Caleb says to me, addressing me directly as he walks over to me after the game. Most of the locker room has cleared out already except for the usual suspects. Carson and I are typically the last ones out, with Caleb always hanging around to make sure everyone's good.

He takes his position as captain to heart.

I glance up at him, not sure what the fuck to say. These guys are all my fucking family, each one like a brother to me. Hell, I spend more time with them than I do with anyone I'm biologically related to.

When my brother and I were growing up, we had that brotherly relationship. Beau looked up to me and followed me around like I was his role model. When he hit his teenage years, everything quickly went to shit. It was like a switch flipped and as soon as he started to have his own issues, he had a chip on his shoulder toward Raven and me.

Raven and I were fortunate enough to not have the mental illness and addiction struggles he had and he felt like he was the outcast of the family. Because we were on the right path in life, Beau took it out on both of us, throwing vicious words at us and even getting physical with me on an occasion or two when I stood up to him and refused to take his bullshit.

He took advantage of our parents and even went to the extremes of stealing money from them and running away as a teen when he was underage. Even still, my mother refused to accept that there was no possibility of helping Beau. She continued to bend for him, until one day, she finally grew a backbone and that's when I saw how much his issues had been weighing on her.

It broke her to have to tell her youngest child that she wasn't going to help him. She wasn't going to extend a hand anymore if he was going to continue to bite. She refused to give him money and told him he had to get his life together and to figure it out himself.

That was after he broke up with Hadley and hopped on a plane to Boston.

He ended up in a pinch with the woman he was staying with and lived on the streets for a few months before he finally saw the light. He's been in an extended rehab facility for the past six months and it's breathed a newfound sense of hope back into my mother.

My father is still reluctant to trust him, but he always stands by our mother, even if her hopes seem far-fetched. She's been insanely proud of the progress Beau has made. It seems as though he's turned to a new page and is getting his life in order.

She thinks I need to make peace with him, though I'm not so sure I can ever bring myself to do that.

Lincoln glances at me from across the room as he and Nash are getting ready to head out. Since Riley had her baby, Nash doesn't hang around late like he used to, but for some reason he's still here tonight. Most likely because Lincoln is dragging his feet.

He's waiting to see what I'm going to say, to see if I'm going to be honest and tell everyone what the fuck is going on.

I don't know what to do. I want to tell them the truth. I don't want to sit with the weight of this secret myself, but then again, I need to know the truth before I come clean about this.

A sigh escapes me and I know I have to wait. "Just a long day," I tell him, forcing a smile onto my face. It barely resembles a smile and my lips fall flatter than I anticipated. I catch Lincoln's eye and he gives me a look of understanding.

Caleb doesn't seem to be convinced and he gives me a look of concern, but he doesn't press the issue. He knows his limitations and even though he's the older brother figure for all of us, he is never one to poke or prod.

Caleb Ford has a slew of his own problems and issues and the last thing he's going to do is make anyone else feel uncomfortable. Hell, he was reserved before he lost his wife and after that tragedy, he pulled back even more.

The man is like a paradox and I'm not quite sure he'll fully open up to anyone else again in his life.

Carson looks at me, his eyebrows pulling together as he tilts his head to the side. He's my best friend and unfortunately, he's nothing like his brother. Caleb won't press but Carson will dig until he gets the information he's after.

He hangs out until everyone else clears out, Caleb giving both of us a wave before he exits the room. Carson waits for me, just like he does every night after a game. I meet him by the door and we head down the hall, making our way toward the exit.

"What's actually going on, Ro?" Carson gives me a look of concern as the glass doors slide open and we both step into the parking lot. "My brother might be cool with being fed bullshit, but I'm not."

I knew this was coming. Carson Ford is a force to be reckoned with. I've known him since we were sixteen and it's a quality I've always admired in him . . . until this moment.

Then again, he is my best friend and I need someone to talk to. I don't want to bother Lincoln with my problems any more than I already have. I appreciate every way he and Nova have helped me thus far, but Lincoln has her and their family.

"Rowan." Carson's voice interrupts my thoughts as we reach my car first. My head slowly turns to look at him, his gray eyes meeting mine. "What's going on, bro?"

My lungs deflate, and my shoulders fall as I let out a deep breath, feeling the heaviness of the situation stacking like bricks on my chest. "You remember your cousin's thirtieth birthday party when I ended up fucking that girl in the closet? Selena . . . Her older brother was one of his friends or something."

"Oh yeah, I think I remember her."

I pause for a moment, staring at him as I attempt to sift through my muddled brain. How the hell do I even begin to explain any of this without sounding like I'm starring in my own reality TV show?

"Do you remember Hadley from the hospital?"

Carson's eyebrows pull together. "Hadley? Wait, she's the nurse who was working there when Riley had Theo, right? The one you said you knew from your hometown?" His brow furrows as I give him a curt nod. "What does she have to do with that night?

Goddammit. I should just save myself and climb in my car and head home.

"She found a baby outside of the hospital and it turns out, I may be her father."

Carson doesn't say a word. He stares at me, his expression completely blank as if his mind is struggling to try to catch up with the information I just threw at him. "What?"

"Yeah."

"Okay, explain to me why you think this baby is yours."

"There was some documentation with her and a note. We're waiting on the results of a paternity test to see if she's my daughter," I explain to him, my voice almost robotic and rehearsed as I force the words out. At this point, I think I'm just becoming numb to the entire situation.

"Rowan . . ." Carson's voice trails off as he stares at me. "So, you fucked this girl, she ended up pregnant, didn't tell you, and then leaves the baby saying you're the father." His face pales. "What in the actual fuck?"

"Yeah, I know." I let out a stiff laugh, the sound abrasive and unnatural. "Apparently she has some personal issues and isn't fit to be a mother."

He snorts. "So, she thinks you're fit to be a father?" He rolls his eyes, shaking his head at me. "I'm kidding. But seriously, what the hell are you going to do?"

I hold my hands up, shrugging as I let out an exasperated sigh. "If she's my child, then she's my responsibility."

Carson's eyes soften, a knowing look passing through his gaze as he gives me an appreciative nod. "Honestly, I wouldn't expect anything less from you. You're a stand-up guy, Rowan, and I admire you for that. I can't begin to imagine the type of mindfuck you're going through right now, yet you're ready to step up and do whatever you have to do."

I stare at my best friend for a moment, knowing it's a compliment but not sure how to even respond. The last thing I need right now is for my emotions to come out of hiding. "Thanks, I appreciate that," I tell him, finally pulling open the door to my car.

"Where is the baby now?"

"She's at my house," I say, my eyebrows pulling together as I watch Carson walking around to the passenger's side of my car. He reaches for the door. "What are you doing?"

"Coming with you."

My head cocks sideways slightly. "For what?"

"Obviously to help you." He stares at me. "I have a niece, Rowan. I know what to do with babies."

"So does Hadley."

A smirk pulls on his lips, mischief dancing in his eyes. "Is she at your house right now?"

"Yes," I tell him, my tone suddenly off. "She's helping me until I figure things out."

"Perfect." Carson shuts the door to my car, backing away with mischief in his eyes. "I'll meet you at your house."

I narrow my eyes, watching as he turns his back to me. "I don't need your help, Ford."

He simply lifts his hand to wave at me, but doesn't bother to look back or say anything in response. I watch him for a moment, a sigh escaping me as I finally lower myself into the car. I'm exhausted and Carson can be a bit of a thorn at times, but I'll welcome any help I can get right now. Lord knows I'm going to need all the help I can get, especially if it turns out that Lucy is mine.

They say it takes a village, but I'm beginning to wonder if it takes an entire hockey team instead.

CHAPTER SEVEN

HADLEY

Standing at the stove, I check the timer, pulling the oven door open as I check on the lasagna one last time. I check the actual time, realizing it's well after eleven thirty, yet here I am, attempting to make dinner for Rowan like I'm some damn housewife. We didn't talk about what time he would be home, although now I'm wondering if I should have asked.

Shit. What if he decided to not even bother coming back?

He has a very particular schedule and routine before a game, I never once considered he might have a ritual after a game too. I don't even know if he eats dinner this late. I have a habit of baking or cooking when I'm stressed, and stressed is definitely an understatement right now.

Relief instantly floods me when I hear the garage door opening and I feel the tension easing from my shoulders. My ears are perked, waiting for the sound of Rowan to come inside. Lucy went down about an hour ago, so she'll be waking up within the next two to eat again. Rowan hasn't asked me to stay tonight, but I can't leave him by himself when I'm not sure he even knows how to change a diaper.

The door to the garage opens the same time the timer on the oven goes off. Rowan walks in, his hair damp and hanging above his eyebrows. His dark blue eyes meet mine from across the room and I ignore the weird feeling in my stomach as I smile at him.

"Hey," I say cheerfully, turning back to the stove as I turn off the timer. "I'm not sure if you ate or not after the game, but I figured I'd make something in case you didn't."

Instinctively, I grab the handle, opening it once more before reaching directly into the oven. I'm sleep-deprived, stressed beyond belief, and distracted by Rowan coming home that I don't even stop to grab one of the potholders.

"Shit," I mutter, sucking in a sharp breath as I quickly pull my hand away from the pan. My gaze falls down to my finger, looking at the redness already blossoming on my skin. I don't know what I was thinking touching the pan without a glove.

"Oh my god, Hadley! Are you okay?" Rowan asks, immediately entering my space as he grabs my hand, inspecting my fingertips. His palm is warm against the back of my hand and my heart picks up pace in my chest—definitely from the burn, not from how goddamn close he's standing to me. "Come here."

Rowan gently pulls me over to the sink, his hand still caressing me as he flips on the facet, turning it to cold before he slips my hand beneath the stream. "Cold water is supposed to be better for burns," he tells me, his voice soft as he doesn't release me.

"Yeah," I murmur, not telling him I already know that as electricity persists on the back of my hand, the burning feeling virtually nonexistent at this point. The faint scent of his body wash infiltrates my senses, my body betraying me as I memorize the way he smells.

Suddenly there's someone behind me, their neck craning as their head pops over my shoulder. "Are you okay? What happened?"

He startles me and I jump, whipping my head to look over my shoulder at the stranger. His dark gray eyes meet mine and he scans my face before looking back at my hand. I remember seeing him at the hospital the night Rowan was there with a bunch of his friends, but I don't think I've ever met him before. His dark brown, almost black hair is pushed to the side away from his face. The tousled, loose curls stop midway down the nape of his neck.

Rowan clears his throat, the cool air replacing his warmth as he pulls his hand away. "She grabbed the pan in the oven without a glove." Rowan gives me a look. "You really should be more careful."

"You don't say," I deadpan, giving him a blank stare before directing my gaze back to his friend. "I'm Hadley," I say, a smile spreading across my lips. "I'd shake your hand, but you know . . . burnt fingers."

"Yeah, I can see that." The guy chuckles, his eyes bright and his smile warm. "I'm Carson Ford. Rowan told me about everything that's going on, so I figured I'd come by and see how I can help."

I glance at Rowan, scanning his face for anything that might give away how much he told Carson, but he's closed off right now. His expression gives away nothing. "If you don't mind, you can take that pan out of the oven," I tell Carson, looking back at him. "Just make sure you use an oven mitt."

"I'll get it," Rowan immediately interjects, his tone tense. I turn off the faucet, turning around to face the two of them as I wrap a paper towel around my fingers. "Ford, go grab some plates."

Carson tips his chin at him, mumbling something under his breath as he walks over to the cupboard and begins to pull out a few plates. He walks across the room, heading through the open floor plan to the dining room as Rowan pulls out the sheet pan.

"Thank you for making food," he says softly, his head turning to look at me. His eyes instantly find me, soft and gentle. "I know this entire situation is fucked up, but I appreciate you doing all this."

"It's really nothing, Rowan," I insist, smiling at him as I finish drying my hands and inspect my fingers to avoid his gaze. There's some remaining guilt inside my chest because in a way, I'm part of the reason he's in this situation. "It's the least I can do right now."

"Whatever you made smells fucking amazing," Carson announces as he walks back over. He pulls open a drawer, grabbing some silverware like he lives here. "They have a spread of food for us after the game, and even though it's good, I'm sure this is a lot better."

A quiet laugh escapes me and I watch the softest smile grace Rowan's lips. He motions for me to go first and the three of us head over to the table. I sit down, Rowan sitting to my left and Carson taking the seat across from me. He wastes no time, scooping some lasagna onto his plate.

"You'll have to excuse Ford," Rowan half grumbles as he helps himself to some food, cutting his eyes at Carson before looking back at me. "He's not as civilized as the rest of us."

"Yeah, right," Carson retorts, rolling his eyes as he reaches for a glass of water. "I'm just fucking starving."

"I promise his manners are usually better than this."

Carson gives him the middle finger and I stifle a laugh, my lips rolling in between my teeth as I bite back a grin. "I'll just take it as a compliment."

Rowan watches me for a moment before he starts to eat. I watch the satisfaction immediately hit him, his eyelids fluttering shut as he lets out a soft moan. "Jesus, this is really good," he murmurs, his eyes opening as he looks directly at me.

"Right?" Carson chimes in. "I may have to fire my chef and hire you instead."

"Nope," Rowan argues, shaking his head at his friend. "She's mine. You can't have her."

Amusement engulfs me and I settle in my seat, digging into my own food as I listen to the two of them volleying back and forth. Compliments tend to make me feel awkward, but I'm actually enjoying this. Rowan's friend is more amusing than I expected him to be and he has no problem giving Rowan shit like the two of them are brothers.

It's comforting to know Rowan has those kinds of relationships in his life, especially because he doesn't have that with his own brother.

After everyone finishes eating, Carson insists on meeting Lucy. Rowan glances at me for backup, but I know he has to do this on his own. I'm not going to be able to stay here forever. I won't always be able to hold his hand.

"I'm going to clean up, but she's in the living room sleeping," I tell the two of them, my gaze meeting Rowan's as I attempt to give him an encouraging look. I'm not sure if he picks up on my nonverbal cues or not, but with the tense look on his face, I don't think he does.

He doesn't protest and he doesn't argue, which is refreshing. Turning around, I walk over to the sink as they disappear into the living room. I busy myself with the dishes, continuously resisting the urge to look over my shoulder. Rowan needs to be able to do this himself. The rest of his life might change after tomorrow and I need to know he can handle this.

I need to know he'll be able to do this without me here.

When I finish up, I walk into the living room just as Lucy is beginning to wake up. Carson and Rowan are both staring at her like she has two heads and they immediately look at me as I walk into the room.

"Well, pick her up," Carson instructs Rowan, looking at him then back to the baby as she starts to cry.

Rowan's eyes widen. "You do it."

"You have a baby in your house and you don't even know how to pick her up?" Carson huffs, shaking his head at Rowan as he slides his hands under her, lifting her into the air before pulling her against his body. "You just have to make sure you support her head and her neck and then her bottom." Carson scrunches his nose. "She almost smells as bad as you do."

"Here, I can change her," I tell Carson, offering to take the baby. Rowan is quiet as he observes the two of us, watching Carson slipping her into my arms. "Oh my gosh, she does stink!"

Carson waves his hand in front of his nose. "Okay, I think this is my cue to go home now."

Rowan narrows his eyes at him, helping me with the changing pad we've been using for now. "I thought you were coming here to help."

"You have Hadley." He shrugs and my heart sinks at the sentiment. He has me here now . . . but that's all going to change. "I think you'll be just fine."

Rowan looks at me and I smile, my chin lowering and lifting. "He's right," I tell him, ignoring the feeling swirling in the pit of my stomach. "We're good. We've got this."

As Carson says bye and heads to the door, Rowan stays, appearing awkward as he stands next to me while I sit on the couch. I glance up at him, watching his eyes widen as he sees the mess in Lucy's diaper. "Do you want to help?"

His eyes widen further, if possible. "I don't—I don't know." He pauses, a nervous laugh escaping him. "How can a tiny person have so much shit come out of them?"

"It's a mystery none of us will ever know."

I give Rowan grace and go about my business cleaning her up. We can start easier with the next diaper, presuming it's just a pee diaper instead of poop. We're going to have to take small, baby steps if I want him to be completely comfortable by the time I have to leave.

Rowan grabs a bowl of water and some washcloths and soap, offering his assistance as I clean her up, but he doesn't dare to touch her. After I finish getting her dried and dressed, I lift her up, motioning for Rowan to sit down beside me.

"Can you hold her for me while I run to the bathroom?"

Fear passes through his eyes. His lips part and he abruptly closes them, anxiety encapsulating his expression. "Can't you put her down?"

I stare at him for a moment. "Rowan. Your entire life might change tomorrow, so you're going to have to be comfortable with her, and that starts with holding her."

"I fucking know that, Hadley," he says softly, his voice cracking. "I don't know what the hell I'm doing. I'm afraid to hold her. I'm afraid to do anything because what if I do it wrong?"

My heart splinters, his words seeping into the

cracks. "You don't have to be afraid.," I tell him, my voice tender as I reach to grab his hand. "I'll show you how to do it."

His eyes meet mine. "Okay." He holds his hands out, reaching for the baby. "Tell me what to do."

"Put your left hand under her head, but while also supporting her neck," I instruct him, his hand radiating warmth as he slides it beneath my palm. "Put your other under her bottom and bring her close to your body." He does as I say, his fear palpable. I show him how to transition her from his hands into being cradled in his arms.

His body is stiff, but she's nestled in the crook of his elbow, staring up at him as she lifts her hands to her mouth. He relaxes the slightest bit, easing back against the couch as he settles with her against his body. He would never believe me if I told him, but he looks as natural as any new father does.

"You're doing great, Rowan," I tell him, my hand resting on his forearm for a moment before I give him a gentle squeeze. "I'm going to go get a bottle for her and then I'll show you how to feed her and burp her."

His mouth relaxes into a soft grin. "You're really giving me a crash course here, aren't you?"

My heart constricts again. "You have to learn one way or another, right?"

"Right," he says, his voice trailing off, his eyes assessing me as if he knows there's something I'm not telling him, but he doesn't comment on it.

I spin on my heel to head into the bathroom before he changes his mind. Tonight isn't the night to tell him

I'm supposed to be leaving soon. These past twenty-four hours have put this poor man through a whirlwind of emotions. The last thing I want to do is make him feel like he's going to be doing this by himself. He needs confidence, he needs to be comfortable with her before I tell him.

Tomorrow, we will know the truth about his future.

Tomorrow, we will know whether or not Lucy is his.

CHAPTER EIGHT

ROWAN

"It's a match."

I stare down at Hadley's phone sitting on the counter, half expecting it to burst into flames. My heart crawls into my throat, the silence stretching between us as I hear the sound of blood rushing through my veins. The simple sentence Cole just spoke feels like concrete layering on my chest.

"Rowan . . ."

My eyes immediately flash to Hadley's. The walls feel like they're beginning to close in on me, my chest constricting as my mouth goes dry. "I—" I start, my tongue sticking to the roof of my mouth as if it's made of cotton. Pushing my palms against the edge of the counter, the feet of my chair scrape against the floor as I get up in a rush. "I'll be right back. I just need a minute."

Her throat bobs as she swallows roughly, her eyes bouncing back and forth between mine. "Okay."

Her friend's voice comes through the phone speaker,

but I don't hear a single word he says as I spin on my heel and make a beeline directly for the back door. My feet don't stop moving until I'm standing on the edge of my deck, staring out into the darkness of the night. The cool air around me burns my lungs as I inhale deeply, attempting to get my breathing under control before I spiral into a full-on anxiety attack.

My knees half buckle as I begin to bend, my senses kicking into overdrive as I drop down onto my bottom. Leaning my forearms against the sides of my knees, I drop my face into my hands, squeezing my eyes shut as I attempt to fight off the panic welling inside.

Everything is going to be okay. This is exactly what I've been trying to mentally prepare myself for the past couple days. Being a father isn't the end of the world.

Or is it?

Fuck . . .

I don't know how to be a dad. I don't know how to take care of a baby, or even another fucking person, for that matter. Hell, sometimes I don't know how I'm even capable of taking care of myself. Lucy is going to grow up in a house with one parent, a father who is gone for days at a time sometimes because of work.

She doesn't deserve this. This isn't the life she should have.

She deserves a loving family with parents who are there for her, parents who are there to raise her instead of having a demanding job that takes up so much of their time. Selena thought she was doing a good job by handing Lucy over to me, but I think she fucked up.

"Rowan." Hadley's voice is soft and warm, the

tender sound moving against my eardrums as she enters my space. "Are you okay?"

I let out a breath, not bothering to lift my head as I cradle it in my hands. "I don't think I can do this."

She's quiet for a beat, the silence encapsulating the two of us. Time stretches and I slowly lift my head, not sure if she's still sitting there. I find her next to me, staring out at the backyard. I study the side profile of her face, my eyes traveling along her jaw and up over her high cheekbones, connecting the freckles that cover the bridge of her straight nose like constellations.

Hadley turns her head to look at me, her bright eyes free of any judgement. "You don't have to, Rowan." She blinks, her expression softening. "There are always other options."

I stare back at her, completely caught off guard by her response. There's zero judgment from her, only support and solutions. She doesn't look at me as if I'm some monster for being completely honest with her in this moment. Hues of brown and green swirl in her irises under the moonlight and I watch the way they melt together.

"I don't know if I can do that either."

The thought of handing my daughter over to someone else also makes me extremely uncomfortable. My daughter. I didn't know she existed until a couple days ago and while this has all been a mindfuck of epic proportions, I'm struggling to evaluate the situation from a neutral standpoint. I'm letting my emotions get too involved and that isn't going to be helpful for anyone.

"What can I do to help you? How can we navigate this to figure out what is going to be the best option for you, but also the best option for Lucy?"

My eyes slowly search hers as if I'm looking for the answers to all my problems. "I like facts. I like logic. I like concrete evidence that can help me see clearly."

She pulls her bottom lip between her teeth as if she's chewing on my words. She bobs her head, her eyes never leaving me. "Should we make a list of pros and cons?"

"No," I tell her, shaking my head. "I think that will end up dragging emotions into this, and that's something I can't do right now. I need it to just be clear-cut."

"Nothing about this is black and white, Rowan," she says softly, her voice a gentle caress. "It can be a gray area."

I shake my head again. "No. I need this to be black and white."

"Okay . . ." She pauses, her gaze abandoning me as she laces her fingers together, staring down at her hands. She lets out a breath before looking back at me. "Let's just talk this all through then. No emotions, just facts."

Okay," I agree, sucking in a deep breath to collect myself as I dip my chin. "The facts. I'm her biological father. I have money, I have a career that pays well, I have a home, I have all of the means to provide for a child."

She tilts her head to the side, her forehead creasing slightly. "Yes, you do."

"I also have a demanding career that takes up a

large chunk of my time. I have a strict schedule that I have to be able to follow, and this isn't something I will be able to do myself. I need some kind of help and I'm not sure where that would come from."

"There is always help available, Rowan."

I'm silent for a moment. "If I don't keep her, what are the options?"

"Adoption," she says matter-of-factly. Again, there's no judgement in her expression, but there's something unreadable that I can't quite put my finger on.

"Will it fuck her up even more when she finds out both of her parents gave her up?"

Her throat bobs. "I don't know."

The question lingers on my tongue and as much as I don't want to ask it, I know I have to. It's my fear, the biggest hang-up I have right now.

"What if I fuck her up?"

Her eyebrows tug together, a frown pulling her lips downward as she studies me for a beat. "You're not going to do that," she assures me, scooting closer to me. Her arm brushes against me, soft and warm as she turns her head to look at me.

"How can you be so sure?"

"Because you're a good person, Rowan. You might not think you can handle this, but I know you can. You're the type of person to help without anyone asking. You'd give the shirt off your back to someone else in need." She stops, her eyes staring directly through me. "You are good and that's exactly why I'm so sure."

Her words sink into my soul as I momentarily lose

myself in those hazel eyes. "I don't know how to do any of this."

A soft laugh escapes her and she leans her head against the side of my arm. "Most people don't," she informs me before letting out a soft breath. "Babies don't come with instructions. You're going to fuck up, but you're not going to fuck her up." She lifts her head and I immediately feel the absence of her warmth against my bicep. "We will figure this all out together."

My forehead creases. "We?"

The softest smile lifts her lips. "Did you think I was going to leave you to navigate all this by yourself?"

"I don't know," I admit, my shoulders rising and falling. "I don't expect you to stay and help me."

Her face momentarily falls, a frown once again taking shape on her mouth, and I want to swipe it away. I want to replace it with that gentle smile again. "Let me help you, Rowan." She rolls her lips between her teeth, wetting them with her tongue. "I have a few more days left for this travel assignment and then I have a three-month break before I'm supposed to go to California for my next contract."

My heart skips a beat in my chest. "I can't ask you to do that, Hadley." I can't ask her to spend her three months off work with me and a baby. She has her own life to live, instead of staying and playing happy family with me.

"Lucky for you, you're not asking me," she says as that smile reappears once again. "I wasn't sure what I was going to do with my time off since my lease is up at the end of the month, so this is perfect. It gives me something to do and I want to help."

I think over the timeline and honestly, it's perfect. Depending on playoffs, there's a little under three months left in the season, so the timing is perfect. If she stays and helps me get adjusted, by the time she has to leave, I'll have a few months off that I can dedicate just to Lucy.

I'll have time to figure out what the hell comes next.

"Are you sure?"

She slowly moves her head up and down, a wistful look dancing in her eyes. "I've never been more sure."

———

I pause as we step back into the living room, glancing around the space as Lucy begins to stir in the bassinet. According to Hadley, it's time for her to eat again soon. A baby's schedule is absolutely insane. Now it makes sense why Nash looks so damn tired whenever he comes crawling into our morning skates.

"I think we need some things."

Hadley glances up at me as she lifts Lucy from the bassinet. She elevates her eyebrows, her mouth twitching. "I think you might be right."

"Do you have any idea where to start?"

A smile blooms across her lips. "Make her a bottle while I change her diaper?"

I grin. "Deal." The anxiety from earlier dissipates as I slip into the kitchen to get a bottle ready.

In a time like this, support is exactly what I need. A

baby was never part of my plan, but life hasn't given me much of a choice now. I know what I have to do and that's exactly what is going to happen. It's up to me to make sure this little girl has the best possible life and I'm willing to take on that responsibility.

Hadley is settling back onto the couch with her as I walk back in, bottle in hand. As I sit down on the couch beside her, her eyes meet mine and she begins to move Lucy to me. My heart crawls into my throat and a pang of anxiety strikes my chest, but I shove it away as I hold my little girl. I get her situated in my arms, popping the bottle into her mouth as Hadley pulls out her phone.

"We can order stuff from Target and pick it up in the morning, unless you want to go shopping in person?"

I raise my eyebrows, feeling the warmth of her against my side, along with Lucy against my chest. "Is it that easy?"

"Well, yeah," she says with a soft laugh, her eyes lighting up. She reaches over to the other side of the couch, grabbing a blanket before tucking it around herself as she eases her legs beneath her body. "It's not like we have to go buy the materials and construct it ourselves."

"Ha ha," I snort, rolling my eyes at her. "You're quite the comedian, aren't you?"

"Finally, you've noticed." She laughs softly as she opens up the web browser on her phone. I pull out my own and begin scrolling to look at baby stuff. Hadley starts listing off the things I need to get, noting that we need one of those little bathtubs because washing her with a bowl of water and washcloth isn't going to cut it anymore.

Hadley peers over my shoulder. "What all do you have in your cart so far?" She looks at my phone and back at me, her face scrunching up. "Rowan. Why are you looking at baby sneakers?"

"She's going to need cool shoes. I can get her a pair to match me."

She lets out a laugh, shaking her head at me. "Yeah, maybe when she's walking. Right now, socks will suffice." She snorts, shaking her head at me. "You have a lot to learn, my friend."

"You're going to teach me, though, right?"

Amusement dances in her eyes and she cocks her head to the side as she lifts her eyebrows. "I'll teach you a thing or two."

The thought sends an electrical current straight to my cock. I adjust myself on the couch in an attempt to hide the effect she's having on me with those words.

Hadley Reed is drop-dead fucking gorgeous and that's a fact that no one else could ever deny.

She directs her attention back to her phone, scrolling through baby things as she fills up the cart. Twenty-seven items later, we've checked out, the baby is sleeping, and Hadley's insisting we watch a movie about aliens. We settle back on the couch, her fingers brushing against my skin as she takes the remote from me. I watch her, curled up in her blanket with excitement in her expression, as she finds the movie she was talking about.

She turns back to me, her soft hazel eyes meeting mine. "Ready?"

I think she's going to teach me more than a thing or two . . .

"Ready when you are."

———

It's in the middle of the night when Lucy wakes up again. Soft sounds come from the bassinet beside the couch and it shakes from her movement as she begins to shift on the tiny mattress. I slowly sit up, glancing at Hadley who's softly snoring on the other side of the couch.

Neither of us planned on falling asleep on the couch, but after we settled down for a movie, it wasn't long before both of us were sleeping. I'm not sure who went down faster, but seeing her now and the fact that she's dead to the world, I can't wake her up.

She's exhausted and she's been doing so much to help me already. Nervousness rolls in my stomach as I look at the bassinet again, hearing Lucy making louder sounds that border on the edge of a cry.

I swallow back my anxiety, knowing I have to do this. I have to do this for myself and for Lucy. Not knowing she was alive until a few days ago has been a complete mindfuck. The idea of settling down always gave me hives and relationships were always off the table. Kids were definitely never part of my plan, yet here I am now . . . a single dad to a little girl that I didn't even know existed.

Rising from the couch, careful not to disturb Hadley, I cover the short distance to the bassinet. My palms feel sweaty as I stare down at Lucy for a moment, careful as I begin to pick her up. The last thing I want to do is anything wrong, and I can't help but feel like I'm going to break her.

She's so small and feels so fragile, yet as I lift her into my arms, I can't help but feel a calming sense of comfort washing over me. I hold her close to my chest, my hand finding her diaper as I remember that was one of the steps Hadley said.

"Always check to see if she needs to be changed or needs a bottle. Those are the two most important things with a baby and are usually the cause of their distress."

Holding Lucy, I walk her over to the small changing area we have set up and do my best job at trying to change her diaper. It's late in the middle of the night and my memory feels fuzzy, but I try to follow everything that Hadley showed me earlier.

Lucy seems content with how I do it and she shoves her hand into her mouth as I lift her back into my arms. I changed her diaper and now it's time for a bottle. Glancing back at the couch, a soft smile lifts my lips as I see Hadley still sleeping peacefully.

I take Lucy into the kitchen and stand along the counter, holding her in one arm as I try to make a bottle with the other. It's a challenge but I hold her close to me, careful not to hurt her. I have one job now and it's making sure this little girl is always safe.

I'm all she has, so I need to make sure I'm the best thing for her.

After fixing the bottle, I carry Lucy and the bottle back into the living room and settle down on the couch with her tucked against me. Her mouth opens immediately as I bring the nipple of the bottle to her lips, and I watch in amazement as she starts to drink the formula.

I think the shock is starting to wear off and I'm accepting of what this is. This is my future now—Lucy is my future and my main concern. She's counting on me to give her the best life I possibly can.

"You're amazing," I murmur, my eyes scanning her face. I can't believe I helped to make her. She's a product of me, carrying my DNA. The thought alone is mind-blowing.

Lucy's eyes blink as she stares up at my face in wonderment. My heart feels like it grows three sizes inside my chest as a warm feeling of contentment encapsulates me. I'm equal parts terrified while also excited to see what the future has in store for both of us.

It doesn't take her long to finish her bottle and I throw the burp cloth over my shoulder, positioning her with her chest against my collarbone as I begin to tap on her back. She lets out a few hearty belches that have me chuckling to myself before I move her back into my arms.

I get her settled back against me, tucked into the crook of my elbow as I stare back down at her again. She fits perfectly in my arm and I lift my free hand to gently stroke the sides of her face.

"I'm sorry I didn't know about you sooner," I murmur, my voice barely audible, but she stares up at me like she knows what I'm saying. "If I would have, I'd have been there the moment you were born."

Lucy's lips part and she lets out the softest sound, almost like a coo. I'm not sure it's intentional, but I'll let myself be delusional for a little bit.

"I promise to do right by you," I murmur, my finger trailing over her nose before I bring my hand down to give her body more support. "I promise I will protect you and take care of you until I leave this world."

The promise feels so definitive, but I feel it deep inside my soul. Lucy deserves everything in the world and I plan to deliver on that. I'll rope the moon and wrangle the stars if that's what she needs.

A smile spreads across her lips, her chubby cheeks lifting as her eyes begin to roll back, her eyelids falling shut. I leave her in my arms for a little while longer, soaking up the quietness of the moment with her in my arms.

My little girl.

The one who is now my whole world . . .

CHAPTER NINE

HADLEY

Rowan stares down at me, his duffle bag in his left hand as I put a breakfast sandwich in his right one. "What's this?"

I stifle a sheepish grin, shrugging with indifference. "I figured you could use some carbs this morning." A frown instantly creeps onto my lips. "You don't have to eat it if you don't want it."

His eyebrows tug downward. "What? No, this is perfect." He smiles at me, his eyes scanning my face as my expression relaxes. "I usually try to eat something before we get on the plane, but it normally ends up being something I can get on the way because I never give myself enough time to make something."

"Well, I guess I saved you a stop this morning."

Something falters in his gaze, something unreadable passing through his dark blue irises. "You did." He dips his chin slowly, his lips parting as if he's going to say something else, but he quickly closes them as he glances around the room at the dozen stacked boxes from our order he picked up this morning. "Are you sure you're going to be okay here with Lucy while I'm gone?"

A smile dances across my face. "Of course. It seems like you're not really leaving me alone anyways."

Rowan asked me this morning if I minded if he gave my number to Nova and her best friend, Riley, just in case I need back up. Nova started a group chat with the three of us immediately and already made plans to stop by this afternoon.

"It just feels like such a fucked-up thing to do, leaving right now," he says softly, glancing down at Lucy in my arms. "I don't know how Coach would feel about it, but I could ask for a leave of absence for personal matters."

"Hey. No." He looks back up to me and I reach for his arm, giving his wrist a gentle squeeze. "This is your job. This is how you pay your bills and how you are going to provide for her. I promise you, we will be fine. Nova and Riley are going to be stopping by later this afternoon and everything will be good."

He slowly tips his chin, still not looking convinced. "I know you can handle it without me," he tells me, his eyes searching mine. "I just don't like the thought of you not having anyone here in case you need something."

"Not all of us are terrified of babies, Ro," I laugh softly. "You have a whole goddamn village. We got this."

After his run to the store this morning, he called and made an appointment with the pediatrician for Lucy tomorrow morning. I volunteered to take her since he won't be here, which he was extremely thankful for. He also set up a babysitter for when I have to work, so we have every single base covered.

"Okay," he half whispers, looking back at the baby and me. He'll be on the road for the next week for a string of away games. "Well, I guess I'm going to go then."

"You should before you're late," I tell him, pushing away the worry that tickles in the pit of my stomach. I have plenty of experience with babies, so I know I have this. I know I can do this. "Have a safe flight, a safe trip, and you'd better make sure you don't let those pucks get in the net," I tell him, a grin pulling on my lips as I point my finger at him.

"Whatever you say, outlaw." He chuckles with amusement. "But only because you told me not to."

Rowan's eyes drop down to Lucy and he inches closer, his face lowering to hers. She stares up at him, her eyes wide, mouth falling open. "Bye, little Lucy," he says softly, his hand lifting to stroke the side of her cheek. "Be good for Hadley until I get home. I'll be back as soon as I can."

He turns his head, looking up at me, and he's so incredibly close, I can smell a hint of mint from his toothpaste. My eyes trace the vein-like lines around his pupils. "She can't understand me, can she?"

I laugh quietly, shaking my head at him. "No, but it's the sound of your voice that is most important. As her vision gets better, she'll be able to recognize you just from seeing you, but it's important for her to hear you now."

His gaze latches onto me for two heartbeats and I'm momentarily lost in those blue orbs. Damn him for being so attractive. And damn him for having a baby, because seeing him with her is literally melting my heart.

Rowan turns his head to look back at Lucy. "I hate having to leave you, but I know Hadley will take the very best care of you." He lowers his lips to her forehead, kissing her gently. "I love you, little Luce, and I'll see you in a few days."

He straightens his body back upright, his gaze landing on me once more. He stays for a moment longer, as if he doesn't want to leave, before he pulls himself away. I watch him as he disappears through the house, the sound of the door shutting behind him as he enters the garage.

I look down at Lucy in my arms and she stares back at me, her eyes roaming across my face. "Looks like it's just the two of us." Her nose crinkles, and she moves around in my arms, lifting her little arms to stretch her body. Her mouth opens with an exaggerated yawn and I find myself doing the same.

"Good idea," I smile at her, glancing at the various boxes of things and back out at the living room. "We'll take a nap and then tackle the nursery."

———

"I don't know how the hell he knows where anything is in his toolbox."

I glance up at Riley as she walks back into the room

with two different screwdrivers. I lift an eyebrow at her as I hand Nova one of the slats for the crib. "Believe it or not, I haven't looked in his toolbox yet."

Nova snorts and I realize there's definitely an unintended innuendo hanging in that sentence. "Give it some time."

"Yeah, right." I laugh, shaking my head at her. The two of them came over a few hours ago and we immediately got to working on putting the furniture together. The furniture that Rowan specifically told me not to touch.

We ran out of time this morning to get things put together before he left and he told me he would do it when he got home. He felt guilty leaving without having Lucy's nursery set up, but I assured him we would be fine. I didn't tell him my plans of doing it anyway, but what he doesn't know won't hurt him.

"How is he adjusting to this?" Nova asks as we finish up the crib, both of us rising to our feet as we carry it over to the wall. It's a crib with a changing table attached to it, so that's one less piece of furniture we need to construct.

"As well as anyone can adjust to something like this," I tell her, taking the crib mattress from Riley as she slides it across the wood floor to me. She adjusts the baby carrier strapped around her body, her son's little head rolling to the side as he readjusts against her chest.

The room is quite the sight right now, but it's coming together. We now have the crib all put together, and Nova and I managed to carry the glider into the room and tucked it in the corner. We have the dresser half put together and then that's it for now. It's not much but it's a start for the little one.

Posey, Nova's daughter, sits in the center of the room, reading a book upside down to Lucy as she sleeps on the mat we got her for the floor.

"He's going to be a great dad," Riley says as she runs her hand over Theo's head. "He has such a big, soft heart." She smiles, her gaze meeting mine as Nova and I start back on the dresser. "I overheard him talking to Nash one day about how he never wanted to go through what we went through." She pauses, a wave of pain washing through her eyes. "After Theo's traumatic birth, I think it really scared all the guys about having kids."

"Oh, yeah," Nova bobs her head up and down. "Lincoln's going to be like a damn helicopter when we decide to have babies."

"At least Rowan doesn't have to go through any of the birth process," I chime in, shrugging innocently as the two of them look at me. "I mean, that part is already over."

Riley chuckles. "This is true. I'm not so sure he wanted kids, but I think this will be good for him." She smiles at me as Nova and I flip the dresser over. "He's lucky to have you here to help him."

"Are you planning on staying here with him full-time?" Nova asks me as we move the dresser to the other wall. Riley walks over with a stack of little baby clothes and we begin to fill the drawers.

"I'm not sure yet," I admit, the thought idling in the back of my mind. "My lease is up in two weeks and I didn't plan on staying, so I need to see if I can extend my lease. I have three months until my next travel assignment, so I need to figure out what I'm going to do."

Rowan told me to take the guest room beside Lucy's nursery, so I put my bag in there before the girls got here earlier. I've spent the past few nights on his couch, so it feels weird to occupy an entire bedroom. I think he meant for me to use it just while he's away, but I don't know. I have my own apartment, but my lease will be up soon and I'm not sure what my plans will be after this.

Originally, I planned on continuing to travel. After feeling so stuck for so many years in Cedar Ridge, I just wanted to see what else the rest of the world has to offer.

"I'm sure he'll just tell you to stay here," Riley says as she lifts Theo from the carrier and unstraps it from her body. "It would honestly make the most sense."

"It does," Nova adds, finishing up the drawers before turning back to me. A soft smile lifts her lips. "Rowan's going to need all the help he can get and I think you might be the perfect person for the job."

I let out a laugh, settling down on the floor in front of Posey and Lucy. "I didn't think my nursing career would have me turning into being someone's nanny."

"Sometimes life takes the most unexpected turns," Riley tells me, the glider shifting as she sits down to nurse Theo. "Enjoy the ride, girl."

CHAPTER TEN

ROWAN

"Coach, can I talk to you?"

We're all filing off the ice after our morning skate and I know I need to bring this up with him. My life is changing significantly with having a baby and while it shouldn't affect my work life, I still need him to know in case there's an emergency or anything comes up.

Lucy is my top priority, over everything.

Coach Landry glances at me, cocking an eyebrow without a smile. "Come with me, Taylor."

The rest of the guys head into the locker room and I follow after Coach Landry, stepping into a separate hallway so we're out of earshot. He heads farther down the hall, just for good measure, before he turns around to face me.

"What's going on?"

I swallow roughly, my nose scrunching as I suck in a breath. "I've had some changes in my personal life that I wanted to make you aware of."

Coach gives me a blank stare. "I don't particularly care about your personal life unless it affects your position as a goalie." His face is like stone. "Is it going to affect your ability to work?"

"It shouldn't, but there's always a chance there could be an emergency." I pause, letting out a breath. "I'm also not sure if it would gain any media attention or not."

He looks less than pleased. "What's going on, Taylor?"

"I've recently found out I have an infant daughter and she's been left under my care while I try to get custody of her."

Coach Landry stares at me, his lips parting, his eyebrows pulling together. "How the hell did you end up with a baby?" He lets out a ragged breath, shaking his head. "You know what, forget I asked that. I don't even want to know."

"It's complicated."

"Yeah, I'm sure," he deadpans, his jaw working the muscle along his jawline. "I will let the general manager know and anyone else who needs to be informed of this. Like everyone else, you will have any needed family privileges, but as I'm sure you know, this is a job, so you have to leave your home life at the door when you get here."

"Yes, sir." I duck my chin in agreement. I know how this goes, even if I've never experienced it myself. However, even though this is a job, they do make exceptions if there is an emergency or anything like that.

Coach Landry's chest rises and falls as he lets out a sigh. "We need you here, Taylor. So whatever support you need, we are here to help you." He pauses, his lips pursing. "Do you need a babysitter at all? My daughter Mia has been helping out some of the families when they need someone to watch their kids."

"Is she done with college already?"

"I'm not sure what she's doing," he tells me, shaking his head. "She finished her bachelor's degree, but now she doesn't know what she wants to do." He tilts his head. "We're not here to talk about her, though, unless you need help with babysitting."

"I'm going to just go ahead and be honest with you. I got her number from Nova, who's actually helping me out a bit while we're away right now."

He gives me a look that I can't quite decipher. "Okay." He motions for the two of us to head back down the hallway, to where the rest of the guys are. "Well, if you need anything else, you know where to find me."

"Thanks, Coach," I tell him, holding my hand out to shake his. I'm a bit surprised by his offer, but his hot and coldness isn't unusual. He's extremely hard to read and borders on the line of being a full-time grump, but every now and then, he has a habit of surprising you.

Coach Landry releases my hand and I watch him disappear before heading into the locker room. All heads turn to look at me, almost as if they're waiting for me to announce that I was in some kind of trouble or something.

Carson's gaze meets mine and his brows pinch together with concern.

This isn't how I planned on telling everyone the truth, but here we are.

"I'm not in trouble, guys." I chuckle, raising my hands up as I start to walk over to my spot. "You're all still stuck with me."

"Thank fucking God!" one of our third-line wingers exclaims.

"What did Daddy Landry have to say then?" one of the other guys asks.

I don't sit down, shifting my weight on my feet as I glance around the room at all the guys. Carson, Lincoln, and Nash all know the truth. No one else does.

Fuck.

"I needed to tell him about my daughter in case anything ever happens or I need any time off."

The room goes silent and I want the ground to swallow me whole. Caleb is the first to look at me. "Since when do you have a kid?"

"Since a few days ago when I found out about her." I let out a breath, shaking my head. "Look, I don't want to go into any further detail, but I just wanted to let you guys know so no one is in the dark."

"Congrats," our backup goalie says as he walks over to me, slapping his hand on my shoulder. "Daddy Rowan."

A nervous laugh escapes me before the room breaks out in excited chatter. At the end of the day, the guys all only care about what is good for each of us. They're here to offer their support without any judgement at all.

I catch Lincoln's eye and he gives me a nod of approval.

I jerk my chin back at him before settling down on the bench as everyone falls back into a conversation that doesn't center around me and my drama. It feels good to get it off my chest, like I'm not having to hide it anymore.

These guys are all my family and an important part of my life.

Just like Lucy.

HADLEY

Holding my phone in front of Lucy, I show her sleeping form to Rowan before turning the screen back to me. "See. She's still alive and the house is still standing."

Rowan's forehead creases. "Is she in a crib?" His eyes flash to me and he lifts his eyebrows at me. "I told you to leave all of it and I would get it when I got home."

A smile tugs on the corners of my lips as I stare back at him through the screen. He's lying on the white sheets in the hotel bed, his hair damp and tousled from the shower. My eyes travel down his throat, lingering on the thin white gold chain around his neck before traveling along his collarbones.

He isn't wearing a shirt and I'm momentarily distracted. I can't see his fully bare chest, but I can see the tops of his pecs. I shouldn't be looking at my ex's brother like this, but goddamn, it's hard not to. He's always been the more attractive one and the kinder of the two, but Rowan Taylor has always and will always be unavailable.

My relationship with his brother wasn't something I really planned on happening. We had been friends growing up and at one point we crossed that line where things shifted into a relationship. We became exclusive and I just wanted to help Beau more than anything. After watching him struggle for so many years, I just wanted to see him happy.

I knew I'd never be the one who could fully do that for him, but it was worth a try.

"Hadley."

Rowan's chiseled face comes back into focus and his eyes are narrowed on me. "Are you okay?"

"Yeah," I tell him, a nervous laugh escaping me as I rub the back of my neck, not bothering to divulge my thoughts to him. "Sorry. I know you said not to put the stuff together, but it needed to be done. The girls helped me earlier and it was actually pretty easy."

"Can I see it?"

"Nope." I shake my head at him, a mischievous grin dancing across my lips. "You can see it when you get home."

He stares at me for a moment, his lips twitching as he shakes his head at me. "Now, that's not fair. You're really going to make me wait that long?"

I slowly move my phone away from my face, moving it in a sweeping motion around the room. It ends up being a blur, a whirlwind of sorts before my face is back in the center of the screen. "There." I give him a smile of satisfaction. "You got a little preview now instead."

"Preview, my ass," he huffs, his nostrils blowing wide as amusement infiltrates the depths of his blue eyes. "More like a tease."

"I'm sure you're not used to that, huh?"

As soon as the words fall from my lips, I want to take them back. My eyes widened slightly as Rowan's darken. Something unreadable settles in his expression, his eyes lock on me. I want the floor to swallow me whole. Heat creeps up my neck, spreading across my cheeks.

"What do you mean by that?"

Goddammit. "Um, I don't know," I quickly say, attempting to recover from sheer embarrassment, but my efforts are futile. "I didn't mean anything by it."

He dips his head to the side, his eyes hooded, though his stare doesn't waver. "I'm so not sure I believe you."

"It literally meant nothing, Rowan. You just seem like the kind of guy who's probably used to getting what he wants instead of being teased."

What the fuck.

Someone needs to slap duct tape over my mouth because clearly I don't know how to shut the fuck up.

"Hm," he murmurs, tilting his head to the side as he assesses me through the screen. He lifts his hand and pinches his necklace between his forefinger and thumb. My gaze drops down, watching the way he drags his fingers along it. Something about the movement has me transfixed, my breath hitching as I watch him move them back and forth.

The sound of his throat clearing pulls my attention away from his necklace, my eyes immediately flashing to his. His mouth twitches, a smirk lifting the corner. "I'll let you go so you can get some sleep."

It takes a second for my mind to register what he's even talking about. They flew into a different time zone, so he's two hours behind us right now. I look at the time on my phone, ignoring the heat traveling across my face, realizing it's close to midnight.

I have to get up at five tomorrow morning and Mia, Rowan's coach's daughter, will be here at six to watch Lucy while I'm at work.

"Yeah, I should probably do that."

I don't know what the hell is wrong with my brain tonight. It must be a combination of sleep deprivation and exhaustion. Regardless of what it is, I think I should keep FaceTiming to a minimum with Rowan. Or at least keep our conversations focused only on Lucy.

"Thank you again for helping me and taking care of Lucy," Rowan says softly, his gaze penetrating mine through the phone screen. I watch his mouth move, the smile that lands on his lips causing my heart to skip a beat. "Sweet dreams, outlaw."

CHAPTER ELEVEN
ROWAN

My gaze is focused on the player who's heading straight toward me. From the edges of my vision, I see two defensemen both skating backward, each of them moving their sticks in an effort to deter the center from getting any closer. Time slows down and everything moves in slow motion, but in reality, this is all happening within fractions of a second.

There's less than ten seconds left in the last period and we're only up by one. I cannot let the puck get past me. I can't let the other team tie this game up. We started off the season stronger than ever, but we had a little bit of a losing streak a month or so ago which has set us back a bit in points. We started off as the number one seed in our division for playoffs, but how quickly that has changed.

We're now more toward the middle of the pack and if things get tied, we still get a point even if we lose in overtime. We need all the points we can get. We need this one. These guys need to have a fighting chance for the playoffs, even if we don't make it out of the first round.

The center moves around one of the wingers, shifting to the left as I drop down in an effort to block his shot. I can't tell which corner he's attempting to pick, so I close the space between the post and my body. My eyes flick to his, seeing his gaze immediately go to the top right corner.

It happens so quickly, but I see the puck soaring through the air. My stick is on the ice, but I shift my body upward, my arm extending as I reach with my glove. The puck hits the center of my palm and I stare him down, effectively stopping his shot.

The ref blows the whistle, play stopping with three seconds left on the clock. The center digs his edges into the ice, coming to an immediate halt just to the side of me. He looks less than pleased and satisfaction fills me as I drop the puck onto the ice.

"Motherfucker," he mutters, skating past me to head to the face-off dot for play to begin again. The ref grabs the puck, skating to where everyone is waiting. This is my job, this is what I'm here to do. I'm the last line of defense and I'll do everything in my power to protect my fucking house.

Everyone gets into position and the ref drops the puck. Caleb wins the face-off, sending the puck to Gray. He skates with the puck, but the whistle blows, the horn sounding through the area signaling the end of the last period.

The guys hop over the bench, everyone skating over

to the net where I'm standing. They all come up to me, each of them either hitting the top of my helmet with their glove or pressing their helmets against mine.

Carson comes over, his hand landing on my shoulder as he kisses the damn top of my helmet. "Good job, bud."

After they all come to me, we form two lines, skating past one another as we slap hands, our fingertips dancing against one another's in a stupid little handshake-slash-high-five Carson started. This win puts us two points closer to securing our seed in playoffs, which is exactly what we needed. The entire locker room is buzzing with energy as we all head inside to get undressed.

I strip down and head into the showers, washing the sweat and dirt from my body before changing back into the suit I wore here. The home team has a spread of food set up for us in one of the rooms, so I stop by there to grab a plate before finding both Ford brothers, Lincoln, and Nash all occupying a table.

Lincoln is on a FaceTime call with Nova, Nash is talking to Riley, and Carson and Caleb are talking about the game as I sit down. Caleb usually talks to his daughter before the games, but he doesn't normally call after in case she's asleep. His late wife's aunt typically takes care of his daughter for him and she tends to go to bed early, so he doesn't bother calling when it's this late at night.

Especially with the time difference, we're two hours behind the time at home. I glance down at my phone, wondering if I should even bother with Hadley. I talked to her earlier today, but it was a short conversation. She called me while she was on her break, just to check in and to let me know that things were going well at home with Lucy. She had to work yesterday and today, so Coach Landry's daughter, Mia, was with Lucy both days.

She's in her early twenties and just finished up her internship with the team. From what I was told, she went to school and got a degree in journalism. She was supposedly exploring different options and didn't love the media side of hockey. I overheard her talking to Nova one day about how she has no idea what she actually wants to do and since she graduated, she's taking some time off to see if her heart is really in it or not.

Her taking the time off has worked out perfectly and when I put feelers out to find someone to help while Hadley's at work, she jumped on board immediately. According to Hadley, her first day went seamlessly, so I hope the same was true for today.

I stare down at my phone, noting the time. It's close to eleven o'clock here, which means it's already one in the morning at home. I'm torn between whether or not I should text her. Calling her isn't an option because she's too polite to ignore my call to tell me that she was sleeping.

Fuck it.

I know it's late, so I hope this doesn't wake you up. I just wanted to check in and make sure you and Lucy were okay.

It takes me a moment before I force myself to actually press send. She's off work tomorrow, so I'm not sure if she's awake or not anyway. Lucy typically wakes up every three to four hours in the middle of the night for a bottle, so I know Hadley will be up at some point and see my message then if she is already asleep.

Just as I'm about to set my phone back down, it vibrates in my hand and I see a message flash across the screen. Lincoln and Nash decide they're going to go wait in the bus, leaving me and the Ford brothers still at the table. I glance at Caleb, who's talking to Carson about his daughter, Sydney, so I direct my attention back to my phone.

Luckily for you, I'm still awake. The evening was uneventful, although Lucy had some bad gas, so she was a little fussier than normal.

Oh no. Is everything okay now?

HADLEY

Oh, yeah. I let her soak in the bath for a little bit and did a little massage on her stomach which seemed to help. Her schedule got a little messed up from it, so she only laid down like thirty minutes ago.

I feel a pang of guilt for leaving Hadley there alone with Lucy, not that I would be of much help if I were there. Hadley definitely knows a fuck of a lot more about babies and what to do with them than I do. I don't know what the hell I would do without her right now, honestly.

I'd probably have to give up my entire hockey career or scramble around to try and navigate this all on my own.

ROWAN

I'm glad she settled down. Thank you for being there and taking care of her for me.

HADLEY

You don't have to keep thanking me, Rowan. I want to help you. I was the one who offered.

ROWAN

I know, but I just want you to know that I really appreciate it. I appreciate you.

HADLEY

I appreciate your appreciation.

But seriously, you can stop thanking
me now lol.

I smile as I read over her words, stifling a laugh. It's clear that compliments and moments like this make Hadley a little uncomfortable, but I can't help myself. She's truly a godsend.

And she deserves all the fucking praise in the world.

ROWAN

Okay, I'll stop verbally expressing my gratitude.

HADLEY

You don't need to do anything else to express it. It's noted.

Good game tonight. That save at the end of the game was wild.

ROWAN

You watched the game? I didn't know you like hockey.

HADLEY

I don't know if I do. I don't know anything about the sport, but I figured Lucy could watch so she can see what her daddy's up to while he's not home.

Something in my chest feels lighter and I can't help myself as I chuckle. The thought of her showing the game to an infant who clearly has no idea what is going on makes me smile. It's the thought that counts more than anything.

She sends me a picture of Lucy propped on the

chaise lounge of the couch in a rounded pillow, staring at the TV. My heart clenches as I smile at the photo. I'm still trying to wrap my head around the fact that I'm a father. I have a little girl who now relies on me for everything.

ROWAN

I wonder if she'll want to play one day.

As conflicting as everything is, I can already feel the attachment growing.

"What are you smiling about?" Carson questions me as he and Caleb both look at me.

I look up at him, my grin growing wider as I show the picture to Carson and Caleb. "Hadley sent me this picture of Lucy from earlier."

"This is still fucking crazy to me that you have a baby." Carson laughs, shaking his head. "She's actually kind of cute. She doesn't have that alien look that some babies do."

Caleb raises an eyebrow at him, giving his brother a disapproving look before directing his attention back to me. "Who's Hadley?"

Carson chuckles and I resist the urge to kick him under the table. "She's his brother's ex-girlfriend."

Never mind that. I drive the toe of my sneaker into Carson's shin. He lets out a yowl, pushing his chair back as he lifts his leg to cradle it. "Fuck, that hurt."

"We've known each other for years. She was friends with my brother and they dated for a little bit," I explain, annoyed with Carson that I even have to offer this part of the explanation. "She's in between jobs right now, so she's going to help me out until the season is over."

"That's good," Caleb says, slowly ducking his chin and lifting it. "The first few months can be exhausting, so take all the help you can get. You'll adjust to everything and it will all become second nature."

"It's definitely been an adjustment," I admit, laughing softly. Caleb knows all about having to do things on your own. He lost his wife in an accident and hasn't settled down with anyone since. He's been living the single dad life, but he's fortunate to have such a great support system.

"It will get easier," he assures me, slowly pushing his chair back as he begins to rise to his feet. Carson does the same and I follow suit as we all get ready to head to the hotel. "Have you spoken to an attorney about custody?"

My breathing halts, my stomach immediately dropping. "What do you mean?"

Caleb stares at me for a moment. "You need to legally gain full custody of Lucy. If you don't and her mother decides to come back in the picture without anything in place, she can fuck you. She could take her from you completely."

Nausea rolls in the pit of my stomach. "I didn't know that."

"Call your lawyer," Caleb instructs as we make our way outside to the bus. "Get it taken care of when we get home. You have a stable income and a good job, so you should be okay. The only thing that could potentially implicate you is our schedule."

"What do you mean?" I repeat.

"I mean, it would look better if you were there all the time with her." He pauses, his lips pursing. "Or if you weren't single."

A worry I didn't know even existed follows me onto the bus and settles in the seat next to me. I suck in a deep breath, forcing myself to calm down before finally looking at my phone again. There are two unread messages from Hadley.

HADLEY

Maybe she will or maybe she won't.

But if she does, I know she'll have the best teacher.

I read over her messages three separate times, pushing away the thoughts of lawyers and legalities. Hadley offers a distraction and I welcome the smile that drifts across my lips.

I don't know what the fuck I'm doing with a baby, but I have a feeling all of this is going to be okay. It's all going to work out.

And I owe it all to Hadley.

CHAPTER TWELVE
ROWAN

Lifting Lucy from the car seat, I situate her in my arms, resting her bottom against my lap as I look across my lawyer's desk, my eyes scanning his face.

"How was your trip? I saw you guys did pretty well in your last game," he says as he shuffles a few papers on his desk.

Clearing my throat, I bob my head at him. "Yeah, it wasn't too bad. We just got back this morning, and I appreciate you being able to meet me on short notice like this."

"Well, you got lucky," he admits with a chuckle before lifting his mug to take a sip of his drink. "My appointment after lunch was canceled, so I had some free time. You said this is about a custody issue?" He tilts his head to the side. "I didn't know you had a kid."

"Neither did I," I explain, before giving him a half lie, half truth about Lucy. I tell him that her mother dropped her off with me, leaving out the part about Hadley being the one who practically baby-napped her.

"What did she leave with the baby?"

"Just a diaper bag with some things, her birth certificate, and a note saying that I'm the father." I pause, my lips corkscrewing. "I did get a paternity test done, but I don't have the results for it."

His eyebrows scrunch together, but he doesn't dive into it further. "Let's get an actual test done, so we have it on record. You can get one after you leave here and mail it in. Just put my address for the official results to come in." He pauses, letting out a breath. "We need to speak to her mother. If we can get her to sign over her rights, that will make this a lot easier."

"I don't think that will be a problem."

"If you don't want to take the papers to her, we have an appointed assistant who will do it for a fee," he explains to me, as he writes some things down on a notepad.

"I'll pay whatever is needed."

He looks up at me, a knowing smile on his face before he nods. "Okay. I'll have to conduct some interviews with friends and family about your character and ability to provide a stable life for her." His eyes are on the notepad, his pen moving across the paper. "I know you're not married, but do you have a girlfriend or anything? You being in a committed relationship will help support your case. A fiancée would be even better."

"Of course," I say with ease, my head dipping with

understanding, but internally, I'm panicking. "I, uh—I have a fiancée."

What the fuck?

Why the hell did I just say that?

"Oh yeah?" He lifts his gaze from his notepad.

I jerk my chin. "Yeah. Her name's Hadley."

He looks extremely pleased and I want to punch myself in the face. "This is perfect. If we can get her on the stand during court, this should be a seamless process."

I stare back at him as he tells me how they will figure out where Selena is and get things underway, but in reality, I'm barely hearing a single word he's saying.

And even after I leave the appointment and head to the store to get a paternity test, I'm still hung up on one thing.

The fact that I just told him Hadley and I are engaged.

CHAPTER THIRTEEN

HADLEY

ROWAN

Can you stop by tonight after you're
done at work?

HADLEY

Of course. Is everything okay?

Rowan was supposed to get in earlier today from their time on the road and Mia said she would stay with Lucy until he got home. I brought all my things with me to work and was planning on going back to my apartment afterward. Since he's home, I didn't think he would want me to stay, although we haven't discussed the specifics of this nanny situation yet.

I don't imagine he'll want me to stay at his house full-time and I don't want to go ahead and assume he will. The last thing I want to do is take up space in his home. I left my landlord a message in hopes that I'll be able to extend my lease for another three months. I'm supposed to be out at the end of next week, but since I've been renting month to month, I'm hoping he'll let me stay.

If not, I don't know what I'm going to do or where I'm going to stay.

ROWAN

Everything's good.

"What the hell am I going to do without you here?"

I snort, pulling the cupcake away from my mouth as I chew the bite I took and swallow it. "Probably the same thing you did before I came here."

Cole rolls his eyes. "Well, yeah, but that was pretty fucking boring."

Janet cuts her eyes at Cole, making sure he notices her disapproval at him swearing. He gives her a sweet smile before walking over to the table to get a drink. It's my last shift at Aston Medical Center and Cole got the entire unit on board to throw me a little goodbye party.

It's bittersweet, really. I knew I wasn't going to be able to stay here forever, but I'm also excited for what comes after this. I know I have the next few months of helping Rowan out and then it's on to the next assignment. I can only hope the people there are as welcoming as they have been here.

I've made friends here in Aston and I hate the thought of having to leave.

"What can I do to convince you to stay?"

I tilt my head to the side, looking at Cole. "They told me they're only going to be hiring internally until further notice. Tell someone to hire me and I promise I'll stay."

"Maybe your nannying gig turns into something full-time," he suggests, wagging his eyebrows at me. He winks at me for good measure and I know exactly what he's hinting at. There's no place in my life for a man and a baby, especially not my ex's brother. I'll stay and help Rowan, but it can't be anything more than that.

It's just a temporary arrangement.

I give him the middle finger, laughing as Janet now directs her scowl at me. An apologetic smile lifts my lips, but she still doesn't look pleased as she exits the room, leaving Cole and me together.

He lets out an exaggerated sigh. "You're really going to leave me alone with her?" He gives me a pitiful look. "She hates me."

"I think she hates everyone."

Cole walks over to me, throwing his arm around my shoulders. "She probably hasn't had a healthy dose of vitamin D in a long time."

Whipping my head to the side, my eyes slice to his as I try to give him a scolding look but instead my face cracks, laughter bubbling in my throat as I shake my head at him. He's absolutely ridiculous and that's exactly why we're friends. "Sex doesn't solve everyone's problems, Cole."

"Maybe not, but you know what they say." He gives me a sheepish grin and a shrug. "An orgasm a day keeps the shitty feelings away."

My eyebrows pinch. "You totally just made that up."

Cole laughs, pulling me toward the nurses' station with him. "Oh, totally."

———

After a relatively normal shift, I stop by to clock out one last time and head out to the parking lot to where my car is. Cole offered to wait for me, but I told him to go ahead. It's his and Damien's anniversary tonight and they had plans for dinner. We're already getting out of here a little later than planned, so I don't want to keep him from going to celebrate.

I head over to Rowan's house, feeling a heaviness weighing on my chest. It's weird to think I won't be going back to Aston Medical Center for another shift. Being a nurse is a thankless job, honestly, but that place was one of the best I've worked at thus far. The staff was amazing, the facility was top of the line, and working with babies has always been my dream job.

It's not easy to find nursing contracts for a specific field, so it just felt like this one was meant to be. But as always . . . all good things have to come to an end. This job was just another step in my journey and even though there is a part of me that's upset, I'm excited for what's to come after this.

I walk up to the front door of Rowan's house, lifting my hand to knock on the door, when it's pulled open before I even get the chance. A soft gasp escapes me and a gentle smile lifts my lips as I meet Rowan's gaze. His deep blue eyes land on me and I take a moment to soak up the sight of him.

He's wearing a plain dark gray hooded sweatshirt and black joggers and there's a tiny baby tucked in along his left arm.

"Hey," he says softly, his voice tender and warm as he smiles back at me. "I didn't mean to surprise you. I saw your headlights when you pulled in." He moves out of the way, holding the door open for me. "Come in."

It feels weird not just coming inside and making myself at home after the significant amount of time I've spent here lately.

"How was your last day?" Rowan asks as he shuts the door behind me.

I kick my shoes off, turning around to face him and Lucy. "It was bittersweet. I'm not sure I was ready to say goodbye to them, but I'm excited to spend the next few months helping you out and then whatever comes after that."

Rowan falls silent, shifting his weight on his feet as an awkwardness fills the air surrounding us. "I'm sure they'll miss having you there."

"Yep." I awkwardly pop the *p* sound at the tail end of the word as I shove my hands into the back pockets of my scrubs.

He doesn't speak and I count three solid heartbeats in my chest as his eyes slowly travel across my face, moving from my left eye, across my nose, down to my lips, and back to my right eye. "I have something for you."

My eyebrows pull together. "What?"

"Come," he says, motioning for me to follow him.

My footsteps are soft and light as I follow him into the kitchen. There's a basket sitting on top of the island, along with a bouquet of flowers in a clay vase. "I wasn't sure if I was supposed to get you something for today being your last day."

Rolling my lips between my teeth, I bite back my smile as I blow a soft breath through my nostrils. "You didn't have to do that," I tell him, excitement bubbling in my stomach. "If I'm being honest, I do love gifts, though."

He tilts his head to the side, watching me for a moment before he slowly nods. I can feel his gaze on me as I sit down at the island, pulling the basket closer. Inside, there's a soft blanket, a pair of slippers, and some chocolate. Just a few things that make me smile.

I reach for the vase, moving it closer to me so I can smell the flowers. The clay is so smooth and the gloss covering it makes the surface almost slippery. I lift it up, looking at the swirling shades of gold and brown.

"This is beautiful." I pause for a moment, feeling something etched in the bottom of it. I lift it higher, seeing there's an RT etched in the bottom, along with the year. My eyes flash to Rowan's and I remember how into sculpting he was in high school.

Beau used to talk shit about it, but I always thought it was pretty cool.

"Did you make this?"

He drags his top teeth over his bottom lip. "I did." He tips his head forward. "I have a pottery shed out back."

"I didn't know you still did that." I smile at him, setting the vase back down and wrapping my hands around it. I remember how his mother proudly displayed the things he made around their house even after he left home. "What all do you have in your shed?"

A smirk lifts his lips and mischief dances in his eyes. "Wouldn't you like to know."

"Well, yeah." I laugh, shaking my head at him. "That's why I'm asking."

"Maybe I'll show you one day and you can find out for yourself."

"I'd like that," I admit, looking down at Lucy as she stirs in Rowan's arms. "May I?" I ask him, meeting his eyes again.

"You never have to ask, Hadley," he says softly as he moves over to me. He moves the baby away from his body, holding her out to me. The backs of his hands brush against my palms, sending a spark of electricity, lighting up my nerve pathways. My heart tumbles over itself and I catch the scent of his cologne.

Oakmoss and cedar.

I've decided that's my new favorite scent.

He moves his hands away, turning away from me as he walks over to the fridge, pulling out a drink. "I talked to my lawyer this morning."

The sentence comes out of nowhere and I stare at the side of his face. "Oh?"

"Turns out if I don't legally have custody of Lucy, her mother can come back and essentially take her any time. Even though she left a note, we still need it to be in writing." He pauses, taking a sip of his drink. "Okay, it would be a little more complicated than that, but I would have to fight her in court for Lucy then, essentially." He leans back against the counter, planting his hands on the surface as he crosses his ankles.

"How do you legally obtain custody? Does her mother have to sign over her rights?"

He ducks his chin, removing his hands from the countertop as he crosses his arms over his chest. A deep breath escapes him. "I'm paying my lawyer to serve her with the papers and to get her to sign, but it's more than just that. I have to prove to the courts that I'm suited to have full custody."

"How do you prove it?"

The muscle in his jaw tightens as he drops his arms away from his chest. "They'll look at my finances and my living conditions to make sure I can provide for her." He moves, closing the distance between himself and the island I'm sitting at. His hands grip the edge of the counter. "The only concern is my job and how much time I have to spend away from her."

"You have to show them that she'll have a stable home life," I muse out loud, my eyes dropping down to Lucy. A gentle smile lifts her chubby cheeks and my heart warms.

"Right . . ." His voice trails off and I look back at him, only to find his gaze solely focused on my face. His expression gives nothing away. "I lied to my lawyer."

My forehead creases. "About what?"

"About you." He lifts his hand, running it through his hair as his eyelids fall shut and he sucks in a deep breath. I watch his shoulders fall as he exhales and looks back at me once more.

"I told him we're engaged."

CHAPTER FOURTEEN

ROWAN

Hadley doesn't say a fucking word.

She doesn't make a fucking sound.

She just stares at me.

"I'm sorry," she starts, shaking her head as she lets out a soft laugh. "You did what?"

I swallow roughly over the lump lodged in my throat and shove my hands into the front pocket of my hoodie. "I panicked. He started talking about stability and my job and he brought up being single and I fucking panicked. I didn't mean to say it, it just came out."

"And you didn't once stop and think to correct yourself?" She raises both of her eyebrows at me and slowly gets up from where she's sitting.

"I—No."

Fuck, fuck, fuck. I messed this all up.

Hadley walks around the island, silently handing Lucy to me. She doesn't speak a word as she reaches for the basket, pulling it into her arms as she stares me down. "What the fuck, Rowan?"

"I know, I know," I tell her, running my hand through my hair again. "I fucking know."

"You do know this is more than you just telling a lie, right?" She shakes her head at me, her eyes wide. "If they send someone out to your house, it has to look like I live here. If they question any of your friends or family, they're going to have to go along with this lie." She lets out a breath. "Did you once think about the fact that you're dragging everyone into this little charade?"

"Obviously, I didn't think about much, Hadley." I scoff, feeling like a fucking idiot. "I told you, I panicked."

"You can't ask everyone to lie for you."

I stare at her, feeling the weight of her words on my shoulders. She's right. It's not right for me to expect anyone to do something like that, especially when it's going to involve them lying to the court. Hadley will be leaving in three months, and then what?

"I will just explain the situation to my lawyer and figure out a way to prove to them that she will have stability here."

Hadley plucks a bar of chocolate from the basket and rips it open. "How good are you at pretending?"

My eyebrows pull together as I watch her lift the whole thing up to her mouth, taking a bite with no regard to the perfectly measured squares. "What?"

"Do you think you'd be able to make it believable?"

She throws me off-balance with her question and for

a moment, I'm not sure I heard her correctly. "Could you?"

She chews the bite of chocolate, swallowing as she shrugs. "Maybe." Silence stretches between us and Hadley sets the basket back down on the counter before she looks at me again. "How do we do this?"

My eyes widen. "Wait, you're agreeing to do this? I thought you were mad about it."

"Oh, I am," she concurs, bobbing her head as she takes another bite of the chocolate bar. "What you did was careless and stupid, but you panicked. I get it." She reaches in the basket and hands me an unopened bar. "If me pretending to be your fiancée makes it easier for you to get custody of Lucy, then I'll do it."

"Hadley, you don't have to. I shouldn't have put you in a position like this and I can just tell my lawyer the—"

She holds her hand up. "Rowan, stop. We're going to do this, okay?" She gives me a knowing look. "We're going to make sure you don't have to worry about having custody of Lucy in the future, okay?"

I let out the breath I didn't realize I was holding, relief instantly flooding me as it chases away the anxiety. "Okay."

"We need to figure out how we're going to do this, though," she says as she glances down at her scrubs and back up at me. "I'm going to run home and get showered and changed, and then I will be back and we will come up with a plan."

"Okay," I repeat the word, dipping my chin again. "I'll order delivery from somewhere."

"Perfect," she says with a tender smile that sparks something in my chest. "I'll be back in a little bit."

She leaves the basket and I stand in the center of the kitchen as I watch her walk down the hallway, into the foyer, and to the front door. My feet move without my brain's permission and I stop just as I step into the hall.

"Hey, Had?"

She turns back to look at me, her soft, hazel eyes finding mine from the front door. "Yeah?"

"You will be back, right?"

A soft laugh escapes her. "Yes, silly. I'll be back before you even get the chance to miss me."

I watch her as she slips out through the door, leaving Lucy and me by ourselves. An unusual feeling of dread pricks at my skin. The thought of missing her is uncomfortable. How quickly she's become someone I find myself wanting around. She's been the pillar that's been keeping me standing since Lucy came into my life over a week ago.

And in a few short months, she'll be walking out of that door again . . .

Except that time, she won't be coming back.

———

Hadley's curled up on the couch with her brand-new blanket wrapped around her body and her new slippers sitting on the floor. We both grabbed slices of pizza and took them out into the living room after getting Lucy settled in her bassinet. We have the baby monitor set up in her room, but with how often she wakes up, it just makes it easier having her close by.

"I don't think I'm going to be able to convince the guys that this engagement is real."

Hadley chews on a piece of pizza, bobbing her head as she swallows her bite and takes a sip of her water. "Yeah, I figured that would probably be a hard sell. I don't think you should be asking people to lie for you, but I think being honest with them about the situation is best."

"They won't have an issue with it," I tell her, knowing my boys. They'd be the first to step up with some bullshit fabricated story, as long as it isn't hurting anyone. They already know about Lucy and the current situation.

"Okay, so there's one group of people." She pauses, tilting her head to the side. "What about your family?"

I chew on the inside of my cheek, immediately feeling guilt. "I haven't even told them about Lucy yet."

She freezes, her eyes widening as she stares at me with a shocked expression. "You . . . haven't told them."

"No," I admit, shaking my head at her as I finish my slice of pizza. "It's not exactly the easiest conversation to have over the damn phone."

"Hmm," she murmurs, screwing her mouth. "Actually, that might not be a bad thing. You could drop both bombs on them at once. Two birds, one stone, you know?"

"That could work. If I hit them with two shocking things at the same time, maybe they'll cancel each other out."

Hadley stares at me for a moment before her face cracks. Laughter spills from her perfect lips and I watch the way she tilts her head back. The sound that comes from her penetrates my eardrums and I store it in my brain for later. I love hearing her laugh.

"That might be wishful thinking, but I don't know that you really have any other choice." She lets out a sigh and shrugs. "Unless, you want to try the same approach as your teammates?"

"I think it's better if they don't know the truth . . . at least not right now." I toss my plate onto the coffee table. "I'll tell them the truth about Lucy and when it's time for you to move, I'll just tell them things didn't work out or something." I turn my hands over in defeat. "I'll worry about that when the time comes."

"Okay, so this seems like a solid plan, so far."

"What about your apartment?" I ask her. "You're going to have to move in with me for it to be believable."

She swallows, her slender throat bobbing with the movement. "My lease is up at the end of the week. I was going to see about extending it, and I still can if you don't actually want me here. We could just make it look like I live here and then I can just come when you need me to—"

"Hadley, stop. Move in with me," I say in a rush, not bothering to think my words through before I speak them. "It makes the most sense. It saves you money, it solidifies the appearance of our fake relationship, and then you don't have to worry about going back and forth."

"Are you sure?" she asks, her eyes bouncing between mine.

"I'm one hundred percent sure." I pause, my eyes now searching hers. "The real question is whether or not you are. Are you positive this is what you want to sign up for? It's just temporary. As soon as Lucy's custody is assigned, we can pretend this never happened. According to my lawyer, it should be handled before you leave."

She stares at me for a moment and time feels like it stretches from seconds to minutes to hours before she finally speaks.

"That little girl needs to be with you, Rowan." A smile spreads across her perfect lips and warmth spreads beneath my rib cage. "Let's do this."

CHAPTER FIFTEEN
HADLEY

Standing in the doorway of my apartment, I give it one last glance, making sure that I've collected all of my belongings. Thankfully, I rented one that was fully furnished, so I only have a few boxes of things, along with a back seat full of clothing and shoes. Rowan already left with my boxes and left me to finish up.

It's another bittersweet moment where I'm closing another chapter to move on to the next. This little apartment wasn't much, but it served its purpose. It was comfortable and cozy and was my own space. Now I'm moving into Rowan's and I'm not sure how I feel about it.

I would be lying if I said I wasn't still mad at him. I can't believe he actually told his lawyer that he has a fiancée. That I am his fiancée. I understand why he panicked and why he said it, but Jesus Christ. What a situation he's put me in now . . .

And now I'm moving into his home to really try and save face.

This is all just temporary and in a few months, all of this will be in my rearview mirror. I do like Rowan. I enjoy his company and he's highly entertaining, not to mention his daughter is the sweetest little girl. I've grown quite fond of the two of them, so my feelings of irritation are a bit conflicting.

I want to stay and I want to help him, but I also know I can't overstay my welcome.

We can get through the rest of the hockey season and then Rowan will have the time to figure out what comes next for him and his daughter . . . and I'll be on a plane to the other side of the country.

After locking the door and loading the rest of my belongings in my car, I make my way over to Rowan's. He's standing in the garage with Lucy strapped to the front of his body in a baby carrier. When I told him we needed to get one, he looked at me as if I had two heads. Seems like maybe he's come around to the ease of having your hands free while wearing it instead.

"Hey you," Rowan greets me with a smile on his face as he plants his hands on his hips. "So, I'm not sure if you want me to take these things all up to your room or what you'd like to do. We can keep the boxes of things you don't want to unpack in the garage." He pauses, shrugging with indifference. "Or, if you do want them all open, we can find somewhere for every-thing to go."

I stare at him for a moment, a little shocked by what he's saying. "I don't need everything in the boxes," I tell him, shaking my head at the idea of me taking over his entire house with my own things. "I just acquired a lot more things in the past few months than I thought I would have."

He lets out a soft chuckle and he absentmindedly lowers his face to Lucy's head, smelling her soft dark hair. "Well, if you decide to change your mind, the offer still stands."

Sunlight dances across his face, bringing out the shimmering hues of blue swirling in his irises. His dark hair lays in tousled waves, stopping just above his eyebrows. His eyes scan my face before glancing back at my car. I pull my attention away from studying his striking features and look back to the vehicle.

"Let's get the rest of your stuff in so you can get settled." He walks past me, the scent of his cologne infiltrating my senses. "And then there's somewhere I want to take you."

I follow after him, my strides much shorter than his. "Oh yeah?"

"Yes." He chuckles, glancing at me over his shoulder as he begins to lift some of my clothing from the back seat. "And no, I'm not going to tell you where we're going."

"I didn't even ask."

He elevates his brows at me. "Not yet. You were about to, though." He winks before walking past me again. "You might think I don't, but I know you, Hadley Reed."

My stomach flutters as I hang on to that sentence, the words swirling around in my brain. I tuck his words away into the crevices of my mind before I grab my own bag of clothes and head into his home.

My new home.

———

I look at Rowan from the corner of my eye, watching him pacing outside of the truck. We pulled up in town and found a parking spot along a side street just as his mother called him. He said he texted her earlier this morning to let her know there was something he wanted to talk to her about. Out of respect and privacy, I decided to stay in the car with Lucy while he talked to her.

And judging by his facial expressions right now, I think I made the right call.

I can't read his lips because he keeps moving, but every now and then his eyebrows scrunch together or his chest heaves as he sucks in a deep breath. From the outside, it doesn't look like the conversation is going well, but it's honestly hard to tell.

Although, I can't imagine how uncomfortable he must feel, having to tell his mom a truth and a lie.

Grabbing onto the backs of the front seats, I lurch myself into the back seat as I hear Lucy beginning to make noise. She's awake and looking around with those bright eyes. I stare at her in wonderment, completely amazed by this little person.

In my line of work, I usually only get to see the babies for the first few days and then they're sent on their way with their families. I first started working in the NICU before I went into travel nursing and that was a completely different experience. The babies there were always so sick and even if they did get to go home, most times they still had a lot of challenges to overcome.

But then there's Lucy . . . sweet little Lucy Taylor.

Her hair is as dark as her father's and her eyes look like they might be the same color, but it's still too early to tell. There's a pang of guilt in my chest, striking my heart like a fatal blow at the thought of not being around to watch her grow and see her transform.

She's going to be her father's little mini-me.

A few minutes pass and Rowan walks back over to the truck, tucking his phone in his front pocket. He moves to the back first, getting out the stroller while I get Lucy covered back up. He comes to the door and pulls it open, watching me for a moment before lifting the car seat out and setting it into the jogging stroller.

I crawl back into the front seat, grabbing my purse before half stumbling out onto the sidewalk. A ghost of a smile drifts across Rowan's lips and he ducks his head to murmur something to Lucy before we fall in step with one another.

"Sorry that took so long," he says softly as we dodge a small group of people waiting outside of a cafe. "She didn't take the news very well."

I glance at him, offering him an apologetic smile. "I'm sorry, Rowan. I'm sure it's a lot for her to try and process right now." I pause for a moment, my footsteps halting as he turns toward a store. I look up at the sign, reading the name but not fully paying attention to it. "Did you tell her about us?"

He inclines his head, pulling open the door for me to go in first. I take the stroller from him, pushing Lucy into the store as he follows us. "She was pissed. She now thinks I've kept the whole relationship a secret from her and she thinks we're moving too fast."

I stare at him for a moment, my face cracking as laughter spills from my lips. "Dear God, if only she knew."

Rowan chuckles before dragging his teeth over his plump bottom lip. "She has no idea, but that's fine. She believed me, even if she wasn't happy about it." I watch him for a moment as he lifts his hand and drags it through his hair. "She has to look at her schedule, but she wants to come visit within the next few weeks."

My stomach falls onto the floor. "What?"

He runs his tongue over his teeth. "Yeah. I haven't been home since before the season started and she hasn't been here in over a year or more. We're due for a visit and she feels now is the perfect time." He shrugs. "She wants to meet her granddaughter . . . and my fiancée."

"Right," I say slowly, tipping my head as I finally take a look around the store, realizing we're standing just inside the doors of a jewelry store. I slowly turn around, taking it all in before my gaze meets Rowan's.

"You need a ring," he says quietly, his eyes scanning my face. "To make it more believable."

My heart stalls in my chest for a beat or two and my breathing ceases. "Right."

"Do you have any idea of what kind of ring you would want?" Rowan asks, his hand finding my lower back as he guides me deeper into the building. My body doesn't protest and I move with him.

As a young girl, I used to dream of one day having that perfect life. My parents weren't the best example for how a marriage or a relationship should look, so I've always wanted what they didn't have. Although, after a few failed relationships, I gave up that dream. Marriage and children weren't something in the cards for me—at least not anytime soon.

"No."

"Well, let's take a look and see which ones you like."

Rowan leads me over to the counter just as Lucy begins to stir again. A woman walks over to us, a bright smile on her face as she looks at me. "How may I help the two of you today?"

"We're here to look at some engagement rings to see what she might like."

The woman smiles even brighter as she looks at Rowan. "That sounds perfect. Come with me," she says, motioning for me to follow her to a glass case. Rowan takes the stroller, walking over to where the woman stops.

She begins to pull a few different rings out for me to try and see how it looks on my finger. It feels foreign and slightly abnormal sliding the large stones over my knuckle. Every single one just doesn't feel right. She bows her head and doesn't argue and instead brings over a small tray of various rings that aren't as big.

I look up at the woman to thank her when I see she

isn't even looking at me. She's staring at Rowan, watching him lifting Lucy up into his arms. Irritation licks my veins and I ignore the rock in the center of my stomach. I know the look on her face right now. I've seen it from too many women when they see Rowan Taylor.

Rolling my eyes, I direct my attention back to the tray, immediately finding a ring that catches my gaze. It's very simple, teardrop-shaped diamonds with small stones along the band. I lift it from where it's nestled in the velvet cushion, sliding it over my finger as I stare down at my hand.

"I like that one," Rowan says softly as he looks over my shoulder at the ring on my finger. "It's very much you."

Turning my head, I look at Rowan. "It is, isn't it?"

He looks directly at me instead of the woman who's been eye fucking him the past twenty minutes. "We'll take this one."

Tearing my gaze from his, I look back down at the ring on my finger.

The ring that means absolutely nothing.

CHAPTER SIXTEEN

ROWAN

The clay is soft and pliable in my hands as I press my foot down on the peddle. The wheel begins to spin and I slide my hands down to the base of the ball of clay, cupping it with my palms as I start to shape the vase.

It's still early in the morning, much earlier than I normally wake up, but I couldn't fall back asleep after Lucy woke up. I've been keeping her in my room in the bassinet, but every time she wakes up, it's like an alarm clock to Hadley.

She's been here for a little over two weeks now and each time I find her standing in my doorway, rubbing the sleep from her eyes before we rock, paper, scissors on who gets to go back to sleep. When Lucy woke up around six, I didn't even bother challenging Hadley. Instead, I told her to go back to bed and that I'd handle the baby.

Lucy thankfully only stayed awake long enough to eat before she drifted back asleep. She's been waking up closer to nine in the morning before she has her longer periods of staying awake, so as soon as she fell back asleep, I decided to slip out into my shed.

With everything that's been going on lately, I haven't been in here in a while and I just need it. It's my outlet. My own little hobby that's reserved just for me. It's somewhere I can go and be productive and constructive, yet I'm able to let my mind just go blank and be clear. I have all the creative freedom when it comes to throwing and molding clay.

After finishing the outside shape, I move my hands to the top and begin to slide my fingers into the clay to form a hollow area inside. I glance at the baby monitor, noting that Lucy is still in the exact same spot she was in when I laid her down an hour ago. Relief washes over me and I focus on the sound of the music playing through my AirPods as I begin to finish sculpting the vase.

Vases are my favorite to make, but, honestly, I just let my brain decide what I'm creating after the process starts. Only when I sculpt without the wheel do I like to have some kind of a plan for what I'm doing.

I'm alone in the zone with no concept of time as I finish up the vase and let my foot off the pedal. I'm careful and deliberately slow as I move it off the wheel, rising to my feet to take it to the small kiln tucked in the corner of the shed.

As I turn around, the air leaves my lungs in a rush as I'm startled by the sight of her. Hadley doesn't notice me at first and I take the moment to watch her as she inspects a shelf of different vases and mugs. Her auburn hair is pulled back in a French braid, the end of it landing in the center of her back. Hairs fly free from the braid and I smile, realizing she must have just woken up and came out here.

She slides her hands into the front pocket of her oversized hoodie as she leans forward to look at one closer. Her fuzzy, cloud-covered pajama bottoms almost drag on the floor, but she has them tucked in her boots. Her outfit is a sight to behold, but goddamn, she's a sight I don't know I'll ever grow tired of indulging in.

The clay is starting to dry on my hands and I balance the vase in one hand as I wipe my fingers on my pants before plucking an AirPod from my ear. The music abruptly stops.

"Hey, outlaw. Are you planning on stealing one of those too?"

Hadley freezes, but she doesn't stand up fully. Instead, she grabs one of the mugs from the shelf and slowly turns around as her eyes meet mine. "Maybe," she smiles a devious grin. "What are you going to do about it?"

"Well," I start, letting out a soft laugh as I walk over to the kiln and lower the vase inside. "Considering I've been an accomplice in your most recent illegal activities, I suppose nothing."

"I guess you aren't the good boy you've made everyone think you are, huh?"

Warmth builds in the pit of my stomach and I ignore the rush of blood that goes straight to my cock as those words tumble from her lips. I close the distance between us, taking the mug from her as I go to set it back on the shelf. "Is that what you think of me?"

"I don't know what I think of you," she admits, her voice soft, yet hoarse and laced with something that resembles lust. I'm aware of how close she is to me as I slowly turn back around. My nostrils spread and I smell the faint scent of vanilla and berries.

My gaze drops down to her mouth and then back up to her eyes, my own lips parting in response, but I'm cut off before I get the chance to say anything. The sound of a soft cry comes through the monitor speaker, meaning Lucy woke up a little earlier than I planned. "Shit."

Hadley lets out a shallow breath, almost as if she were holding it. "Stay. I'll get her," she offers, her chin tipping as her expression becomes unreadable. She forces a smile onto her lips, but it's tight and almost appears conflicted.

"Let me clean up out here and I'll come in and make breakfast."

The tightness of her smile dissipates and now it's genuine, lighting up her soft hazel eyes. "Deal."

After I finish in the shed and get washed up, I find Hadley walking around the house, bopping Lucy up and down as she pats her back. I watch her for a moment, admiring the ease of her movements as Hadley burps her like a fucking pro. I'm still getting the hang of things, but I think Hadley might have the magical touch when it comes to Lucy.

"I'm convinced you're a sorcerer of some sort."

Hadley smirks. "I prefer sorceress."

"You're a baby whisperer."

She laughs softly, adjusting Lucy in her arms so her back is against Hadley's chest. "It's an art, really."

I drink in the sight of her, my eyes tracing the constellations of freckles across the tops of her cheeks. "Yes, it is." I allow myself another lingering gaze before I finally pull my attention away from her and head over to the fridge. I get everything out to make eggs and set it down on the counter. "I wanted to go over schedule stuff with you then, if that's okay."

"Sure," Hadley says with simplicity as she walks around the room with Lucy. "Can I do anything to help you with breakfast?"

Shaking my head, I glance over at her as I start to crack the eggs into a bowl. "Nope. I got all of this handled."

Hadley doesn't argue. She stays in the kitchen for a little before disappearing with the baby. When she returns, she has Lucy in one arm and the mat for her to go on the floor in the other. Lucy kicks her feet around, making cooing sounds as soon as she sees me.

I'm not sure how much she really understands the world around her or how good her vision is yet, but she seems to know who I am. And something about that revelation makes my heart feel like it's melting inside my chest.

I finish making breakfast and pile it onto a plate

before setting it down at the table where Hadley's sitting. She has Lucy on the floor playing with some of the toys as she tries to do tummy time. So far, she seems to hate that position, but Hadley has been very insistent on the fact that tummy time is super important.

"This looks amazing, thank you," Hadley smiles up at me as she lifts her fork to take a bite. I set my own plate down, but abandon it as I walk over to the fridge and grab a calendar from the side of it. Stopping by the one drawer, I pull it open and pluck out the small velvet box I picked up yesterday. I take the box and the calendar to the table, setting it down as I tuck the ring into the front pocket of my sweatpants.

I flip open the calendar to this month and grab a pen as I begin to write things down. We've fallen into a bit of a routine with the way my game schedule and practices go, but things are about to get a little more intense as we get closer to playoffs.

We've been fortunate enough that we had two weeks straight of home games followed by a few away games that didn't require us to fly, so I've been able to be home more lately.

"We're leaving next Wednesday morning," I explain to her, writing all the dates down on the calendar. Today is Friday, so we have a home game tomorrow and Tuesday, and then we leave the next day. "We only have three games, but each one is in a different city and with the way they're spaced out, I won't be back home until the following Wednesday night."

Hadley chews a bite of her eggs before washing it down with water. "Okay, what comes after that?"

I slide the calendar over to her for her to see. The next few weeks are going to be a little crazy, but thankfully we have almost two full weeks off because of the All-Stars competition, the game and then a world competition that has enlisted quite a few players from the league.

"Okay, this is perfect," Hadley says as she bobs her head up and down and looks up at me after looking at the calendar. "Look at that nice little stretch of away games where Lucy and I will have the house to ourselves."

I catch the mischievous look on her face and shake my head at her. "Yeah, but what about those two weeks that we have no games? We'll still have things to do, but you'll be stuck with me here."

"I think we'll manage," she tells me with her eyes glimmering as she finishes her breakfast. "Did you find out when your mother is going to be coming?"

Ironically, she texted me this morning to give me her flight information. "She's flying in tomorrow morning so she can be here for the game tomorrow night and then she'll be heading home on Monday."

Her eyes widen slightly. "Wait, like, tomorrow, tomorrow?"

"Yes," I tell her, chuckling softly. "It will be fine. You know my mom, you know she likes you."

"Yeah, but that was before she knew I was engaged to her son . . . and not the one I used to date." She gives me a look that I can't quite discern. She lets out a breath, slowly rising to her feet. "I should probably clean and stock the fridge before she gets in."

She begins to move around the table, her legs moving to walk past me, when I instinctively reach out for her. My hand wraps around her delicate wrist, gaining her attention as she comes to a halt. My grip isn't tight, but I don't let her go as I shove my other hand into my pocket, pulling out that velvet box.

"Here," I tell her, my voice gruff as I slip it into her palm and curl her fingers around it. "I picked it up yesterday and figured you might want it before my mom gets here."

Her gaze drops to mine, her eyes distant as she stares at me. "Thanks," she says quickly, ducking her chin as I release her. It's almost as if we both forget about the fake engagement until it's right in our faces. I know this isn't what Hadley wants—and if I'm being honest, it's not what I want either.

I'm encapsulated by a blanket of guilt and regret. My lips part as she walks across the kitchen, but words fail me entirely.

What the fuck can I really even say anymore?

CHAPTER SEVENTEEN

HADLEY

Nervous doesn't even begin to explain how I'm feeling right now.

Honestly, the thought of his mother being here any minute has me ready to throw up.

"Hadley, don't hate me."

As I open the door from the bathroom, I find Rowan standing in the middle of the hallway with a laundry basket filled with things . . . things that look like my belongings.

My eyebrows pull together. "What's wrong?"

"I have to move all your stuff to my room."

My eyes flash to his, widening as I stare at him. "Why?"

"Do you really think my mother is going to believe we're engaged if she sees that you're sleeping in my guest room?" His eyebrows lift, waiting for me to give him an answer that is different from the one we already know to be true. "If we are going to sell this engagement thing, it has to be believable."

"So, I'm going to have to stay in your room, with you, while she's here." I let the words sink in, feeling something in my stomach and chest that I know I have to ignore. Dear God, I cannot even begin to consider giving those feelings any attention.

They will get me nowhere fast.

"Yep," he says, popping the *p* with his lips. He begins to walk past me, carrying my belongings into his room. "My bed is big enough for two."

I follow after him, hot on his heels as we walk into his bedroom. He comes to a halt and I let out a breath as I almost collide with his back. "I'm not sleeping in your bed."

He sets the basket down, turning around, and I realize how goddamn close I'm standing to him. I have to tilt my head back to look up at him. His eyes shimmer from the sunlight shining through the window and I notice the almost black rings around the perimeter of his irises.

"I promise I don't bite," he says quietly, winking as he reaches toward my body. My breathing stops, my heart coming to a standstill as I anticipate his touch. He grabs my necklace, his fingertips brushing against my skin as he slides the gold strand, repositioning the heart charm to the front. "Unless you ask me to."

He lets go of my necklace, not taking a step away as he stares down at me, his gaze penetrating mine. My heart kicks into overdrive but again, I have to shove every little feeling back down into a box. I clear my throat, pulling myself out of whatever daze he just pulled me into.

"I promise that won't happen," I tell him, straightening my spine as I square my jaw. Tension sizzles in the air, but I refuse to crack under it. I know better than to play with an electrical current.

Rowan chuckles, brushing past me as he heads toward the door. "Sure thing, outlaw."

There's a loud knock coming from downstairs, followed by the sound of the front door opening. "Hello? Is anyone home?"

Spinning on my heel, I quickly meet Rowan's gaze. He simply smiles and waves for me to come with him. "Shit." I grab the small velvet box from the laundry basket, popping it open before sliding the ring along my finger.

"Yeah, shit," he says, his expression unreadable as his gaze drops down to my hand. He stares at the ring with a pregnant pause before looking back at me. "It's showtime."

Sasha Taylor is just as I remember her from the last time I saw her. It's hard to believe it's been a few years. When I dated Beau, he made sure to keep me out of sight of his family, which, to this day, I still don't understand why.

"It's so good to see you again, Hadley," Mrs. Taylor says as she pulls me in for a hug. She smells like lavender, just as I remember from when we were younger. It feels like I'm stepping back in time for a moment, except things are so different now.

Rowan Taylor isn't just someone I'm admiring from afar, sharing silent glances within the hallways of his childhood home. No . . . Now I'm admiring him from up close as I help him take care of his infant daughter and pretend to be his fiancée.

"It's good to see you too, Mrs. Taylor."

"I see old habits die hard." She laughs as she releases me and takes a step back. "You make me feel old and you're not a teenager anymore. Please, call me, Sash." She turns to Rowan. "Where's my grandbaby that I have yet to meet?"

I see Rowan wince as he grabs the chain around his neck and adjusts it, but he quickly recovers. As if on cue, Lucy lets out a soft cry and we all walk into the living room, finding her waking up from where she was sleeping in the pack and play. Sasha walks right over with Rowan, watching him as he lifts Lucy into the air and hands her to his mother.

She stares at her for a moment, tears brimming along her waterline as she pulls her in close to her body. "Oh my gosh, look at this precious little thing." She trails her fingertips over her cheeks. "How amazing." She looks at Rowan. "I don't even know if I can be upset with you over this anymore."

"I'm going to go get her a bottle," I tell the two of them, giving them some time to themselves as I duck out into the kitchen. I can hear their voices as they talk amongst themselves about the situation with Lucy as I get everything ready. I take longer than normal, giving them some extra time.

The last thing I want to do is feel like I'm imposing

on their conversation when it's really meant to be between the two of them.

It takes me a good five minutes to get Lucy's bottle ready and when I walk back into the living room, Rowan immediately looks at me with a smile on his face. Lucy's wearing a different pair of pants, but I don't comment on it or ask what happened as I hand the bottle to his mother so she can feed her.

I take a seat on the opposite end of the couch and Rowan walks over to me, lowering himself down onto the cushion beside me. His thigh presses against mine, his hand landing on my knee as he looks over at me with a reassuring smile. I'm surprised by the action but I know what he's doing. We have to make this believable.

If the courts want statements or to question anyone from Rowan's life, they have to be convincing enough. We don't have to worry about any of his friends. When Rowan told them that we got engaged so he could get custody of Lucy, no one questioned it. They all get it. They know what could potentially be at stake here if Lucy's mother were to decide to come back into the picture.

His family, however, is a completely different story and we're at an advantage with them living farther away. It's an easier sell and shouldn't be difficult to convince them that this is a real engagement. And then it eliminates the guilt of asking them to lie.

Instead, it's just the two of us lying.

Sasha tears her gaze away from Lucy's face and I can feel her staring at Rowan and me. I know I can't let my expression give anything away. All I have to do is pretend. I let my eyes roam across his face, memorizing the way his eyebrows shift, the strong line of his jaw, his perfect lips. A smile lifts my own as my gaze lands on his deep blue eyes.

He's a work of art.

His face softens, his lips parting as a gentle breath escapes him.

"So, the two of you," Sasha starts, pulling us out of our own private moment and back into the living room with her. She knows how toxic my relationship was with Beau, so I'm grateful that she doesn't even bring it up. "I won't lie, this was all a little unexpected."

Rowan nods, turning to look at his mother. "Honestly, it was unexpected for us too." He pauses, glancing at me with a tender look. "We ran into each other about six months ago and one thing just kind of led to another."

Sasha looks back and forth between us, the softest of smiles cresting her lips. "When you know, you just know, right?"

Rowan smiles, tipping his chin at her. "Something like that," he tells her, looking at me again as his eyebrows jerk upwards. "Honestly, I don't know where I'd be without Hadley right now," he tells his mother as he directs his gaze back to her. "She has helped me with Lucy without any judgement, which I know has also been a difficult adjustment. It has been for both of us, honestly."

"The fact that her mother didn't tell you about her until she gave her up still blows my mind," Sasha admits, her voice barely audible as she shakes her head. She looks back at me. "Thank you for being here for Rowan and sticking by his side. I know this must not have been easy for you at all."

My breath catches in my throat, my heart stumbling over itself. "I would have never left him to figure this out on his own."

"Thank you for taking care of both of them."

Unwanted tears spring to my eyes and Rowan squeezes my thigh. I lay my hand over his, the recessed lights in the ceiling catching on the diamond on my finger as I wrap my fingers around his. Rowan's throat bobs as he swallows hard, the muscle in his jaw twitching as he stares at the ring.

"You don't have to thank me, Sasha," I tell her, my gaze finding hers once more as I smile. "It's truly my pleasure."

She smiles at me, bowing her head as she looks back down at Lucy. "Such a sweet, beautiful girl."

"She is, isn't she?" Rowan murmurs from where he's still seated beside me. I look over at him, catching his unwavering gaze as his eyes burrow holes through my own, tunneling directly into my soul. There's a warmth inside my chest and a tingling feeling trailing up my spine.

I take a mental picture of the way he's looking at me and tuck it away inside my mind for safe keeping. I store it for a later date, for a time when I'm going to need that memory to get me through the day.

For a time when I won't have him right here in front of me.

———

I stare down at the mattress against the center of the wall in Rowan's room. He's on the other side, going about his business as he disappears into the bathroom to brush his teeth. I already went and did my nighttime routine before slipping into a pair of fuzzy pajama bottoms and an oversized t-shirt.

His mother is sleeping in the bed I've been occupying. After she came and while she was busy with the baby, Rowan changed the sheets while I moved my toiletries to his bathroom. There couldn't be a trace of my existence in that room.

And now here I am, trying to figure out where I fit in his bed instead.

"I can take the floor if you would prefer that," Rowan says softly as he strolls back into the room from the bathroom. I didn't notice him at first and I lift my gaze, immediately meeting his from across the bed.

He must have discarded his shirt while he was in the bathroom because now he's just in front of me in a pair of low-hanging sweatpants. I immediately pull my gaze away from his chiseled abdomen.

"I don't want to do that to you," I tell him, shaking my head as heat begins to creep up my neck. "I could always sleep on the floor instead. Or I could just go down to the couch and give her an excuse in the morning if she sees me."

Rowan stares at me for a moment, a look of disapproval sliding across his features before he lets out a soft breath and shakes his head. "You're not sleeping on the floor or the couch," he says in a huff, although there's a lightness to his tone.

I don't move as I watch the muscles in his arms flex as he grabs the covers and pulls them back before climbing into them. My breath feels like it's caught in my throat and all I can do is watch him.

"Get in the bed, Hadley," he murmurs, pulling the covers back for me on the other side. It's a king-sized bed, so it's definitely big enough that we can sleep without being close to each other. "Remember my promise? I don't bite . . . unless you ask," he adds with a soft chuckle.

My heart pounds erratically in my chest as I weigh my options before ultimately deciding to climb into the bed with him. Rowan moves farther away and the distance feels like it stretches. There's room for two other people between Rowan and me, but I grab one of the extra pillows and place it between us on the mattress.

Rowan watches me with amusement before my gaze meets his again. "What's this for?" He lets out a low chuckle, the sound vibrating through my spine.

"In case you decide to get handsy." I bite back a smirk and shake my head. "I'm kidding. This is more for me so I don't accidentally cuddle you," I explain as I lower my head onto the pillow. "I've been known to do it in my sleep and I don't want to subject you to that."

His eyes do a slow scan of my face as a sheepish grin pulls on his lips. "I might not be opposed to that." He rolls over, reaching for the light. It flickers off, leaving me in the darkness. "Good night, outlaw," he says softly.

"Good night, Rowan."

Rolling away from him, I pull the covers up over my shoulder and close my eyes as I try to get my heart to calm down. I count my breaths, attempting to count sheep to fall asleep and pretend Rowan isn't behind me.

He's too close and too distracting . . . but he's comforting at the same time.

A few moments pass before his voice breaks through the silence again. "Hey, Hadley?"

"Yeah?" I whisper into the darkness. I hold my breath for a beat, waiting to hear his voice again. Just when I think maybe he fell asleep, he speaks .

"For the record, a pillow wouldn't stop me from getting to you."

Holy shit.

He doesn't say anything else, settling deeper into the pillows as I lie staring at the wall, eyes wide, adjusting to the dark. We both lie in silence and I'm acutely aware of his presence. I listen to the sound of his breathing as it begins to grow even, transforming into a soft snoring sound as he falls asleep.

Me, on the other hand . . . I don't think I'll be falling asleep anytime soon.

This is going to be a long night.

CHAPTER EIGHTEEN

ROWAN

We've been gone since Wednesday and I swear, these past four days have been the longest year of my life.

"Did you guys want to go out tonight?" Carson questions the rest of the guys as he walks back into the dressing room. We've been on a bit of a winning streak these past few weeks and today we won 5–0.

The entire room is buzzing and the energy from the boys is contagious. Since our game was in the middle of the afternoon, we still have all of tonight to do whatever we want before we have to hop on the plane early tomorrow morning.

Just as the guys start to chime in, my phone vibrates from the front pocket of my pants. Pulling it out, I see that it isn't the name I wanted to see on the screen.

RAVEN

Are we still doing dinner tonight?

I forgot I told my sister that I'd meet up with her

while I was in town for the night. I didn't get to talk to her after the game, but I caught a few glimpses of her face from the bench and she was not happy with the way things were going for her team. This is my sister's second season as the assistant coach for the Bridgewater Bears and she's really been helping to turn their franchise around.

ROWAN

Sure. Did you have a place in mind?

RAVEN

Yeah, I've already made a reservation for 7 p.m. Meet me in the parking lot.

ROWAN

Sounds good.

"Taylor, what about you?"

I glance up at Carson who's looking at me expectantly as I lock my phone screen and place it back in my pocket. "Not tonight. I'm supposed to meet Raven for dinner."

"The Bears' assistant coach?" Gray, one of the wingers, questions me from where he's sitting. He lets out a low whistle. "I wouldn't mind meeting her for dinner."

I look over at him as he rises to his feet, joining a few other guys waiting by the door. "Yeah, she's my sister, asshole."

The color drains from Gray's face and he gives me an apologetic smile. "My bad, I didn't know that."

Carson snorts, rolling his eyes at Gray before

looking back at me. "If you decide you want to meet up with us after, just let me know."

I jerk my chin in agreement as I also climb to my own feet. We all funnel out of the dressing room, down the hall, and make our way out into the parking lot to find the bus. I stand off to the side, watching them all file on, each of them finding a seat. My sister must be parked somewhere in their underground garage, but I have no idea where I'm supposed to find her.

A horn beeps from behind me as I lift my hand to wave at the guys as the bus begins to drive away. I look over my shoulder, my body slowly turning around as I see a black Benz stopping behind me. The tinted window rolls down, revealing my sister sitting behind the steering wheel.

"Get in, loser."

I walk directly over to the driver's side, attempting to pull open the door, which is inevitably locked. "Let me drive. I don't trust you not to get us killed."

Raven lets out a snort, rolling her eyes at me. "Get the fuck out of here." She laughs, shaking her head. "My city, my car, my rules. Get in or we're going to miss our reservation and then you're going to have to deal with me being hangry."

I stare at my sister for a moment, attempting to keep a neutral and stoic expression, but I fail. Laughter escapes me and I give her the middle finger before walking around the front of the car and climbing into the passenger's seat. The interior of the car is perfectly clean and looks like she just rolled off the lot with it.

Raven Taylor is such a type A person, I shouldn't be surprised by this at all.

"Good game tonight," she says as she pulls out of the garage and onto the street. "You played your ass off. You were practically standing on your head tonight."

I glance over at my sister, pulling my seat belt across my body as I smile at her. "Yeah, well, your guys didn't make it fucking easy." I chuckle, reaching toward the screen in the center of the car to change the music. Raven swats my hand away.

"They played well, but not well enough."

"Don't be so hard on them," I tell her, studying the side of my sister's face. She's almost two years older than me, although we look more like we could be fraternal twins. Same color eyes, same color hair—she's just definitely the prettier and more feminine of the two of us. "Look at the team you guys were up against."

"Jesus, you're so cocky sometimes, it's disgusting." She laughs, shaking her head before looking at me from the corner of her eye. "But you're also entirely correct."

"You've been doing a great job with the team, so try not to be so hard on yourself," I tell her, the seriousness hanging in my tone as the atmosphere changes. My sister is one who strives for perfection, which I think contributed to her downfall with playing professionally herself.

She played in the women's professional league for a few years before it blew up in her face. She was contin- uously pushing herself too hard and past the limits of safety. After tearing muscles in her thigh and calf, she lied to the team doctors, telling them she felt fine, when she in fact was not fine.

She hid the pain for a few games before she ended up injuring herself past the point of no return. She could have continued to play after rehabilitation, but if she got injured again, it could have resulted in very serious damage. I know it was hard for Raven to make the decision, but she ultimately decided to step down from her pro career and transitioned into a position of coaching instead.

"You do realize who you're talking to, right?" she reminds me, raising her brows as she pulls up along the street where the restaurant is. It's a dark, almost black-colored brick building and looks equally as dark inside. She lets out a sigh. "Oh, little brother. I wish I had your attitude and positivity. Unfortunately, I'll probably continue to beat myself up until the day I die."

I stare at her for a moment as she kills the engine. "It sounds like it's pretty miserable to be you."

She attempts to punch me, but I duck out of the way, her fist meeting the air as I quickly scramble out of the car. I hear Raven laughing, mumbling a string of curses under her breath, before she follows suit and meets me in front of the restaurant.

"I've missed you and that black cloud you drag along with you," I joke, pulling her against my side as I ruffle the hair on the top of her head, pulling pieces from the tight bun she has it pulled back in.

"Pfft," she says, pushing me away as she attempts to smooth out her hair again. "That fucking thing follows me around."

"No, it doesn't, Rae," I tell her, shaking my head as I pull open the door for her. "You cling to it like a security blanket and refuse to release it."

Raven cuts her eyes at me as she walks past. "Listen, bro. If I wanted a therapy session, I would have called my therapist, not you."

She doesn't comment any further as she steps up to the host and tells the young woman her name before we're led through the swanky French restaurant, finally reaching a table along the wall. I also don't bother to say anything else because I'm just glad to hear she's still seeing her therapist.

We both settle into our seats, retrieving the menus and scanning the words until our server comes over with a bottle of water and two glasses. He pours each of us a drink before asking if we want anything else to drink. We order a bottle of wine before returning our attention back to the menus.

Raven brings up some of the selections and we spend a few moments discussing food. I see the persisting questions in her eyes and I know she's chomping at the bit to get into the nitty-gritty things right now.

When the server returns again, he pours the wine, takes our order, and disappears again through the restaurant. Raven waits until he's far enough away that there's no one who could potentially be listening to our conversation before she dives in without any remaining hesitation.

"I've heard the story from Mom, but it's your turn to explain."

I've been avoiding this conversation with my sister since I told my mom about Lucy. I told her, knowing she would inform the rest of the family, even my brother who's currently in a rehabilitation facility. There were no secrets in the Taylor family, and I've been able to starve Raven of any additional information, telling her I wanted to talk to her in person instead.

Well, here we are in person now.

My movements are deliberately slow as I take a sip of my wine before diving in. I give her the entire story from start to finish and I'm left winded after I get it all out. I will say, there is a bit of relief that comes with getting it all out in the open like that.

Raven stares at me. "Jesus fucking Christ, Rowan."

"I know," I agree, bowing my head at her as I let out a sigh of relief, but it's also a bit exasperated. "I know, it's a lot."

"I don't even know what topic to touch first." A wave of emotion washes over her expression. "Like, do we talk about your surprise baby or the fact that you're engaged to our brother's ex-girlfriend?"

I blow out a breath through my nose. "I mean, I don't even know."

"Does Beau know? Does he know about you and Hadley?" She stares at me, her gaze burning through mine. "I didn't even know you were seeing her."

I don't know how far to take this lie. Raven lives in a different city. She's always been the one person I've trusted with my entire life. The one I could always confide in. It just feels wrong to lie to her, so instead, I decide to water it down a bit.

"It's new," I tell her, shrugging my shoulders. "I told Mom we had been dating for longer so she would be on board with the engagement. When Hadley and I found out about Lucy, she understood the importance of me gaining custody of her."

She tilts her head to the side. "Wait, so are the two of you actually engaged or not?"

"We are, but only because she agreed it would look better for my case."

Raven visibly relaxes, leaning back in her seat as she lifts her glass of wine to her lips and takes a sip of the red liquid. "Okay, I understand why you would have lied to Mom and I might like Hadley even more for this." She pauses, her lips pursing. "I'll be honest, it's weird because she dated Beau. I don't know her like that, but from what I do know, she's always seemed very kind and caring."

"She is," I assure her. "She's amazing with Lucy and she's been a huge help to me."

Raven stares at me. "You didn't answer my question about Beau. Does he know?"

I shake my head at my sister, the guilt layering in the pit of my stomach. "I haven't talked to him in at least a year."

After the night I found Hadley in tears, I wrote Beau off. I'd had enough of his shit and I was sick of always cleaning up his messes, even in our adult years. He left that day for Boston and ended up getting himself into a whirlwind of trouble that landed him at rock bottom.

According to my mom, he was the one who put himself into rehab and based on that initiative alone, it gave my mother hope. She truly believes he's making the right changes to get his life on track.

"You should talk to him," she encourages, her expression softening as she leans forward, placing her forearms on the table. "I was reluctant to do it, but he's been doing really well. He has a few weeks left in rehab and then he'll be moving in with Mom and Dad for the time being."

Irritation licks at my heart. "Why? So he can just take advantage of Mom and Dad's kindness a little more?"

Raven shrugs. "I don't know, Ro. I'm not saying he's changed and things will be different when he gets out, but it seems like he's trying and that's all we can hope for, right?"

My sister has been the one with the most resistance toward Beau. The two of them butted heads for years, so this change of heart with her has me shocked. She's never agreed with his behavior or actions, but it seems as though something changed.

"All I'm saying is, talk to him." She shrugs again with indifference. "If he's still the fucking asshole you remember, then write him off for good."

I lift an eyebrow at her. "Is that your plan?"

"I guess." She takes another sip of her wine. "I'm giving him a chance to show me he can change and be better. And if he can't, then I don't need to see or talk to him again."

I mull over her words, considering her advice. Reaching out to my brother isn't really what I want to do because it's going to open a box of emotions and uncomfortable feelings. We've never had a good relationship, but what if there's a chance that could change? If he's doing better, perhaps there's room for improvement in all aspects of his life, including his family life.

"Enough about that asshole," Raven says with a laugh, breaking through my thoughts as she holds out her hand. "Show me some pictures of my baby niece. We play you guys in Aston after the break, so you'd better believe I'm going to need to see her in person then."

Laughter falls from my lips. "I figured."

I open up my photos, immediately going to the album I've created for pictures of Lucy. The first one that pops up is a picture I took of Hadley holding her when she didn't realize I was watching. She's standing in the center of my kitchen, wearing a loose-fitting t-shirt and a pair of cotton shorts. Her face is lowered to Lucy's, their gazes intertwined as Hadley smiles down at her.

My heart clenches and something resembling homesickness wells in my chest.

Fuck . . .

I miss them both.

CHAPTER NINETEEN

HADLEY

Holding Lucy in my arms, I stare out at the glass at the end of the tunnel, feeling my stomach in knots. This is the first game I've ever been to and it's been an experience to say the least. When Rowan asked me to come, I wasn't sure if I wanted to. Being in the public like that, it opens up a lot of discussions.

Rowan was known to be a bachelor and even a bit of a playboy. No one figured he would settle down, so it's been a bit of a shock to everyone who works closely with him to see him with a baby and now a fiancée.

What a secret life it looks like he's been living.

Rowan ushered Lucy and me into the wives and families' room, assuring me we'd be safe there. And thankfully, he was right. No one bothered us there. The women who were in the room already knew the situation and everyone has been so kind. I didn't receive a single dirty look from anyone or have any bad feelings until this moment.

"Are you okay?"

I look over at Nova as she steps up beside me, her hand holding on to Posey's as Riley follows behind with Theo strapped to her chest. Rowan told me I could stay in the room the entire time if I wanted to, but I know he wanted us to come watch him—not that Lucy has any clue what's going on. He's transitioned into the proud father role and I can't deprive him of that, even if it means I'm subjecting myself to public scrutiny.

"I think so," I tell her, my voice quiet as I let out a deep breath. "Do we just walk down there?"

Riley dips her head. "They're about to start warm-ups, so we are able to go down to the glass and watch them. We're in a protected area, so no one can get to us or the kids. It's a safe place for families before the game."

"Rowan said we go up to the suite level to watch the game then?"

Nova chimes in. "Yeah, we have a box up there where we can watch without having to deal with other people. I had an incident in the stands before, so Lincoln's a little particular on where I sit."

Riley bites back a grin and laughs. "What she means is, Lincoln doesn't want to have to worry about her while he's on the ice."

"That makes sense." I smile at the two of them, attempting to reach inside to find some kind of confidence. These women are used to all of this, but I unfortunately am not. "Do you think anyone is going to notice?"

Riley's eyebrows pinch together as she glances at me as we begin to walk down the tunnel. "Notice what?"

"Lucy and me."

"Without a doubt," Nova tells me, wrapping her arm around my shoulders as she gives me a gentle side hug. "It will be okay. Rowan can deal with the media. Just stay off social media. The fans can be vicious, especially the ones with crushes on the players. Some will be supportive, but there will be some who say fucked-up things."

"Mommy." Posey tugs on Nova's hand and Nova releases me as Posey's eyebrows lower. "We don't say 'fucked up.' That's a bad word."

"Oh my gosh." Riley laughs, immediately covering her mouth as I do the same.

Nova gives Posey a big smile and lifts her into her arms, tucking her against her side. "You're right, baby. I shouldn't have said that."

"It's okay, I won't tell Winky," she tells her mother, bobbing her head eagerly as we reach the end of the tunnel. I can't help but smile at her nickname for Lincoln as we step out into the light. She's the exact comedic relief I needed in this stressful moment.

The cold air surrounds me and I pull Lucy closer against my body. We're the only ones in the gated area that's mainly hidden by the seats and the three of us walk up to the glass with our babies. I see Rowan immediately and he looks like he's exactly where he needs to be. His gear makes him look massive and I watch as he blocks a few shots as the guys all warm up.

Some of them begin to skate around and Rowan begins to move, digging his skates into the ice before he looks over to where we're standing. His eyes find me from across the distance and suddenly my surroundings begin to fade.

All the fans in the crowd, the people gathered around to watch them along the glass. None of those people matter. I see his lips relax into a smile as he stares at Lucy and me where we're standing. I know people are going to talk. They're going to wonder who the woman is that he's skating over to right now, but I don't even fucking care.

Rowan slows to a stop as he reaches the boards, lifting his helmet as he pushes it up over his head. Nash and Lincoln stop by Nova and Riley, but I'm not worried about them. Tilting my head back, I look up at Rowan, unable to fight the smile drifting across my mouth.

He holds my gaze for a moment before dropping it down to Lucy. I move her in my arms, holding her up to see him, the light from above catching on the diamond on my ring finger. Rowan moves his face closer to the glass and there's nothing but adoration written in the man's expression.

"Who is that?" I hear a voice, but I'm not sure where it's coming from.

"Since when did Taylor have a baby?"

"He has a baby?"

My brain starts to move a mile a minute and I want to pull Lucy back to my body. I want to shield her from the people asking questions, along with tucking myself back in the safety of the wives' room. As I watch Rowan, who has no idea of the chatter going on around, I know I can't do that.

All he can see is Lucy.

His eyes flash to mine and my heart is a puddle at my feet.

"Do you want me to take a picture?" Nova asks me, while also asking Rowan as she holds her hands up with her phone, making the motion of taking a picture.

I look at her and back at Rowan, silently asking him if that's what he wants. He pulls his hand from his glove, holding it under his arm as he removes his helmet completely from his head. We got some pictures earlier before anyone was allowed in the building, but this is different.

This is their first picture together at one of his games. The first picture of them where there are currently thousands of people around who can see.

"Sure. I'm not sure how I should stand to hold her for him since he can't."

Nova's expression is soft as I turn around to face her. "He's going to want you in the picture too, babe."

Riley looks over at us with a smile on her face as my heart crawls into my throat. I take a step backward, stopping as my back hits the boards. Lucy is awake, so I move her to an upright position, holding her against my body as I support her chest and her bottom at the same time.

Rowan is on the other side of the glass and he half bends down so the three of us look like we're all standing together. Nova smiles, taking a few pictures before she looks pleased.

"I'll send them to you and you can show him then," Nova tells me as I turn back to Rowan. His eyes meet mine once more, a tenderness settling within the deep hues of blue in his irises before he's called back to warm up.

He winks at me, sending a shiver down my spine, before he slides his helmet back over his head and puts his glove back on. I watch him as he turns around, heading back over to the net as the guys all begin to line up.

"Holy shit, is that Rowan Taylor's fiancée?"

"Ew. She's probably just another woman he's sleeping with."

Reality comes crashing down around me, but I knew this was a possibility. Ignoring the whispers from the fans, I stare out at the ice, keeping my attention solely on Rowan before it's time for us to head up to the suite.

We all knew eventually this would have to come out to the public. It's not like it's big news or anything like that, but the fan base for some professional sports teams can be crazy from what I've heard.

Rowan warned me that if people caught wind of it, it could go a few different ways. There could potentially be people sticking their noses in business that isn't theirs. The media could have a heyday with it and run rampant through the headlines, spreading rumors. There's also the potential that no one would really notice or things could just blow over quickly and we wouldn't get a lot of attention from the media.

Regardless of what happens, Rowan wanted Lucy and me here to support him and truly, that's the only thing that matters.

For the next few months, we're a team, and I plan on being the best teammate he's ever had.

Even if it ends up costing me my heart.

CHAPTER TWENTY

ROWAN

Press after the game turns out to be less of a dumpster fire than I was expecting.

After managing to cinch another win, I'm the one who ends up having to talk to the media afterward. Much to my surprise, I'm not pressed about details on Lucy and Hadley. A few questions are brought up in regard to them and I set the record straight with limited information. I confirm that Hadley is in fact my fiancée and that Lucy is my daughter.

The interview was cut short by Coach Landry interjecting and I wasn't able to answer the question about how I managed to keep it a secret this long.

And now Hadley is silent the entire fucking way home.

I don't know what I said or did wrong. I didn't even know she caught the interview, but she must have been watching it as it was broadcast on the TVs in the wives' room.

We pull into the driveway and she sits with her

hands clasped in her lap as the garage door slowly slides open. I glance at her, hoping she'll look at me, but when she doesn't, I pull the car into the garage, letting the door close behind us.

As I turn off the engine, I glance in the rearview mirror, and I see Lucy's still asleep. Hadley turns her body slightly, the Aston Archers jersey she's wearing shifting as she undoes her seat belt. It makes a sound as it slides away from her body.

"Where did you get this?" I ask her, tilting my head to the side. "Whose name is on the back?"

Hadley looks at me, reaching for the door handle. "I got it at the game." Her tone is off and her voice is clipped. "It's yours."

My eyebrows pull together, confusion washing over me. She was silent the entire car ride and now this is just not like her at all.

Reaching for her, my hand wraps around her wrist before she gets the chance to fully open her door. It slams shut and she whips her head to the side, looking at me with her eyebrows raised. "I'm tired, Rowan."

"Tell me what's going on. The silence is fucking killing me, Had."

Her eyebrows lower, pulling together in the slightest movement as her expression softens. "It's nothing."

"To me, it's something," I tell her, my hand still wrapped around her wrist as my gaze probes hers.

She falls back against her seat, my hand sliding closer to hers as she drops her eyes down to the ring on her finger. "I overheard some fans talking in the crowd tonight during warm-ups when they saw Lucy and me," she says quietly, her voice barely audible.

"Baby, no . . ." I murmur, the tips of my fingers drifting across her palm before I lace them through hers.

Heat creeps up my neck and my heart stalls in my chest as I realize I just called her baby. I clear my throat, attempting to brush past that little word . . .

"Don't listen to a fucking word any of those people are saying."

"I was trying to ignore them, but I overheard a woman make a comment about how I'm probably just another woman you're sleeping with," she admits, her eyes meeting mine as I slowly stroke the side of her thumb. "Riley and Nova both warned me that it's probably best if I stay off social media for a while too."

Fuck.

My stomach sinks, yet at the same time, I'm enraged at the thought of someone making Hadley Reed feel like she's insignificant. Like she's less than anything.

"We both know the truth. Everyone who knows us knows the truth." I squeeze her hand, my eyes desperately searching hers. "You're not just another woman I'm sleeping with. You're more than that—so much more than that."

Her throat bobs as she swallows hard. "How do you live under such a microscope like this? How do you deal with the negative things people say?"

"I ignore them. Fans are always disgruntled about one thing or another. If we're on a losing streak, they're quick to point the finger and blame someone. If we lose and it's my fault, no one talks about when defense fails to do their part." I let out a sigh, resisting the urge to pull her across the center console and into my lap. "Some can be supportive, but there are also ones who tend to get jealous because they're envious of what you have."

A laugh slips from her lips and it's harsh and jagged as she shakes her head at me. "I don't think they'd be envious if they knew all of this was fake." She pauses, tilting her head to the side. "What are you going to do if people ask questions when I leave?"

But I don't want you to leave.

"I haven't thought that far ahead yet," I tell her with honesty, my voice low as my eyes drift over the freckles across the bridge of her nose, memorizing the pattern. I want to set the record straight so it doesn't look bad on Hadley when she leaves, but I don't know if I can.

The thought of telling anyone that Lucy isn't hers just feels wrong.

Because deep down, even though that little girl isn't biologically related to her, Lucy *is* hers.

Lucy stirs in her car seat, letting out a small sound and at first, I don't look away. My gaze is locked on Hadley's with my hand still wrapped up in hers. Her palm warms my own, her fingers like silk entwined with my own. She lets out a soft breath as she tears her stare from mine, glancing at the clock.

"We should get Lucy inside," she tells me, her gaze sliding back to mine. Her fingers are still laced through mine and fuck, I don't want to let her go. I'm not ready for this blip in time to be over. "It's time for her bottle and then we should probably lay her down."

I swear, every time she says 'we,' it's like my heart forgets how to function.

"Okay," I agree, yet we still don't move. It's almost as if we're both just hanging on to the last threads of the moment passing between us. "Just promise me something?"

Her eyes slowly search my expression, the intensity lingering in her gaze. "Anything."

"Promise me you won't listen to the outside noise, Hadley. The world can be a cruel place with vile people, and you are more, okay?" I don't know how to get out what I'm trying to say and now I'm stumbling over my words. "You're just more."

The softest smile lifts her lips. "Nice save, Taylor."

I stare at her for a moment, my heart doing that stupid little skip again. When it comes to Lucy and Hadley, I'll make as many saves as I have to. Words fail me and I simply wink at her because it's all I can do with how tongue-tied I feel right now.

Lucy makes another sound of discontent in the back, effectively severing the moment.

"Your daughter is very demanding," Hadley chuckles softly as she abandons my hand. Her eyes twinkle, her gaze stays a heartbeat longer before she finally reaches for the door handle.

I'm acutely aware of the absence of her warmth and I watch her with a smile drifting across my lips as she gets out of the car and opens the back door. The soft sound of her voice penetrates my eardrums from the back seat and I close my eyes, savoring the sound as she whispers sweet words to Lucy.

I don't know what the hell she's doing to me, but goddamn, I think I might like it.

———

Holding Lucy in my arm, I slip the bottle into her mouth, settling down on the rocking chair in her room. I make sure she's comfortable against my body and I slowly begin to rock, staring down at her little face. Her mouth releases the bottle as she stares up at me. Milk dribbles from the side of her mouth and I quickly catch it with the burp cloth before it dirties her clean pajamas.

"Oops," I murmur softly, a chuckle rumbling in my chest as she pushes her tongue against the nipple, half playing with it. "You have to drink your bottle, Luce," I explain, trying again. "It's late and Daddy still needs to get a shower."

She doesn't take the bottle and continues to stare at me. Suddenly a smile erupts across her face and she lets out a cooing sound.

My heart swells in my chest as I watch her with wonderment. "You just want to give me a hard time tonight, don't you?" I shake my head at her.

Lucy still stares at me and we stay like that for a few minutes. My eyes scan her face, memorizing every last detail of my little girl, and it seems like she does the same with me in return.

"Luce, it's bad if I can smell myself," I explain, even though she doesn't know what I'm saying. Most days I shower at the rink, but today I just wanted to get home and now I'm regretting it.

She coos again, her hands moving back up to her mouth.

"If you want to stay like this all night, I won't object." I smile at her, warmth washing over me as it mixes with sadness. "I don't feel like I get enough time with you, anyways."

Lucy just stares, half smiling as she starts to suck harder on her fingers. Knowing her signs, I give her the bottle back and she starts to suck on the nipple, filling her stomach as she drinks steadily. It only takes about ten minutes and an empty bottle for her to be fully in a milk coma in my arms.

I move to burp her, but the movement causes the gas to escape her and she lets out a loud belch. She smiles in her sleep and I laugh to myself, careful to be quiet enough that I don't wake her as I lay her down in her crib.

After she's settled, I allow myself a few more moments to soak up the tenderness of her before I slip out of her room and step into the hall. Hadley inhales sharply, quickly stepping out of the way as I almost collide with her.

"Oh my god, I'm sorry!" Hadley exclaims in a hushed voice. "I didn't even hear you coming out of Lucy's room."

My breath catches in my throat as I realize she's

standing in front of me in a robe and a pair of slippers. Her legs are bare and the sharp V cut in the front makes it look as if she's wearing nothing beneath.

I notice a pink tint creeping across her cheeks as she rolls her lips between her teeth.

"I thought you were in bed."

She lets out a nervous laugh. "I ended up taking a bath instead, but I'm on my way to bed now."

I swallow roughly, watching her carefully as I feel the blood rushing to my cock. Goddamn her and goddamn the effect she has on me.

"Let me get out of your way then." My voice is strained and gruff as I slide out of the way, letting her pass me. She smells like vanilla and raspberry and the smell infiltrates my senses, immediately swirling to my brain.

She smells good enough to fucking eat.

I wonder if her pussy tastes as good as she smells.

Jesus fucking Christ, what is wrong with me?

"Good night, Ro," she says softly, just before she slips into her bedroom.

"Good night," I mumble, although I'm not sure she hears the word as her door shuts.

The sound of Hadley's voice caresses my eardrums and I loiter in the hallway, staring at her door before forcing myself to go to my own room. I want to walk to her door and knock on it before slipping inside with her, but I know I can't.

My feet begin to move and I head to my bedroom then into my en suite bathroom, shutting the door behind me. I turn on the shower, the hot water immediately hitting the floor as I strip out of my clothing and throw them into the hamper.

The glass door slides open as I pull on it and step inside. There's a massive bathtub in the corner of the room and then there's a stand-up shower. I step into the hot water, feeling the beads of liquid rolling down my back. Tilting my head back, I let my eyelids fall shut, inhaling deeply as I feel the heat soothing my tired muscles.

I find my shampoo on the shelf and work it into a lather on my scalp, washing away the sweat and dirt before I move on to my body. My mind drifts to the thought of Hadley, seeing her in the hallway wearing nothing but a robe. I didn't expect to see her like that, but now that I have, I cannot erase the memory or the thought from my brain.

I need to scrub it away, but I can't. Trust me, I try, but as I rub the soap along the length of my cock, it only grows harder over time. If only I could have my way with her . . . if only I could allow myself to give in to that temptation just one fucking time.

I don't know which is hotter . . . seeing her in a robe or seeing her wearing my jersey tonight. When we parted ways at the rink earlier this evening, she was only wearing a sweater. When I saw her in my car after we were leaving, that's when I noticed the jersey.

And fuck . . . what I wouldn't give to see her in that instead of a goddamn robe, with nothing underneath. Only her skin for me to touch and tease and fuck and please.

Thinking about her this way isn't what I should be

doing. She dated my brother and she's only here to help me get custody of Lucy. It's not supposed to be anything more. She has a career, she has a life outside of these four walls. After everything is squared away and it's time for her to get back to work, she's going to leave us.

Imagining her wearing nothing but my jersey may not be right, but she can't read my thoughts. She can't see me in the shower right now with my cock in my hand, hard as a fucking rock for her. What she doesn't know will never hurt her.

Sucking in a deep breath, I tilt my head back, my eyelids falling shut as I imagine her standing outside of the shower door. She slides it open, her eyes finding mine as she grabs the bottom hem of my jersey, lifting it up over her body, before tossing it onto the floor behind her. My hand wraps tighter around my cock and I slowly start to stroke it up and down as I continue with my fantasy.

Hadley pulls her hair free from her ponytail, her auburn hair cascading in soft waves down the middle of her back. It shifts around her body as she enters the shower, closing the door behind her as she shuts the two of us in there together. She moves closer to me, her body pressing against me as she wraps her hands around the back of my neck.

Hot water streams down her taut body and one of my hands falls to her waist, gripping her hip as the other slides through her hair, along her scalp. I grab a handful of auburn hair, jerking her head back as my face drops down to hers. My lips immediately find hers.

She tastes like mint and I kiss her deeply, my tongue plunging into her mouth as it dances with her tongue.

Hadley kisses me back with a ferocity that has my toes curling before she pulls away. She stares up at me, mischief dancing in her hazel orbs before she begins to move down my torso, her lips leaving a trail of delicate kisses as she lowers herself onto her knees in front of me.

"Goddamn, look at you," I murmur, my hand stroking the side of her face as she wraps her hand around the shaft of my cock. She blinks twice, her lips parting before she inhales the tip of my cock. A low groan rumbles in my throat, my hand sliding to grip the back of her head as she licks along my length. My eyes fall shut again, my head tipping back.

Her tongue is like silk on the underside of my cock and she takes me deep, the tip hitting the back of her throat as she gags around me. Her gaze finds mine, her eyes glistening as she sucks the girth of my dick, her lips swollen and wet around me. She starts to bob her head, pulling me in and out of her mouth as she sucks me hard.

My hips start to shift, moving in tandem with her as I start to fuck her face while she fucks me with her hand and mouth. "Fuck," I moan, the sound vibrating off the shower walls. "You're so good, Hadley. So fucking good."

Warmth builds in the pit of my stomach, my hips instinctively bucking as I tighten my hold on her hair and her scalp. She starts to suck faster, her head moving back and forth. My balls constrict, drawing closer to my body as she drives me closer to the edge of ecstasy. Her plump lips suck me harder, pulling me in and out of her mouth, her hand moving with her so she's stroking every inch of me. She sucks my cock like she was fucking made for it.

She bobs her head a few more times, faster and harder before she suctions her lips around my length, sending me over the edge. A volcano of warmth erupts inside of me, spilling into my veins as it fucks my system. It's like a wildfire I can't stop and I'm entirely consumed by it.

By her.

I thrust into her mouth again, my orgasm pulling me into the abyss. I lose myself in her mouth, spurts of cum shooting down the back of her throat. She takes me, swallowing every last drop as I ride on this high, soaring through the clouds.

Her movements slow and I open my eyes, lifting my head to look back down at her, when I realize it was all my imagination and reality crashes around me. Hadley isn't here, she never was here with me. She's not on her knees in front of me with my cock down her throat. Instead of her lips, it's my hand.

I just jerked off to the thought of Hadley, knowing damn well I shouldn't have.

Water streams down my face, blurring my vision as I release my cock and let out a frustrated sigh. I wash myself off again before washing my cum off the side of the shower wall. Shutting off the water, I step out into the cold air, hoping it will provide some relief, but it doesn't.

Nothing about this helped me in any way . . . If anything, I'm even more curious now to see how she would actually look on her knees for me. I drag a frustrated hand down my face.

I might actually be fucked.

CHAPTER TWENTY-ONE
HADLEY

I like Rowan home.

He's been home for a little more than a week now, since they have a two-week break from games, and although he still has had some other obligations like practices and appearances, he's been here a lot with Lucy and me.

I like the simplicity of the early mornings where one of us is fixing coffee while the other sits and gives Lucy her bottle. The quiet moments before the rest of the world is awake, when it's just the two of us orbiting around one another. Sometimes we sit in silence, each of us lost in our own thoughts, while the others we're lost in conversation together, musing about the wonders of the world.

He offers me the sense of security and peace I was sure I would never find in another person. Too bad Rowan Taylor can never be mine.

He took over with Lucy this morning so I could go for a run and when I got back to the house, he was busy in the kitchen making breakfast with Lucy strapped to his chest. I allowed myself a few minutes to absorb the moment, to take in the sight of him as he hummed some tune while moving around the room with her.

Seeing him with her in the tender moments where he thinks no one is watching him has my heart feeling like it could explode. There's something about watching a man with a baby that has a way of making your hormones kick into overdrive.

Who am I kidding? I've always been attracted to Rowan Taylor.

And in a way, in another life, it feels like all of this could have been real. And we would have been happy . . .

After breakfast, I disappeared upstairs to shower while Rowan kept Lucy with him. She's been starting to stay up for longer periods of time and sleeping longer at night, which I think both of us are grateful for. Although, there's a bittersweetness to it. It only means that she's growing, which is great, but that also means my time here is growing shorter.

The clock has been ticking and there's less than five weeks left until I have to move on.

I stand alone in the shower with my own thoughts, ignoring the pain inside my chest as I try to not focus on having to go. I can't stay here any longer than we agreed to. The last thing I want to do is insert myself in someone's life where I don't belong. The hockey season will be coming to an end and Rowan will have more time to take care of Lucy himself.

He has a hearing in a little over a month, so his

lawyer has diligently been working to make sure they have everything in order for him to fully gain custody. Everything will be tied up by the end of March and then I have no choice.

There will be no further need for me here.

The water in the shower has since grown cold and I force myself to turn the water off, wringing out my hair before stepping out into the cool air. I grab my towel from where it's hanging, wrapping a microfiber one around my hair before drying my body.

It doesn't take me as long in the bathroom as it did in the shower. In less than twenty minutes, my hair is semi dry from the blow-dryer and pulled back in a clip and I'm slipping into a pair of leggings and an over-sized crewneck sweatshirt. The house is quiet as I step out into the hall, the only sound I hear is the white noise machine coming from Lucy's room.

She must have gone down for her morning nap.

I walk over to her room, peeking in through the door. I see her little body lying in the center of the crib, sleeping peacefully. Rowan really got lucky with her. She's rarely ever fussy and is typically a very happy and peaceful baby. She's been tolerating tummy time, is able to roll over, and, unless she's really tired, she can support her own head for the most part.

It's been an amazing privilege to watch her grow and to see how much she has gotten bigger in the past two months alone. As much as I've enjoyed it, I think my favorite part of this experience has been watching Rowan grow. He was thrown into a situation he wasn't expecting and he really stepped up. He's become the best father Lucy could ever ask for.

When I finally make my way downstairs, I find the kitchen clean and orderly, but no Rowan. Anxiety wells in the pit of my stomach and I quickly walk around the rest of the house, looking for him, but finding him nowhere. I walk over to the glass doors that open up to the backyard and I look out at the shed situated in the back corner of the yard.

It's hard to tell if there's anyone inside, but Rowan has been spending time out there since he's been home. I've made sure to keep my distance from the shed because I haven't wanted to overstep or go into his safe place, but I have to know if he's in there for my own peace of mind.

I slide my feet into a pair of shoes and slip out into the cool air. The sun is shining this morning and it's warm against my skin, a contrast to the coldness around. It's definitely been warmer the past few days than it has in months, but I should have grabbed a coat as an extra layer against the air.

The grass crunches beneath my feet as it's still a little crisp from the early morning frost. I make my way across the yard, glancing back at the house for any signs of him inside as I reach for the handle of the shed door. I pause, knocking just for good measure, but when no one answers, I find myself turning the knob and letting myself inside.

It's warm inside the shed and I close the door behind me, my eyes surveying the space and relief washing over me when I see Rowan on the opposite side. He's wearing a pair of earbuds and he's sitting at the pottery wheel, staring down at the mound of clay on top, almost as if he's trying to figure out what he wants to do with it.

I watch him in silence, knowing he can't hear me anyway because of the music that's beating against his eardrums. He dips his hands into the bowl of water beside him, then slides them along the mound, moving it into more of a cylinder shape. My breath catches in my throat as I'm transfixed by his movements, watching the way his hands begin to mold the clay as he presses his foot on the pedal, causing the wheel to spin.

He's skilled with his hands and his attention is laser-focused on the clay as he continues to move his hands upward, sliding his fingers into the center of the cylinder he created. The movement is sensual, sending a rush of warmth to the pit of my stomach as I watch him with a fervent burning inside my body.

He tilts his head to the side, turning his head a fraction of an inch when I see his movements falter. He moves just enough to see me over his shoulder and I'm frozen in place. I can't help but feel like I've interrupted an intimate moment he was having by himself, although I might be the only one in this room who thinks anything about what he was doing was intimate.

Lifting his foot from the pedal, the wheel slows to a stop and he turns his body to look at me, wiping his clay-covered hand on his dirty pants before he plucks both AirPods from his ears. His eyes smolder as he stares at me, his gaze sweeping down the length of my body before resting on my eyes. "Come here."

There isn't a single coherent thought that goes through my mind. My feet move on instinct, closing the distance between us as I walk directly to him, stopping by his side. He pushes his feet against the floor, sliding his body back as he makes room on the bench in front of him.

"Grab an apron unless you want to get dirty."

My mouth goes dry and my brain short-circuits. "I don't mind getting dirty."

"Good," he says in a low tone, his voice hoarse. He reaches for me, his clay-covered hands grabbing my hips before he pulls me closer. I turn to face the other direction, throwing my leg over the bench as he lowers me down in front of him.

He's so goddamn close, his warmth rolls off his body in waves, penetrating my back as he scoots closer. His chest and abdomen are solid as he leans against me, my body moving forward with his as he reaches around me. The veins are visible in his forearms and hands, his muscles taut in his arms as he grabs the cylinder he was working with and crushes it beneath his palms.

"What are you doing?" I ask him, my voice husky, almost sounding foreign as I watch him squish it back into a ball. He slides his hands back into the bowl of water, wetting the clay and my hands, before he slides his palms along the backs of my hands.

"Starting over," he breathes against my ear, the sound of his voice vibrating against my spine. His body is just barely pressed against me and I revel in the way he feels with his arms along my own. He positions his head over my shoulder, his cheek light against my own as he moves my hands to the ball of clay. "Press your foot on the pedal."

Following his instruction, I find the piece of metal on the floor and slowly begin to push it down, the sound of the wheel spinning filling the room as I feel the cool clay beginning to move. Rowan keeps his palms plastered to the backs of my hands, his fingers spreading mine as he slips his own into the spaces between them.

Neither of us speak a word and my eyelids fall shut as I find myself consumed by him. He invades every single one of my senses, seeping into the marrow of my bones. His solid arms melt into me, his skilled hands moving ours together to mold the clay as it spins beneath our palms and fingers.

The insides of his thighs press against me, the stubble on his cheek rough against my own, yet it's a feeling I find myself craving. The warmth of his breath against my neck. The smell of his cologne and body wash. He's everywhere and I lose myself in the moment, letting my senses absorb and memorize the way he feels.

His hands press mine into the clay, movements slow as we stroke it, working from the bottom to the top, creating the shape of the vase. As we reach the top, his fingers slide along my knuckles, guiding me on where to put them. "You have to push them deep inside, but you don't want to go too fast," he murmurs against my ear, the sound vibrating throughout my body as warmth builds in the pit of my stomach. "Gentle and slow."

I follow his lead, letting him guide my fingertips into the clay as we begin to mold and shape the inside. Our fingers move together, in and out, as we stroke the inside of the vase, smoothing out the surface with tender yet firm touches.

"Beautiful," he breathes, his lips brushing against my ear. "Just like that, baby." A shiver travels down my spine as he speaks, my breath catching in my throat. "Do you want to take over?"

I shake my head. "No," I murmur, not sure if he can hear me. My heart pounds erratically in my chest, the warmth spreading between my legs. He shifts his hips behind me, his cock rock hard as it brushes against my lower back through his pants. Holy shit. I'm momentarily surprised by his girth and him being hard, but I'm equally turned on. I want him to do more than throw clay with me. "I want you to do it with me."

"Mmm," he half moans, the sound sending a shock of electricity to my core. Moving together, our fingers work to finish the shape of the inside before he guides my hands back along the outside, smoothing the exterior of the vase. "You're doing so well."

Holy fucking shit.

He moves my hands back down to the base of the vase, moving upward once more in a slow fashion. "You can ease your foot off the pedal." His voice is rough and I can still feel his hardness pressing into my lower back. "We're finished."

The apex between my thighs tingles and I slowly lift

my foot from the pedal, the wheel coming to a stop as we still have our hands wrapped around the base. Neither of us move at first and I'm acutely aware of the close proximity of his chest against my back. My brain registers every single part of my body he's touching.

"You did great for your first time," he breathes, his lips brushing against my ear again. He slowly moves his hands away from me and a rush of cool air drifts across the backs of my hands, replacing his warmth. "I have to move the vase and let it dry before we can do anything else with it." He rises to his feet, not even bothering to hide his erection. I tilt my head up to look at him, his eyes smoldering as they collide with my gaze.

"It's too wet." He pauses, his tongue darting out to wet his lips, and something in my stomach flutters. "To put it into the kiln," he adds, his voice rough as he turns his back to me, walking over to the shelf where a few other pieces are drying. He sets it down, slowly turning back around to face me, propping his arm against the side of the shelf as he leans against it.

His gaze finds me across the small space. I'm completely transfixed, my body frozen in place as I stare at him from where I'm still sitting on the bench. My hands are covered in clay, but I know I can wash that off.

It's him, the imprint he's left on me, that I know I'll never be able to wash away.

"I have to head out," he says slowly, desire hanging in his tone as the electrical current refuses to waver between us. I glance at the time on the clock hanging on the wall, remembering he had a meeting today that he's already late for.

"Shit, I'm sorry."

He pushes away from the shelving unit, closing the distance between us as he steps in front of me. I tilt my head back to look at him and he reaches for me, leaving a streak of clay along the side of my temple as he brushes a lock of hair away from my face.

"We'll just have to finish this later."

My breath catches in my throat and he pulls away, retreating as he turns around and slips out of the shed. I stare after him, long after he's gone, attempting to get myself under control before I have to head back into the house.

I need a cold shower after whatever the hell that was . . .

Or some alone time with my vibrator.

CHAPTER TWENTY-TWO

ROWAN

Fuck, she's beautiful.

Hadley holds Lucy up, her lips moving as the softest sounds escape her, and Hadley pulls her back down to her chest. Her eyelids flutter shut as she holds my daughter tightly, pressing her face against the side of Lucy's before she moves her away.

"Are you sure she's okay with you for the evening?" I ask Nova for the third time as Hadley hands over Lucy. Lincoln sits on the couch with Posey tucked in against his side, a gentle smile on his lips as he watches the three of us passing the baby around.

"Yes, Rowan." Nova lets out a soft laugh, shaking her head as she takes Lucy from Hadley. "I promise, she will be perfectly fine." She looks at Lincoln with a smirk before glancing back at me. "This will give Lincoln some more practice with a baby."

My eyebrows lift at her before looking at my friend. "Whatcha need practice for, bud?"

Lincoln gives me a sheepish grin. "Just for possible future ventures."

"To answer your question, no, I'm not pregnant," Nova tells me, rolling her eyes, and Hadley chuckles. "But like he said, for future ventures."

My heart soars at the thought for Lincoln. After watching how he's been with Posey, it's going to be something else to see him with a tiny baby. I don't know what his and Nova's plans are, but I know they've been wanting to grow their family.

Nova walks over and hands Lucy to Lincoln, getting her settled in his arms before she turns back to the two of us. "We decided on a date," she informs me, a smile blossoming across her face. "July twenty-eighth."

The two of them had been going back and forth on dates and locations for what has felt like a damn lifetime. "Fucking finally." I snort, laughter following the sound. "Did you decide where?"

"Turks and Caicos. It's completely short notice for everyone, but we just had to pick a time and a place and everything else will happen the way it's meant to," Nova says, glancing back at Lincoln with a tender gaze. "Neither of us want to wait any longer than we already have."

I look back and forth between the two of them, the connection and love they have is palpable.

It's not something I ever imagined I would want in life, but I can't ignore the longing in my chest.

Hadley moves into my peripheral vision, always stealing my attention, as I turn my head to look at her. I take a moment to drink her in, just like I did before we left the house. Her heeled boots give her a few extra inches, but even still, she just barely reaches my shoulder. Her auburn hair falls down her back in soft waves against her cream-colored sweater. She's wearing a black skirt that shows off her tanned legs.

And fuck me for the blood rushing to my cock again.

It would be really fucking cool if I could stop getting hard every time I take a second to appreciate the way she looks.

My secret trick when this happens is to think about the one time I saw Gray almost cut off the tip of his finger. We were playing a stupid game in our twenties that was alcohol-induced, where you spread your fingers and tried to hit the spaces between them with a knife.

Idiotic, I know, but that's what happens when you throw a group of young guys together and expect them to make great decisions in their downtime between hockey games.

Gray just nearly missed his finger, but caught the side of it and sliced off a layer of skin.

"Rowan, are you okay?"

I'm pulled immediately from the memory and my cock isn't hard anymore as my expression relaxes and I give Hadley a confused look. She's staring back at me with concern. "Yeah, I'm fine."

"Are you sure? You looked like you were in pain or like you were going to get sick." Her face is filled with concern. "We don't have to get dinner, we can always do it another time."

"What? No," I say in a rush, shaking my head at her in assurance. "I promise, I'm fine. I was just thinking about something else."

She doesn't look like she's buying it and I hear Lincoln stifle a laugh as he lifts his eyebrows at Nova. "Okay, if you're sure," Hadley eventually says, stepping closer to me.

"I'm positive." I glance back at Lincoln and Nova. "Thanks, guys. We'll try not to be too late."

"You kids just be safe and have a good time," Nova calls out to us, her gaze linking with mine as Hadley gives her a wave and starts to walk ahead.

"Don't forget to wear a—"

Lincoln's words are cut off as Nova quickly shoves her hand against his mouth. I cut my eyes at him, not sure if Hadley heard him or not as she's already walking out the front door. Lifting my hand, I give Lincoln the middle finger, muttering a string of curses at him before I break out into a jog to catch up with Hadley.

"Are you sure you're okay?" she questions me once more as we get into the car.

I turn to look at her, meeting her look of concern. "Yes." I pause, a cheeky smile forming on my lips as I tilt my head to the side. "Are you trying to get out of going to dinner with me?"

"No." She bites back a grin, shaking her head as I see that darkness washing over her gaze again. "I didn't know if you were having second thoughts of possibly being seen in public with me."

"Why the fuck would I have second thoughts?"

She shrugs as if it's nothing. "I don't know. It just seems like it would be easier to explain us no longer being together if no one actually sees us."

There it is again. That stupid goddamn reminder that this is all going to end sooner than I want it to.

"I told you, I'll worry about that when the time comes," I tell her, swallowing back the dread that surrounds that thought. "Until then, I want the entire world to know you're mine."

Something unreadable dances in her eyes. "Even if it's fake?"

I'm beginning to hate that word and the concept behind it.

Pulling my bottom lip between my teeth, I tilt my head in agreement, blinking once before allowing myself the opportunity to fully drink her in. She's fucking breathtaking.

"Even if it's fake."

———

I can't keep my eyes off of her the entire night and I find myself doing and saying whatever I can just to hear the sound of her laughter snaking itself around my heart.

Dinner didn't last nearly as long as I wanted it to and as we find ourselves coming down to the end of the night, I can't bring myself to walk her back to my car. I know we have to go pick Lucy up and get home, but I need just a little bit longer . . . just one more fleeting moment with her.

"Are you ready to go?" I ask as we walk out the

restaurant, immediately wanting to kick myself for even asking.

Hadley lifts her head to look at me, her eyes resting on me. She pulls her bottom lip between her teeth, raking them over her flesh as she shakes her head. "Are you?"

My eyes scan her face and I swallow roughly as I take a chance and extend my arm, holding my hand out for her. "Come with me?"

Her lips part, her eyes shimmering beneath the moonlight as she wordlessly slips her palm against my own, weaving our fingers together. There's a park nearby that has a pond in the center with a walkway around the perimeter. It's the first place I can think of to take her and she falls in step beside me as we head in that direction.

As we reach the park, the sound of a violin and an acoustic guitar dances around us, the gentle breeze carrying the melody from the gazebo on the other side of the pond. I glance at Hadley from the corner of my eye, watching a wistful smile drifting across her face.

Ignoring the path around the pond, I let her lead me directly to the water, reveling in the way her hand fits perfectly in mine. She stares out at the ripples caused from the fountain in the center, the same wonderment in her expression as she tilts her head back to look up at the stars.

"There're so many stars tonight," she says quietly, her eyes scanning the constellations. I tip my chin, looking up as I find the ones that look similar to the freckles across the tops of her cheeks. "We're so small in the grand scheme of things."

I find a cluster of stars that reminds me of her freckles. "What do you mean?"

"There's so much about this life and this world that we know nothing about, that we may never know about in this lifetime." She pauses, turning her body to face me, her fingers still entwined through my own as I move my eyes to hers. "In a way, we are all insignificant, you know?"

"No, I don't know," I tell her, shaking my head as I pull my hand away from hers, both hands snaking around her lower back as I pull her closer to my body. "I promise you, you're not insignificant, Hadley. Not to me, not ever."

She lets out a soft laugh, the sound warming my soul as she lifts her arms, linking them around the back of my neck as she begins to sway to the melody shifting around us. She moves closer, turning her head to the side as she rests her cheek against my chest. "I meant in terms of the grand scheme of life."

I hold her close, feeling her entangling herself in my soul as she listens to the sound of my heart beating in my chest. Lowering my face to the top of her head, I breathe in her scent, clinging on to the moment before it slips away.

"Can I tell you a secret?"

"Always," she tells me softly.

"I couldn't care less about the bigger picture, not when I already have everything I'll ever need." I pause, letting out a breath, my voice dropping lower. "The moon can keep the stars and the sun can keep the clouds."

"But then what do you get to keep?"

You. I just want to keep you.

I pull away from her, my gaze yet again settling on hers. "Everything that's supposed to be mine."

CHAPTER TWENTY-THREE

HADLEY

"My sister thinks I need to call my brother."

The words that fall from Rowan's lips momentarily have me pausing from the dishes I'm washing in the sink. I glance over my shoulder at him as he steps up beside me, reaching for a hand towel to start drying the plates, leaving the bottles and nipples to air dry.

This is the first Rowan has even brought up his brother and I've been wondering when this topic would finally come up. My relationship with Beau was complicated to say the least and I also know that Rowan has had a similar experience with his brother.

"Do you know what's going on with him?"

I haven't spoken to him since we broke up over a year ago. Even though I was upset when it happened, it was more from a place of feeling like I failed and disappointment. Beau Taylor was once my friend, but when he broke up with me, it was the clean break I needed from the toxicity and chaos that came with him.

Rowan finishes drying, putting the bottles back in the cupboard before turning to face me as I dry my hands. "Raven said he's in rehab right now, and supposedly he's doing really well." He pauses, hanging the hand towel on the stove. "Honestly, I'm not sure I really care."

"Does he know about us yet?"

He shrugs with indifference. "I would imagine so because my mother has a habit of gossiping, but what can he really say about it? At the end of the day, he fucked things up with you, and he and I barely have a relationship. He's done nothing but take advantage of our entire family. I don't need his permission to be with you."

My heart stumbles over itself and I quickly pull it back into place, back into a steady beat because I can't take those words to heart. We both know this isn't real, he just failed to mention it in conversation right now.

"I don't really think he would care anyways," I admit, walking across the kitchen before heading into the living room. I start to pick up some of the baby's things that are thrown about the couch from our mad dash to get her into the bath after she had a blowout earlier.

I accidentally kick one of Lucy's toys under the couch. I lower myself onto my knees, glancing up as I see Rowan stopping in the doorway. He extends his arms above his head, the muscles tightening as he grips the top of the doorframe, his body leaning forward slightly.

He drops his chin closer to his chest, watching me

down on my knees through the pieces of his hair that fall across his forehead. Holy fuck. I forget what the hell I'm even down on my knees for, other than for him.

What the hell is wrong with you, Hadley?

His shirt rides up, lifting from the tension in his shoulders, revealing a few inches of the bottom of his torso. I've seen him without a shirt on before, but I try to force myself to forget how he's built until I'm rudely reminded again.

"Why do you think he wouldn't care?"

I stare at him for a beat, my mouth completely dry. "What?"

"My brother. Why wouldn't he care that I'm with you?"

My memory of what we were talking about is instantly jogged and the mention of his brother pulls me out of my stupidity. I reach under the couch, finding the toy and retrieving it before I rise back to my feet.

I thought he looked good while I was down on my knees, but standing face to face with him while he's looking at me with a darkened gaze is an experience I wouldn't mind happening more than once.

"Things with Beau and me were weird. We were friends and then I was trying to help him with things while he was working on getting medications straightened out. One thing led to another and then we ended up dating." I let out a breath, pulling my gaze from his as I finish straightening the living room. "I thought that I loved him, but knowing what I do now, it was never love between us. I was a convenience for him and he was someone I thought I could help. Your brother never loved me."

When I look back at Rowan, he's still staring at me, the muscle in his jaw tightening as he watches me with an unreadable expression. "My brother's a fucking idiot," he says slowly, his tone low, yet the sound of his voice is soft. "I'm sorry he treated you like shit."

I shake my head at him, sucking in a deep breath before releasing it. "It's fine, really. I moved on from that long ago and I've been working on moving past the little bit of a mental hiccup it gave me."

Rowan drops his hands away from the doorway and slowly stalks toward me. He reaches for me, taking the blanket I'm folding from my hands and tossing it back onto the couch. His fingers slide beneath my chin as he tips my head back for my eyes to meet his. "Did he hurt you?"

I swallow hard, my heart pounding faster. "No. He never laid a finger on me."

"I'm not talking about physically, Hadley."

My heart stops in my chest. "He wasn't always kind, but he has his own struggles, Rowan."

"Don't you dare make fucking excuses for him," he grates the words out, his pulse in the side of his neck visible as it throbs. "Regardless of the shit he was struggling with, none of that is ever an excuse to hurt someone. What did he say to you?"

"The things he said about himself hurt worse than what he would say about me."

Rowan stares at me and I can feel the heat and anger radiating from his body. His throat bobs as he swallows hard and he moves closer, his palm sliding along the side of my neck as he gently cups it with his hand. "What did he say to you, baby?"

"At first, there were just little comments about things I was doing wrong, but over time they became cruel." I pause for a second, letting out a shallow breath. "He cheated on me and he liked to compare me to other women from his past."

His jaw clenches. "What did he say, Hadley?"

I swallow roughly. "Just that I wasn't as good as most of them. That I laid there like a dead corpse and just took it." Tears spring to my eyes and I hate the thought of having to speak these words out loud. "He just had a habit of making me feel small and pretty insignificant."

Rowan doesn't move. His eyes burn into mine, his fingers soft along the back of my neck. "Nothing he said to you is true, Hadley. My brother is a piece of shit and I'm so sorry for everything he did to you. You are not small." He pauses, his throat bobbing as he swallows. "You are so fucking far from insignificant." He shakes his head. "You're more than he ever deserved and he knew that. He views himself so poorly, he has an incessant need to drag everyone down with him."

"I know," I tell him, even though there are still moments where his vile comments circle in my brain. They have a habit of creeping in during moments of self-doubt. "I've let the past with him go. I've moved on and had to find it inside myself to forgive him."

I've forgiven Beau for everything bad that happened between us. I know he wasn't mentally stable and I don't fault him for any of it. All I can do now is hope that things have taken a turn for the better for him.

His eyebrows immediately pull together. He tilts his head to the side, his eyes searching my face. "After the mental fuck he put you through, you can just forgive him like that?"

"I can," I reply, tipping my chin forward as I reach up to place my hand on his solid chest, just over his heart. "Holding on to hate and blame does nothing. Just because I forgive him doesn't mean I like him or want anything to do with him. It gave me the peace I needed to move past it." I pause, a gentle smile drifting across my lips. "For what it's worth, I think you owe yourself the chance to forgive him for your own sense of peace."

The vehemence within his stare rocks me to my core. His lips part, his tongue darting out to wet the bottom one before he rolls them together. "What if I can't?"

"Then at least you can say you tried," I say, pressing my palm harder against his chest before I retreat and let my hand fall away. "That's all you can do."

CHAPTER TWENTY-FOUR

ROWAN

My eyes scan the shelf, slowly making their way to the one pot that has yet to be touched. After Hadley and I made it together, I let it dry out and put it in the kiln. That was a couple weeks ago and we still have yet to glaze it.

Life has been a bit of a whirlwind as we're approaching the end of the regular season and lately, the exhaustion has been hitting me a little harder than normal. Around this time is typically when I find myself having to push even harder through the fatigue that runs through my muscles and my soul.

I hang on to every last shred of adrenaline that helps to bury the exhaustion I'm truly feeling. It's like a blanket—like a facade. It creates a false sense of being able to continue and then when the season finally comes to an end, I crash.

It truly is an unhealthy lifestyle, but I know it will only last a few more short years. The average for careers in the professional league is supposedly only five years.

There's a soft knock on the other side of the door and I glance over my shoulder as Hadley steps inside. She's wearing a pair of sweatpants and a matching sweatshirt, holding two mugs in her hands and the baby monitor tucked underneath one arm.

Since we had a few away games and I have a week at home again, Hadley insisted on taking care of Lucy tonight since I was with her most of the day. I took the opportunity to disappear into my pottery shed. It's my little safe haven and where I can come to unwind. Where I can silence the outside noise and just work with my hands as I block the rest of it out.

After talking to Hadley about my brother, she advised me to take a few days before deciding what I wanted to do. I took a week instead and still don't know what I'm going to do. A part of me feels like I should call him, but there's a hesitancy. A lack of belief that he could be on a better path.

Hadley walks over to me, her footsteps light as she hands me a mug filled with what looks like tea and milk.

A soft smile dances across her lips. "Without any issues, like normal." She laughs quietly, her face lighting up. "She's predictable, just like you."

"What's that supposed to mean?" I question her, tilting my head to the side as I take a sip of the steaming liquid and set it down on my workbench.

Amusement passes through her expression. "There are certain things you do that I've noticed."

"Like what?"

"Well," she starts, setting her mug down next to

mine as she begins to walk between the two shelving units, inspecting the pieces I have sitting for another day. As she begins, I follow after her, trailing behind until we're both between the shelves. "You always drink a glass of water with salt in the morning. You are ritualistic with most things. You blow inside of cups before you use them, just in case there's dust in them. And when you need a moment of quiet, I know I can either find you out here or on the ice."

My breathing ceases and my heart promptly crawls into my throat as I hang on to every last one of her words. I move closer to her with everything she said floating around in my head. She turns to look at me, her back to the wall of the shed. I'm transfixed on her, completely swept away in her undertow. Hadley's been slowly slipping under my skin, and fuck me, she's there.

My hand finds the underside of her jaw and I tip it back, those hazel eyes immediately colliding with my own. Her lips part and my fingertips dance along her skin, memorizing the way she feels.

This entire time, she's been watching and observing, taking notes on every single thing that makes me tick. Maybe I'm under her skin, just as much as she's under mine. I don't know what to say, but I know exactly what I want to do.

Every thought melts from my brain and our surroundings vanish as my eyelids flutter shut and my mouth crashes into hers. The sharp intake of her breath surrounds me, consuming me as I let myself feel the cascade of emotions that hit me at once.

Her lips are soft beneath my own and she doesn't move away. Her delicate hands find my sides, gripping my shirt as I slide my hands along the side of her face, pushing my fingers through her hair as I cradle the back of her head. I'm swept away in a whirlwind of her, her mouth moving with my lips as she kisses me back with a tenderness that seeps into the marrow of my bones.

I feel her everywhere. Under my skin, creeping into my heart, permeating my bones, slipping into the fibers of my soul.

She holds on to me, her lips parting as her tongue darts out and tangles with mine. She tastes like chocolate and whipped cream and I savor the overload to my senses, cataloguing every piece of her. Her body shifts, pressing into me, vibrating through every layer of my flesh, melting into me. My heart is on a journey of its own, thrumming to her melody as it threatens to break free from its cage.

I breathe her in, our tongues tangled, lips melting. Time is suspended, hanging precariously in the air, and everything around us ceases to exist. The only thing I know—the only thing that matters—is her. The way she feels pressed against my body, her mouth moving with me.

In the past two months, she's opened my heart to possibilities that I never thought would happen. She came barreling into my life with a baby I had no idea about and now I can't imagine what my life would look like without either of them.

Hadley just feels right. Like this is exactly where

she's supposed to be, right here with me, even if it's only for this short amount of time.

I'm done wasting it.

I'm done denying myself of her.

My lips move slowly against hers, drinking her in before I break apart from her, both of us coming up for air. Her eyelids lift, the swirling hues of brown and green searching mine as she sucks in an uneven breath. My chest rises and falls in rapid succession, my heart pounding away inside my chest, but I ignore it all as I stare down at her, utterly lost in the depths of her eyes.

Utterly lost in her.

"That was . . ." Her words trail off as she lifts her fingers to her mouth, tenderly touching her swollen, bruised lips. A pink tint creeps across her cheeks. "Unexpected."

"Just like you," I murmur, my eyes falling shut as I press my forehead to hers. "Just like you," I repeat, the words falling from my lips like a prayer.

As I pull away from her, I open my eyes, my gaze colliding with hers once more. Hadley glances to her right, releasing my shirt as she picks up a vase. A smile dances across her face as she holds it up to show me. "How about we finish this, just like you said we would." She lifts her eyebrows, releasing me fully as she saunters past.

My body involuntarily turns, watching her as she walks over to the table, inspecting the various glazes I have. Her hair is slightly tangled from my hands, her lips still swollen, and her cheeks flushed. Blood rushes directly to my cock as I wonder how she might look after she's been thoroughly fucked instead of just kissed.

"What color should we make it?"

I stalk over to her, not really caring about the vase, but only caring about what she wants and what her thoughts are. "What color do you want it to be?"

She turns to look at me, her eyes slowly drifting back and forth between both of mine. Her expression is warm, yet there's something unreadable dancing in her stare as she looks back at the glazes. "This one," she tells me, plucking a small bucket of glaze. I read the color, immediately looking at her as she stares back at me. "It reminds me of your eyes."

I cannot formulate a single coherent thought and words completely fail me as she fucks up my feelings with more force than I've ever experienced before. Wordlessly, I take it from her, unscrewing the top, and set it back down. I find two pairs of gloves, handing one to her before pulling my own over my hands.

She's quiet as she watches me pull out a drill and slide it into the liquid, effectively stirring it before I begin to pour a small amount inside the vase. "It's easier if you do the inside first like this," I murmur, swirling it around so the entirety of the interior is coated.

"What about the outside?"

"Grab a brush," I instruct, motioning to a small container on the table. "We'll do a coat now and then it will need two more, spaced out over the next few days."

She bobs her head, pulling out a brush as I wrap my

hand around hers, dipping it into the glaze. I guide her hand to the vase, moving the brush in sweeping motions, showing her how to evenly coat the dried clay.

"I can do that while you're gone," she says softly, her eyes fixated on the vase. "After you get home next week, I'm going to California for a few days to look at apartments while you're home."

My entire body takes a pause and my hand stills before I immediately recover. Our hands continue to move together again, although my spine is board straight and my heart feels like it's going to fall onto the floor. "That's not a problem. I'll see if Mia can watch Lucy during practice and games."

"It won't be long," she tells me, the words tumbling from her lips in a rush. As we finish glazing and I pull my hand from hers, I feel her gaze immediately on the side of my face. "I made a few appointments to look at places, so I'm planning on only being gone for three days."

I swallow roughly, carefully picking up the vase as I force a smile onto my face. It doesn't come close to reaching my eyes and goddammit, it feels unnatural. "You don't owe me an explanation, Hadley. It will be good for me to establish some kind of a routine for when you're not here."

The thought alone feels like a dagger severing my aorta.

"You're right," she murmurs softly, the words barely audible as she plasters her own fake smile on her face. She walks over to the bench as I move to the kiln and it feels like we're already miles apart. She picks up her mug, staring down at the hot chocolate that has since grown cold, a conflicted look in her eyes.

"We'll manage, Hadley," I assure her, watching her as her eyes find me again. "I promise, you don't have to worry about Lucy and me."

"I know." She jerks her chin, the same plastic smile lifting her lips again as sadness encapsulates her gaze. She shifts her weight, almost as if she doesn't know what she's supposed to do. "I think I'm going to head in and get ready for bed."

I want to tell her to stay. I want to sweep her into my arms and never let her go.

I know I can't do that. It isn't fair to her.

I will not be another person in her life who holds her back. She lived that life with my brother and if I kiss her again . . . if I sweep her into my arms, I know I'm never going to let her go.

"I'll see you in the morning," I tell her, the words feeling foreign as they roll off my tongue.

Hadley gives me one last lingering stare before she picks up the mugs without another word and leaves me alone with my pottery and my thoughts.

Hadley Reed was only ever meant to be temporary . . . so why the fuck does she feel so permanent?

CHAPTER TWENTY-FIVE
HADLEY

I stare out the window as the car rolls to a stop, looking out to the horizon. My eyes travel across the water that shimmers in the sunlight. The temperatures here have been a shock compared to what I've grown used to in Aston. I've been comfortable just walking around in a short-sleeved shirt, not having a need for my thick coat I brought along on instinct.

The hospital I'm supposed to be working at is located in the center of the city that borders the coast. On the outskirts of the city is where I've spent the day looking at apartments. With a handful of papers, I climb out of the car, tip the driver, and head toward the small hotel nestled along the sea.

It's a quiet and quaint little place, tucked away from the hustle and bustle of the city. It's like the best of both worlds here, with the Pacific Ocean and the startling warm temperatures.

I'm not sure I could see myself making this my

permanent residence, but it's been a nice little escape from the frigid temperatures in Aston.

My return flight to Aston isn't for two more days and I've been enjoying exploring the city, but there's something about it that just doesn't feel right. Like there's something missing. I miss the way Rowan's house smells like warm vanilla bean and the comfort it provides. I miss accidentally kicking Lucy's toys under the couch and having to blindly reach for them, not sure of what I'm going to find under there.

I miss the familiarity.

I miss them.

As I settle back into the motel for the night, I end up ordering delivery and settle on the bed to eat after showering. It's a small room with one bed, a dresser and TV, and a full bathroom. I don't need any more space than this while I'm here and there isn't anything about it that feels like home.

The only thing I enjoy is being able to have my windows open and the smell of the salt air drifting in from the sea.

I tried to watch the Archers game on the TV, but for some reason I wasn't able to find it. Instead, I ended up settling for a rerun of an old rom-com that I found instead.

My phone vibrates from beside me on the bed and I move quickly to retrieve it as I open up my messages. Yesterday I talked to Rowan when I got here, just to let him know that I made it safely and to check in on Lucy. I would be lying if I said I wasn't checking in on him too.

A smile lifts my lips when I see that it's a message from him. I'm on the opposite side of the country, three hours behind him, and judging by the time, I'm guessing he just got home from a game.

ROWAN

How did today go? Did you see any apartments you like?

HADLEY

It went well. I'm not sure about apartments, but I think I like it here.

After viewing four different apartments today, I didn't see one that I fell in love with, which is okay. I don't have to be in love with the place for it to be my home—even if it's just temporary.

ROWAN

How many are you looking at tomorrow?

HADLEY

I have one scheduled and then I'm looking at two different Airbnbs that said I could rent one of their rooms for the three months I'm here.

ROWAN

I'm glad things are going well for you and that you like it there.

HADLEY

I do, but it's not home, you know?

ROWAN

So, where is home?

I swallow roughly as I read over his message again. I used to think the word referred to an actual place, but now I'm not so sure. I think it's more of a feeling. It's where you can exist beyond the constraints of society; where you feel safe and at peace. Home is where your soul can rest.

And I think that maybe, just maybe, you can find that within another person.

HADLEY

I don't know.

ROWAN

When you do, you'll feel it.

It won't even be a question.

I chew on his words, knowing damn well that he's right, but I decide to point the conversation in a different direction. Now is not the time to unravel the feelings I've been quietly locking away in a vault.

HADLEY

I missed your game tonight. How did it go?

ROWAN

It was good. We won, and had another shutout.

HADLEY

You're insane. I don't know how you do it.

ROWAN

Well, typically I use my body, gloves,
blocker, and stick to stop shots. If I'm
in the correct position at the right time,
pucks don't make it into the net.

That's the gist of how I do it.

I laugh, lifting my gaze from my phone as I realize there's no one laughing with me. It's just me, myself, and I, lying alone on a bed in a motel room in a city on the opposite side of the country. The sudden gravity of the loneliness is overwhelming and my laughter dies off as I swallow back my emotions.

Pulling myself away from the uncomfortable realization, I look back at my phone, the loneliness transforming into longing as a tender smile drifts across my lips.

HADLEY

Smart-ass.

ROWAN

Debatable.

Two more messages come through back-to-back before I get the chance to argue with him. The first is a picture of Lucy. It must be from earlier in the day because the sun is still shining in the background. She's sitting in one of the bouncer seats we got for her, drool dripping from her lips and her arms stretched out as she's trying to reach for the phone.

ROWAN

Lucy misses you.

HADLEY

I miss her.

ROWAN

She's been cranky lately. I think she's sick of me and wants you to come home.

HADLEY

Are you trying to use your daughter against me?

You send me sweet pictures of her so I get on the next plane back to Aston?

ROWAN

I most certainly would never do that.

But . . . would it work?

HADLEY

That depends . . . What's in it for me?

ROWAN

Unlimited baby snuggles and pottery lessons.

My chest and my throat constrict. I didn't anticipate how being away from the two of them would leave me feeling this empty.

HADLEY

Sold.

ROWAN

You're an easy sell.

HADLEY

No, you just happen to have the sweetest baby girl and I may or may not have enjoyed pottery lessons with a certain goalie.

ROWAN

I hope you're not throwing clay with anyone else.

My breathing hitches and the butterflies in my stomach begin to stir. Is he asking what I think he's asking? He constantly throws me off-balance to the point that it's becoming difficult to distinguish what is up or down anymore.

HADLEY

I'm not.

ROWAN

Good.

HADLEY

I think I'm going to get ready for bed. It's getting pretty late and we both have busy days tomorrow.

ROWAN

Okay. Let me know how tomorrow goes then.

HADLEY

I will.

ROWAN

Can I tell you something?

HADLEY

Always.

ROWAN

Lucy isn't the only one who misses you.

My heart stumbles over itself, a cascade of unsteady beats as my breath quickens. I know my heart will never survive the destruction Rowan Taylor can lay upon it, but my sense of self-preservation isn't enough to stop me from telling him the truth.

HADLEY

She's not the only one I miss either.

Abandoning my phone on the bed, I head into the bathroom to brush my teeth and get ready to sleep. I check my phone one last time, disappointment pricking my skin when I see he still didn't respond. Closing my eyes, I settle against the down feather pillows and just as I'm about to fall asleep, a message from him comes through.

ROWAN

I was hoping that would happen.

Sweet dreams, outlaw.

CHAPTER TWENTY-SIX

ROWAN

I reposition Lucy in my arms as I look through the sea of people funneling down into the baggage claim area, my eyes searching for one person in particular. It's only been three days since I last saw Hadley, but I swear, it feels like years have passed.

"She should be coming any minute now, Luce."

Hadley texted me twenty minutes ago to let me know that she had landed safely. She told me where she was supposed to pick up her bag, but she didn't know I already knew. I got to the airport almost an hour ago now and I've been waiting at baggage claim ever since.

Lucy makes a cooing sound, her body shifting in my arms as she reaches her little hands down to play with my fingers. A string of drool hangs from her bottom lip, landing directly on my thumb as she attempts to fold in half to put the digit in her mouth.

She'll be four months old next week and it blows my mind how much growth she has made in such a short amount of time. As someone who never thought I would ever have kids, this entire experience has opened my eyes to so many things and so many possibilities.

Seeing the world through the eyes of a new father has been incredible and wild.

Moving Lucy back into a more stable position, I hold one arm across her chest, keeping her back against the front of my body as my other arm supports her bottom and under her knees. She's a little discontent, which isn't a new thing the past few days. It appears that I don't have the same touch that Hadley has.

"I think I might see her," I murmur to Lucy, craning my neck as I thought I saw the top of her head. I shuffle a few steps to the side, my eyes finding the same auburn-colored hair that's pulled up in a bun. "That looks like her hair."

Lucy makes another cooing sound and I start to move up and down, bopping her along as I watch Hadley step around the couple in front of her. She looks flustered, her legs moving quickly as she does a little skip-like step to get ahead of them.

Her face is flushed, her eyes bright, as she looks past another crowd of people, her gaze finding me through the moving bodies.

"There she is, Luce." I let out a breath of relief, kissing the top of Lucy's head. "Fuck, I missed her." Lucy makes a sound and I wince. "I mean, minus the F-word."

Thankfully, she doesn't understand much yet, but I know I'm going to have to watch what I say in front of her. It won't be long before she starts repeating the same words and I've seen how much fun Lincoln and

Nova have had with Posey repeating the wrong things in public.

Hadley adjusts the strap of her backpack on her shoulder as she walks up to us. She's a little breathless, her eyes shimmering pools of gold and brown and green as she stops in front of me. "Hi."

I stare at her for a beat, my lips crinkling as I feel contentment washing over me. "Hi."

My eyes are transfixed on her as she leans forward slightly, dropping her bag onto the ground as she peers at Lucy. "Well, hello there, sweet girl."

Lucy stares at her for a second before she does a full-body wiggle in my arms with a string of happy coos escaping her. She lifts her hands, not quite reaching for Hadley, but the motion shows exactly what she wants.

She wants Hadley.

Get in line, Luce.

Without any hesitation, I move Lucy away from my body, holding her out to Hadley, and Hadley meets me without any delay. She slides her hands along Lucy's rib cage, just below her armpits, and pulls her close to her chest. I watch in wonderment as she buries her face in the crook of Lucy's neck and Lucy attempts to hold on to her.

They don't share a single strand of DNA. There's no biological attachment between the two of them, yet their connection is so much deeper than that.

Leaning down, I grab her backpack, lifting it over my shoulder before I walk over to retrieve her checked bag. As I turn back around, I find them waiting for me. Hadley holds my baby girl in her arms, her eyes meeting mine as she lifts her face away from her neck. There's nothing but pure joy and adoration written across her features.

Pushing her suitcase, I pause when I reach her. Her eyes rest on me.

"Are you ready to go?"

A smile drifts across my lips. "Let's go home."

———

After we get home, Hadley doesn't protest when I insist on making dinner for her. She ended up showering afterward, to wash off her day of traveling, and returned downstairs in a pair of silk pajamas. She asked to do Lucy's night routine and I didn't once think to object.

Even though I wanted to do it with them, something inside me told me to let her have that moment. It won't be long before she won't be around for bedtimes with Lucy. I want her to have as much time with her as she wants.

I'm lounging on the couch when she comes back into the living room, thirty minutes after she disappeared upstairs. Hadley walks into the room, making her way over to where I am. I'm on my back, my hands tucked behind my head, and I watch her, my neck turning to look at her as she settles onto the cushion beside my head.

"Did she give you trouble?" I ask, tilting my head to look at her. "That took you longer than I thought it would."

She shakes her head, her expression unreadable. "She fell asleep while I was rocking her, but I wasn't ready to put her down yet." She pauses, her throat bobbing as she swallows. "I know I have obligations I have to fulfill, but it makes me sad to think about not being here and seeing her."

I stare at her for a moment, watching the emotion sweeping over her expression before I extend my arms, reaching for her. I know I can never ask her to stay. I can never ask her to give up the things she has planned in her life to play house with Lucy and me.

But that doesn't mean I can't take advantage of every moment I have with her.

"Come here," I murmur, finding her wrists as I pull her over to me. She doesn't object nor hesitate as she settles down on the couch beside me, her body flush against my side. I wrap my arms around her, holding her close as I take a second to breathe in the scent of her. "You can see her whenever you want. Just because you're moving on and living your life, it doesn't mean you can never see her again."

"I know," she mumbles against my chest, her arm tightening around my torso. She shifts against my side, her leg hiking up just enough that I can feel the heat radiating from her center. "I just hate thinking about it and the closer we get to me having to leave, the more it keeps invading my thoughts."

I can't ignore the way the blood rushes straight to my cock. She's been driving me insane for the past couple months and having her this close has me feeling like I'm going to combust. Loosening my arms around her, I begin to trail my fingers along her back, feeling the soft silk beneath my touch. She inhales sharply, her chest pressing against me as she instinctively presses against me.

"You need something to distract you," I suggest, my voice hoarse as I feel the warmth of her body seeping into me. My fingers travel over the skin on her bare arms, the goosebumps erupting across her flesh. In the back of my mind, a million reasons why I shouldn't be doing this knock against my skull.

She's my brother's ex. She's leaving soon. She deserves someone who can give her more than I ever could.

"Is that what you think?" she murmurs, her arm releasing my torso as she places her hand along my collarbone. She begins to move her fingers, trailing them across my chest and down my abdomen. Her touch burns through the thin cotton material of my shirt and I resist the urge to flip her onto her back. "What do you think would be a good distraction?"

My cock down your throat.

"Whatever you want, Hadley," I groan as her fingers brush along the skin above the waistband of my sweatpants. "All you have to do is tell me and it's yours."

She lifts her head, her eyes finding me, almost as if she's trying to decide what she wants to do. She surprises me, lifting her leg as she pushes off the couch. I immediately notice her absence, missing her warmth, but then she throws her leg over my body, her shorts riding farther up her thighs as she straddles my lap.

Both of her hands land on my chest, her eyes

searching my expression as her hair cascades around the sides of her face. Fuck, she's so hot like this. My hands find her hips and I pull her down onto me until she's sitting directly on top of my erection.

"Come here," I growl, one hand snaking up around the nape of her neck, my body lifting as I pull her face down to me. "I changed my mind," I breathe, my lips brushing against hers. "I don't want you to ask. I want you to take whatever the fuck you want from me."

She stares at me for two heartbeats. Her lips part as if she's going to say something, but it's almost as if at the last second, she changes her mind. Her mouth crashes into mine with an intensity that knocks the air from my lungs, sending a jolt of electricity directly to my core.

Her lips are soft yet unforgiving as she kisses me with a fervent need, wanting to take everything I have to give. And fuck me, she can have it all. My mouth melts into hers, taking just as much as I give, my tongue pushing past her lips, past her teeth, to tangle with her own.

She steals the air from my lungs, draining every molecule of oxygen. I drink her in, tasting the wine from earlier in the evening on her tongue. Her hands slide into my hair, her body moving against me as she pushes down, grinding against my rock-hard cock. With one hand gripping the back of her neck, I hold her in place, the urgency behind our kiss tightening my grip on her hip.

Hadley abruptly breaks apart, a ragged breath escaping her as she stares down at me. Her hands leave my hair and she pulls me up, just enough for her to start to lift my shirt up my abdomen. I take over, grabbing the material, stripping it away from my body before tossing it onto the floor beside the couch.

"You too," I moan as she shifts her hips, the friction sending a shock wave to my balls. I reach for the top button of her silk pajama top. The first one slides through with ease and the second one proves to be more challenging. Hadley's hands begin to trace the curves and the planes of my chest and abdomen as I fight against the buttons of her top.

"Do you want me to get it?" she breathes, rolling her hips once more.

Shaking my head at her, I struggle with the third button before doing it a different way. "Fuck this," I growl, grabbing the material in both hands before giving it a vicious tear. The buttons pop, flying in every direction as I rip her shirt open. She inhales sharply, her eyes widening as I push her shirt over her shoulders, sliding it down her arms. "I'll get you a new shirt."

My eyes travel across the planes of her body, memorizing every fucking inch. Lifting my hands, I slide them beneath her breasts, cupping them in my palms as I roll her nipples between the tips of my fingers. "Goddamn, you're so fucking sexy, Hadley."

Her head tilts back, a moan escaping her again as her back arches, her tits almost spilling from my hands. She straightens her head, her eyes flashing to meet mine once more before she lowers her face back to me. Our lips collide and her tongue plunges into my mouth, feeling like silk. She kisses me with haste and urgency before abruptly breaking apart once more.

My heart pounds erratically in my chest and I want to strip away every barrier. I want to feel her completely. My hands find her hips and I lift her off me, springing to my own feet. She doesn't say a word as I step to her, slipping my hands beneath the waistband of her shorts and panties before dragging them down her thighs.

I lower myself to my knees, moving her clothing down her thighs and down to her feet so she steps out of them. My gaze slices to hers before slowly trailing down her body. "Fuck," I murmur, my hands finding her hips once more. I lower a hand to her thigh, my eyes dropping down to her cunt in front of me, as I spread her legs.

"Throw your leg over my shoulder, baby," I order, my fingertips digging into her flesh as my lips graze her pussy. "I want to make you come."

She drops her left hand to my shoulder, holding on to me as she lifts her leg and does exactly as I say, giving me full access to her glistening cunt. My mouth inches closer, a moan slipping from me as I inhale her scent, dragging my tongue along her center.

Hadley's body quivers and she arches her back. Fuck, she's so responsive and I love it. Lifting my hand, I smack her pussy, my hand connecting with her skin with a sting.

"Oh, fuck," she moans, her hips involuntarily moving, her nails digging into my flesh. I moan against her cunt, my tongue working over her, finding her clit as I begin to play with it. Hadley doesn't protest and her other hand lands on the back of my head, her fingers diving through the locks of my hair as I fuck her with my mouth.

I love the way she is right now. She wants to come and I'm the man for the job. If she wants pleasure, I'll give her pleasure. I'll give her whatever the fuck she wants from me, no hesitation, no questions asked.

I'd spend the rest of my life on my knees for her, giving her anything she'd ask for.

My tongue moves against her, alternating between a slow and faster rhythm. I taste her, licking, sucking, fucking, and teasing until she's a mess of moans. Her body writhes above me, the muscles in her leg beginning to tighten as her grip on my hair and shoulder grows firmer.

"I'm so close, Rowan," she breathes, her cunt pressing against my tongue. "Don't stop."

I do exactly as she orders and I don't stop even as she starts to come. My name falls from her lips in a breathless, moan-filled chant. My tongue laps at her pussy, drinking her in, tasting her pleasure on my lips as I make sure she's fully satiated.

She tugs on my hair, pulling my face away from between her legs. I look up at her as she removes her thigh from my shoulder. "Get up, Rowan." She stares down at me, her eyes filled with a deep-seated need as a devious grin slides across her lips. "I want you to fuck me."

Obeying her command, I rise to my feet, my hands reaching for the waistband of my pants as she watches me. Lust dances in her irises and there's a fire burning inside as I slide my pants down my thighs, pushing them down to my feet. My cock is so fucking hard, the thought of being inside her males me feel like I'm going to come on the first thrust.

"What's this?" she murmurs, her gaze dropping down to my thigh as she inches closer. Her fingers trail over the ink-marred skin. "I didn't know you had a tattoo." Her eyes scan the script above both of my knees. Her fingers graze the words written in Latin. "What's it mean?"

Omnia possibilità sunt.

"All things are possible."

"And what's this for?" she asks, her fingers dancing over the date above my other knee.

2018.

"It's the year I was drafted."

Hadley looks up at me with mischief in her eyes. "I didn't think you'd be someone with tattoos."

My head dips to the side. "What did you think I'd be then?"

She lifts her hands back to my chest, her fingers dancing across my skin, setting my nerve endings on fire. My cock throbs and fuck, I'm ready to bury myself inside her. But I'm also curious to hear what she has to say.

"I don't know. I'm still figuring you out," she admits, pulling her bottom lip between her teeth.

"How about I just show you instead?" I murmur, my hands traveling back down to her hips. "Maybe that can help you figure things out."

"I like the sound of that," she says as she reaches for me. I inhale sharply, electricity slithering down my spine as she wraps her delicate hand around the base of my cock, the tips of her fingers don't touch. She slowly begins to pump her hand, moving back and forth along my length.

"I need to get a condom."

Hadley's eyes flash to me. "Have you been tested?"

"Yes." I got tested a few weeks before Hadley came barreling into my life.

"I have an implant in my arm. I want to feel you without anything between us."

"Fuck, okay." I let out a breath, the thought of fucking her raw sending a warm feeling to the pit of my stomach. "You need to get it wet," I tell her, my voice gruff as she continues to stroke my length. "Spit on it."

Her eyes are glazed over and hooded as she draws her lips together, her cheeks moving. She stares up at me, drawing spit into her mouth before she lowers herself, spitting her saliva on my cock. I watch her for a moment, completely transfixed as she slides her hand through it, coating my entire dick.

I reach for her, pulling her back upright as my hands fall to her hips and I begin to spin her around. "Turn around for me and grab the back of the couch."

Hadley listens, bending forward until she's folded at the waist, her hands gripping the back of the couch. I grab my cock, pumping it two times before positioning the tip along her center. She sucks in a breath as I start to push into her, her tight cunt stretching around the girth of my dick. She's so goddamn tight, I feel like I could come on the spot.

She glances at me over her shoulder, taking every inch of my length as she lets out a ragged breath.

"Goddamn, look at you," I murmur, my hands sliding along her spine before I push my fingers into her hair. Grabbing a handful, I pull her head back, her neck craning as I grip her hip with my other hand. "I've been waiting so long to fuck you."

"So, what are you waiting for?" She groans, pushing her ass back against me as she takes me even deeper. "Fuck me, Rowan."

Without another word, I pull back, so just the tip is inside of her before I slam into her. Hadley lets out a cry, pleasure mixing with pain as a moan rumbles in my throat. She pushes back against me as I start to move in and out, falling into a steady rhythm as I fuck her slowly at first.

I want to come, but I want to savor this. I want to savor her.

It isn't long before something in my mind switches. The warmth is turning into a searing heat in the pit of my stomach, my balls constricting closer to my body as my cock feels like it's going to explode. My fingers grip her hip, my hand tighter around her hair as I start to pound into her, fucking her with no mercy.

She takes every thrust and every inch without so much as a whimper in protest. She moans, her body moving beneath my touch as I fuck her relentlessly. Hadley cries out my name as I slam into her, filling her to the fucking brim with my cock.

That's all it takes to send me falling over the edge. I thrust into her again, my chest constricting as my orgasm hits me in full force. I spill myself into her, pumping my cock in and out until every last drop of cum fills her tight cunt.

Hadley collapses forward, her forehead resting against the couch as I release my grip on her hair and hip. Taking a step back, I slowly pull my cock from her, the tingling feeling completely overwhelming as the cool air around us hits my warm, soaked flesh.

I stare at her for a moment, her ass still in the air, her chest rising and falling with every ragged breath, as my cum starts to drip from her pussy. "Fuck, I love you like this." I groan, dragging my finger through my cum, pushing it back into her. "I love seeing my cum dripping out of you."

She slowly pushes away from the couch, her legs unsteady as she turns around to look at me. Soft laughter spills from her perfect lips and she looks at me through glazed eyes. "My legs feel like Jell-O." She smiles, her cheeks flushed. "I don't know if I can walk."

Without hesitation, I close the small amount of distance between us, my knees bending as I slide my hands behind her thighs and lift her into the air.

A gasp escapes her and she stares down at me, her arms sliding around the back of my neck. "What are you doing?"

"You're a fall risk right now," I tell her with a smirk, feeling the warmth of her cum and mine against my stomach. "I'm taking you upstairs to my room." I pause, raising an eyebrow at her. "Unless, you'd rather me take you to yours instead?"

She pulls her bottom lip between her teeth again, shaking her head. "I like the sound of yours better."

"Good."

Because that's exactly where I want her tonight.

I carry her up to my bedroom, but instead of stopping at the bed, I walk her directly into my en suite bathroom, only stopping when we reach the massive tub in the corner. She tilts her head to the side as I set her down on the edge, inhaling sharply as the cool porcelain meets her skin.

"What are you doing?" she questions me as I turn on the water, increasing the heat as it begins to fill the tub.

"Taking care of you."

Hadley watches me carefully as I grab a washcloth and some soap, waiting for the tub to fill more. When it reaches halfway, I help her to her feet, my hands holding hers as she eases down into the water. I watch her eyelids flutter shut as her body slips beneath the hot surface.

As she settles against the back of it, her eyes open, immediately finding mine. "Come here," she murmurs, her hands reaching for me.

I don't protest and she moves forward, making room for me behind her as I settle into the hot water, sinking in. Resting back against the tub, she moves between my legs. My arms snake around the front of her torso, pulling her against me as she relaxes.

She settles with her back against my chest, her head

falling back against my shoulder. I press my lips against her temple, holding her close as I revel in the way she feels and the warmth surrounding us.

Time passes and the water grows warm before I wash her body and my own. I settle with her in my arms again, not wanting to let her go as I hold her against me. I bury my face in her hair, breathing in the scent of her, memorizing the way she feels. We stay like that, wrapped up in one another, until the water turns cold.

Letting the water drain, we get out of the tub and I dry her and myself before sweeping her into my arms again. She doesn't argue as I take her straight to my bed, tucking both of us under the covers. I pull her body close to me, our legs tangled together as I wrap my arms around her.

She's slowly infiltrating my heart and I'm not certain I stand a chance against this kind of warfare.

I need her out of my head and out of my bed, but not tonight . . .

Not until it's time for her to go.

CHAPTER TWENTY-SEVEN

HADLEY

And just like that, Rowan's gone again.

When he first explained his hockey schedule to me, it seemed a little crazy, but he explained that it comes with the territory. He seems pretty well-adjusted to the way things go, but as we've grown closer, I find myself missing him more in the empty moments when he's not home.

Thankfully, they didn't have to travel by plane, so it's just a short road trip to a neighboring state. He's been gone for two days already and we have two more until he's back home.

I know I need to pull back and protect my heart, but it's beginning to feel like an impossible feat.

Standing in my bedroom, I stare down at my bed, listening to the sound of the white noise coming from Lucy's room. She was laid down an hour ago and I took some time to clean the house up before retreating to my room.

The last night Rowan was home, I spent it in his bed

with him. Last night, I fell asleep watching a movie on the couch, and now tonight, it just feels weird climbing into this bed. It's been where I've slept since moving in with Rowan, yet now it feels foreign.

The sheets are cool against my skin and I settle in against the pillows on my side. Something about it just doesn't feel comfortable and I roll onto my other side, attempting again. Shaking my head in defeat, I roll onto my back, staring up at the white ceiling as I listen to the sounds from Lucy's room again.

Abruptly, I sit up, throwing the covers away from my body before exiting the room. I slip into the hallway, my eyes landing on Rowan's door, and I let myself in. His bed is still a mess from the way we left it the morning before he left. It smells like him and I close my eyes, absorbing the scent before I open them and pad across the floor to his bed.

Without a second thought, I slip between the sheets, enveloping myself in every fiber of fabric that his smell clings to. It's not him, but it's as close as I can get. I shouldn't be missing him as much as I am right now, but I think the impending date of me moving is really weighing heavily on my heart.

I've gotten comfortable in the confines of his home with him. I'm used to waking up every morning to the sound of Lucy cooing and the aroma of coffee as Rowan starts his day downstairs. Everything has just become normal to me. It's the familiarity I crave.

Grabbing my phone from my pocket, I see there's a notification for an unread email on the screen. It's already close to eleven o'clock, so I'm not sure what it could be at this hour. When I open the app, I see the first unread message and it's from the one leasing company in the city.

I was approved for the apartment I wanted to rent there in California and they are willing to do it on a monthly basis with me.

Disappointment washes over me and I frown as I look at the contract for me to sign attached to the email. I needed this to happen for me to successfully move without having to stay in a hotel room for an extended period of time. This is the next step in my life and it's everything I was hoping for . . . so why the hell do I feel so damn sad about it?

I exit out of the email, figuring I will deal with it tomorrow, and as I lock my phone screen, it goes black. And then a fraction of a second later, it lights up and a message pops up.

ROWAN

Are you awake?

HADLEY

I am.

ROWAN

Oh good.

I wanted to see how your day was and how Lucy was.

I smile as I read over his message. Rowan checked in this morning and it seems to be a habit of his while he's on the road. He does a quick check-in in the morning and then again before I go to sleep.

HADLEY

It was good and she's always good :)

ROWAN

Are most babies like her?

HADLEY

My experience is limited to newborns, but I think you may have gotten lucky.

ROWAN

I think I may have too…

There's a less-than-a-minute pause and as I'm about to type out a response, another comes from him.

ROWAN

I can't stop thinking about you, outlaw.

My heart stumbles in my chest as warmth floods the bottom of my abdomen. He's not alone in the way he's feeling. After he left, I was left with the memory of his lips on my skin, his hands traveling along my flesh. I haven't been able to get him out of my head since.

HADLEY

Neither can I.

I wait for another message from him and my eyes widen when my phone starts to vibrate as a phone call comes through. Rowan's name is across the screen and I'm momentarily paralyzed. I didn't expect him to call me, but here we are.

"Hello?"

"Hey." His voice is gravelly, low and hushed. "I'm

sharing a room with Carson and he's in the shower, and I wanted to hear your voice."

"I'm glad you called," I tell him, my voice also hushed as I roll onto my back in his bed.

"Are you in bed already?"

I'm silent for a moment, my bottom lip between my teeth as I think of whether or not to tell him where I actually am. "Kind of."

"What do you mean?"

"I'm in bed, but I'm not in my bed."

Rowan doesn't say anything for a second. "Where are you, Hadley?" His voice is stern, a touch of jealousy laced through his words.

I let out a breath. "I'm in yours."

He lets out an audible sigh of relief. "Goddamn, I wish I was there with you," he half whispers, his voice hoarse. "The last time I saw you in my bed, you were naked with my cum dripping down the insides of your thighs."

"If only that were the case right now . . ."

He groans through the phone. "Fuck, Hadley. I'm so hard just thinking about you like that." The sound of his voice vibrates through my body and I slowly move my hand down my abdomen, pushing it beneath the waistband of my sleep shorts and panties. "Can you do something for me, baby?"

"Yes," I murmur breathlessly, my fingers brushing over my clit.

"I want you to touch yourself, but I want to watch you make yourself come."

"What if I told you I already am?" I let out a soft

moan as I slip a finger inside. "How are you going to watch me? Do you have a camera I don't know about?"

"I don't, although that doesn't sound like such a bad idea right now," he admits with a chuckle. "I'm going to FaceTime you, but I need you to be quiet for me, okay? Carson will be out of the shower soon."

The call abruptly disconnects, pulling me out of the moment as I lie awkwardly in his bed with my hand down my pants. Suddenly, my phone starts to vibrate again and I don't hesitate to answer it. It's dark in his room, his face illuminated by the soft glow of the TV.

"I want to watch you come," he murmurs, his voice barely audible as he stares at me through the screen. "I'm going to talk you through it, but only if you promise not to make a sound."

Pulling my bottom lip between my teeth, I bite down, my eyelids fluttering as I tip my head forward.

"Good girl," he breathes, a soft breath escaping him as his chest rises and falls. Light shimmers on the chain around his neck and he stares directly at me. "How do you usually make yourself come? Do you have any toys?"

The pit of my stomach is on fire. "Yes."

He stares at me. "Did you bring any toys with you to my house?"

Heat creeps up my neck, rapidly spreading across my cheeks. "Yes."

"Fuck," he groans, his jaw momentarily tightening, his hand running down his face. He curls it into a fist, biting his knuckles before releasing them. "Go get your favorite toy, outlaw. I want to watch you while you fuck yourself with it."

I stare at him for a moment, not sure what to do before I lay my phone down and rush into my room. My feet move quickly and excitement mixes with anticipation inside me as I find my dildo hidden in the pocket of one of my duffle bags in my closet. Rowan's patiently waiting as I crawl back into his bed and retrieve my phone. Grabbing a pillow, I prop it up as I roll onto my side to face him.

"Goddamn, Hadley. My cock is so hard right now, I might explode." He lets out a ragged breath. "When I get home, I'm going to fuck you so hard, you won't be able to walk straight for at least a week."

I swallow hard, my tongue darting out to wet my lips. "I like the sound of that."

"Good," he murmurs, his voice dropping lower. "Can you be a good girl and be quiet for me while you make yourself come?"

Holy shit. His words send a rush of warmth directly to my clit.

"Yes."

"Fuck, you're so good," he groans, a ragged breath escaping him. "Show me what you're going to use."

I lift my dildo up, nervousness washing over me as his lips turn upward in a smirk.

"Get it wet."

His pupils dilate as I bring the dildo up to my mouth, my lips parting as my tongue slides around the tip of it. If he wants a show, I'll give him a fucking show. Rowan is transfixed, his eyes glued on me as I slowly slide the dildo into my mouth, sucking the length of it as I get it wet with my saliva. Rowan's phone moves and I see the muscles in his chest tighten as he slides his hand down to his cock.

"You're so fucking sexy. Are you imagining my cock sliding down your throat?" He moans, his eyelids fluttering shut before he looks at me again.

I try to answer him around the dildo, but the sound is garbled and saliva dribbles from the corners of my mouth.

"Jesus Christ," he growls, blowing through his nostrils. "Fuck yourself, baby. Pretend your toy is my cock stretching you out."

I press the button, turning on the vibration before moving it down my body, between my legs. I push my panties and shorts down, spreading my legs before sliding the length of the dildo inside me. It vibrates against my insides and I position it with the clit stimulator suctioning around the bundle of nerves. Instantaneously, my pussy clenches around the silicone, a moan slipping from my lips.

"I need you to be quiet for me," Rowan tells me, his voice hushed. "Carson will be out any minute now."

I clamp my mouth shut, rolling my bottom lip between my teeth as I bite down to refrain from moaning. I'm already so close as I move the dildo in and out, fucking myself with the toy as it stimulates my clit at the same time.

"Do you feel as full as you do with my cock?"

I shake my head at him, the muscles in his arm tightening as he strokes his length.

"Use your words."

"No," I breathe, the word falling from my lips without hesitation.

"Good girl," he murmurs, his teeth grazing his bottom lip. "Nothing can fill you the way I do, but this will have to suffice for now." He lets out a moan, his eyes half rolling back in his head. "Are you close, Hadley? Are you going to come for me?"

Biting down harder on my lip, I give him a quick tip of my chin, feeling the pressure building within. I'm on the precipice of an earth-shattering orgasm and I can see it in his expression that he's right there with me. The cords in his neck are visible, the muscles in his chest tightening as his necklace shifts on his skin.

"Fuck, Hadley," he groans, my face screwing up as I feel myself teetering on the edge. "Eyes on me. Look at me while you come."

That's all it takes. Those three simple words fall from his lips and I'm already coming by the time he's finished speaking the second sentence. My pussy constricts around the dildo, a wildfire of pleasure spreading through my veins as I come hard, biting my lip until I taste blood to stay quiet.

I stare at Rowan through the screen, watching his face contort as he loses himself in his hand. He doesn't make a sound, just a mess of hasty breaths as his muscles clench. He slowly finishes pumping his hand, undoubtedly making a mess all over himself under the sheets. I finish and ride out the high, my body tingling as I remove the toy, turning off the vibration.

There's a rustling sound in the background, a light

shining into Rowan's room, and I hear Carson's voice. A smirk lifts Rowan's lips and he slowly shakes his head at me.

"What are you doing to me, outlaw?"

My face is flushed, my body still floating on a cloud of ecstasy, and I can't stop the grin that dances across my lips. "Good night, Rowan."

CHAPTER TWENTY-EIGHT

ROWAN

I don't know why I agreed to this.

I successfully managed to avoid talking to my brother while he was in rehab, which was probably a worse choice than what I'm facing now. At the urging of his sponsor and our parents, he decided to take a day trip to Aston because he wants to come and visit me.

Beau agreed to meet me at Drip N Sip for a short visit since I have practice today. It's a neutral space so if I decide I don't see what everyone else is seeing, I can easily walk away. It's not like I'm inviting him into my home where I live with Lucy. The same home where the very woman he made feel like shit has also been living.

"It will be okay," Hadley tells me, reaching for my hand as she gives me a gentle squeeze. I glance down at her standing beside me outside of the shop as her other hand rests on the handle of the stroller. We decided to come into the city together and she's going to check out some of the stores in the strip while I meet up with my brother. "If you need anything or if you're ready to go, all you have to do is call me."

I stare at her for a moment, and instinctively lean forward, my lips meeting her forehead. "Thank you."

Hadley gives me a smile, then I watch her for a moment as she turns away, pushing my daughter down the sidewalk before disappearing into a store. An exaggerated sigh leaves me and I head into the coffee shop, the aroma of beans wrapping around me as I pause just inside. My eyes survey the small space, eventually landing on my brother sitting in the corner with a mug between his hands.

Not bothering to order my own drink, I head directly to him, taking in his appearance before I sit down. He looks good—better than I last saw him. His eyes are brighter, his skin clearer, and his hair is styled. He's wearing a pair of jeans and a sweatshirt, looking completely normal, yet in a better state than before.

"Hey, Rowan," he says, a soft smile lifting his lips as he looks up at me. I slowly sit down, bobbing my head at him in response as I watch his brow furrow. "Did you want a coffee or anything?"

"I'm good," I tell him in a clipped tone.

His mouth corkscrews and he stares at me for a second before smiling. "Thank you for agreeing to meet up with me. I know I should have called you sooner to talk about things, but it was something I was having a hard time bringing myself to do." He pauses, his eyes searching mine. "It just felt like it was a conversation that needed to be had in person instead."

I swallow before running my tongue over my teeth.

My spine is rigid, my body on high alert, and I know I'm giving off aggressive vibes just from the way I'm staring at him. Rolling my shoulders, I force myself to relax in my seat. A conversation like this is completely uncomfortable but sometimes the only way to get over something is to rip off the Band-Aid.

"I agree," I say, leaning back in my seat as I let my hands rest in my lap. "I will be honest, I didn't want to talk to you, and I'm still not sure I do. With that said, I'm willing to hear whatever it is you feel you need to say."

Beau purses his lips and irritation passes through his stare before it vanishes. "I appreciate that." I'm shocked to see him let it go instead of harnessing it. "Well, I will just get straight to the point. I owe you an apology for the way I've treated you in the past. I know I was not a good brother to you and I took advantage of every single person in our family. I've made a lot of mistakes in my life and one of my biggest regrets will always be the wedge I drove between the two of us.

"I always looked up to you and am so proud of everything you've accomplished and where you are in life. There was a part of me, when I was in the thick of my struggles, that was jealous and envious of you. I wanted what you had. I wanted the praise and the recognition, but I didn't see myself as worthy. I was a piece of shit and all I did was hurt everyone around us. I never felt deserving and I hated that you were."

He pauses, taking a sip of his drink as I watch him carefully. He looks healthy and the way he's speaking has me off guard. These are words I never expected to hear from my brother—not from someone who has always lived in defense mode, ready to strike like a snake.

"I know saying sorry will never make up for the things I've done or the things I've said. I just wanted you to know that I take full responsibility for it all and I'm sorry for ruining our relationship. I'm sorry for the things I did to Mom and Dad and for you having to witness it all. I can't take it back but I can move forward and I hope that one day, maybe we can have a new relationship, something healthy and better than what we had before."

I stare at my brother, unsure of what to say. I'm torn between wanting to forgive him and wanting to remind him of every bad fucking thing he did in life. Hadley's voice slips into my mind, a sound of comfort and the voice of reason.

"You owe yourself the chance to forgive him for your own sense of peace."

"A lot of things have been done in the past and talking about them isn't going to change anything that has already happened," I start, my voice trailing off as I lean forward, folding my arms on the table. "It's hard for me to expect that things will be any different with you going forward, but it isn't fair to anticipate the worst. I want nothing but the best for you, Beau. That's all I ever wanted, but you pushed me so fucking far away."

I let out a deep breath, the uncomfortable feelings from our past resurfacing. "I don't know what a relationship between us will look like now, but I'm willing to try. I'm willing to forgive you and give you another chance."

Beau's expression softens, his eyes damp as he stares at me from across the table. His eyes do a brief search of my own, almost as if he's looking for some kind of lie or a but. A few moments pass between us before he speaks again. "I am sorry. You never deserved the way I treated you in the past and I just want to be a better brother to you."

"Well, all we can do is learn from our mistakes and grow from them."

A gentle smile lifts his lips. "You're so right. I've learned so much since entering rehab and finally getting my bipolar disorder under control. I've been able to process and see clearer and see past myself."

"I'm happy for you," I tell him with nothing but honesty. I may not have been there for him this past year, or past few years for that matter, but I am genuinely happy for him. My brother can be a fucking monster and a prick, but I know deep down inside, there's more to him. That younger version of him who thought I was his best friend is still there.

"You've just always fought against everyone and you were literally your own worst enemy." I let out a breath, letting it go instead of throwing it all in his face. Even from this small interaction, I see a change in him. It's a noticeable difference and I find myself feeling proud of him actually following through on getting his shit together.

There's a sense of relief and that peace Hadley spoke about as I reach inside my heart and find the forgiveness he needs. I can't continue to hold on to the negative feelings I've had for him. The last thing I want to do is contribute to why he doesn't find his way in life.

"I forgive you. There are no hard feelings from me or between us, okay?"

He's silent for a moment before he tips his chin. "Okay. Thank you, Rowan." He swallows roughly. "I want to apologize to Hadley . . . if she'll talk to me."

My breathing ceases and the thought feels like a thorn in my side. I may forgive him for the things he did to me and our family, but Hadley is a sore fucking subject. The last thing he needs to do is open any of her wounds.

"Mom mentioned to me the two of you are engaged and she told me about Lucy," he admits, lifting his mug to take a sip of his coffee. "I'm not mad or upset with you," he adds, an apologetic smile on his face. "I never should have dragged Hadley into my shitstorm of a life and I was never fair to her. I didn't treat her the way I should have, but I know you're good for her. You're everything she deserves."

Words fail me as I stare directly into my brother's eyes. I didn't give a shit what his thoughts would be on the matter, especially after the way he ended things with her. But I'd be lying if I said I wasn't surprised at the way he speaks matter-of-factly and with such resignation and peace.

"You're right. You never should have pulled her into any of your mess." I shake my head at him, biting back the anger that licks my veins. "You treated her like dog shit and she never deserved any of that."

"I know," he says quietly, his head hanging in defeat before he picks it back up and stares at me head-on. "I'm happy that she has you, but I would still like to apologize to her if she is okay with that." He pauses, his eyes bright. "And maybe one day, I can meet my niece too."

The part of me that would have continued to hang on to the anger and negative feelings gets pushed to the back of my mind. There's no way to move forward or to forgive and grow while hanging on to any of that. Beau still has a lot to prove, but if he doesn't get a chance to do that, there's no room for any growth. All it does is provide an impossible roadblock for him and his healing.

"Hadley is down the street right now with Lucy," I tell him, my voice soft as I glance at the door. "Let me text her and see if she wants to talk to you at all."

I pull out my phone, noting the time and that we need to get going soon anyway. I open my messages app and find Hadley's name at the top.

ROWAN

Are you ready to go?

HADLEY

I'm ready whenever you are.

ROWAN

I'm ready now.

My brother wants to talk to you, but I can tell him no if you're not comfortable.

Hadley doesn't respond at first but then her message comes through.

HADLEY

That's fine.

I'll meet you at the car.

I look up at my brother. "She said okay."

Hope passes through his gaze as he drains the rest of his coffee. I rise to my feet and he follows suit, leaving his mug at the small station they have by the trash cans. His footsteps are even and I'm able to get a better look at him while he's standing up. He's filled out and has a healthy amount of weight. My brother looks better than I've seen him in years and just from talking to him, I already have a good feeling about him.

Hadley is waiting by the car with Lucy when we get there. I walk up to her, my eyes meeting hers as I take the stroller from her. "I'll get Luce in the car while the two of you talk."

She stares up at me, her eyes searching my face as a gentle smile lifts her lips. "Okay."

Hadley walks past me, stepping up to my brother, and I turn my body to watch the two of them for a moment. There's a healthy amount of space between them and my brother starts to talk, a string of apologies falling from his lips. I catch some of his words as I lift Lucy and the carrier seat from the stroller and get her secured in the car.

In a way, I know the two of them need this moment. Hadley may forgive him and she may be over him, but there's something about an apology that helps as that final piece of closure.

I fold up the stroller and slide it into the trunk of my SUV before walking over to where my brother and Hadley are. Instinctively, I step up to her, wrapping my arm around her lower back as she leans into me, pressing her body against my side.

"Thank you for your apology, Beau," Hadley tells him, her voice tender and filled with so much kindness. "I know that was a very dark point in your life and I don't hold any of it against you. Honestly, I don't think we were ever supposed to be in a relationship together, so I have no ill feelings toward you for that not working out." She lifts her head, her hazel eyes meeting mine. "Some doors have to close for others to open."

Beau looks back and forth between the two of us. "I know I still have a lot to prove to you both, but thank you for today. I have every intention of making things better between us and I look forward to building a healthy relationship with you," he says, looking directly at me.

"In forgiveness, there's peace," Hadley says, her eyes shifting back to Beau. "I think we all needed this today."

"I agree," he says quietly as he tips his chin at her and looks at me.

"Do you want to see your niece?" I half blurt the words out, almost regretting them until I see the way my brother's face softens. It transports me back to simpler times when he still thought I was the coolest person.

"I'd love that." He smiles, looking back and forth between Hadley and me. We all move to the car and I pull the door open for him to look inside at her. "Oh my goodness, look at her. Thank God she's not as ugly as you," he jokes, glancing at me as he laughs. "Hello, Lucy. I'm your uncle Beau."

He takes another moment or two, talking quietly to Lucy before standing back to face Hadley and me. "Thank you for sharing her with me," he says softly. "We'll talk soon?"

"We will." I incline my head at him, my arm releasing Hadley as she walks over to pull Beau in for a hug. He looks at me over her shoulder, a look of contentment in his expression as he holds her for a brief second before releasing her.

I step closer to him, holding my hand out to him as Hadley watches the two of us. "Drive safe and let me know when you get back home."

"I will," Beau tells me, inclining his head at me. He remains for an extra second, his eyes hovering over us as Hadley silently slides her palm against my own, her fingers tangling with mine as they tighten in a gentle caress.

My brother turns around, leaving the two of us as he heads off in the direction of the parking lot behind the coffee shop. Holding Hadley's hand, I walk her over to the passenger's side. She reaches for the door with her free hand, but I stop her, spinning her around as I pin her against the side of the SUV.

My hand finds the side of her face, my fingers trailing along her jaw as I tip her head back. I lower my mouth to hers, our lips melting together as she kisses me back with a tenderness that snakes around my soul. I kiss her until she's breathless, pulling away and kissing her forehead.

"What was that for?"

A smirk lifts my lips. "Because I wanted to." I stare at her, vigor seeping into my bones. "Thank you for pushing me to do this. I'm not sure I would have talked to him or tried to forgive him without you."

"I didn't push you to do anything," she says softly, her eyes burning holes through me. "I only helped to guide you. This was all you, Rowan. You chose to take a chance and try. You chose to find forgiveness."

My breath catches in my throat, my chest constricting around the emotion that builds inside, and my lips find hers once more.

She might not believe it, but she's the voice that drifts in the back of my mind, assuring me anything is worth trying.

She's always there . . . She's everywhere.

CHAPTER TWENTY-NINE

HADLEY

"Did that guy just buy us a round of drinks?"

I look over at Riley, seeing where she's pointing to a man in a suit over at the bar. Riley and Nova asked me to come out with them for a girls' night and we've done a little bit of bar hopping. We ended up at the Lucky Frog to end our night with one more drink before the guys come pick us up.

Nova and I direct both of our gazes over to the man as he lifts his glass into the air in silent cheers. A smile dances across his face and Riley lifts her glass up at him. He looks to be in his early thirties and he's quite handsome. Strong jawline, perfectly pressed suit, and styled, black hair.

"Ry, what are you doing?"

She takes a sip of her drink, looking at Nova with a shrug. "Being polite." She giggles softly, a sheepish grin on her face. "Trust me, I have no intention of going home with anyone other than your brother."

Nova makes a fake gagging sound. "Okay, we can just leave it at that."

"Drink up, girlies. The boys will be here soon to ruin our fun." She laughs again, the sound carefree as she tips her head back. "It's not every day that some random guy is offering to buy us drinks."

"This is true," I tell her, following suit as I lift my glass to the man and take a sip. "Let's just hope no one slipped any drugs into it."

"Oh, shit," Nova says in a hushed voice as she stares at the drink. She contemplates her choices and drinks it anyway. "The bartender knows Lincoln, so he knows better than to slip anything into our drinks."

"Well, that's reassuring," I tell her with a laugh. "I already know I'm going to be hungover tomorrow morning, so that eliminates a worry I didn't have until half a minute ago." I take another sip, swallowing down the liquor before letting out a sigh. "Thank you, guys, for including me in your girls' night tonight. I don't know the last time I've had something like this and it's been refreshing."

Nova reaches for my hand, giving it a gentle squeeze as she smiles at me. "You're one of us now. Whether you're still in Aston or another state, you're part of the girl gang now."

"And once you're a member, there's no out," Riley says with a grin. Her words are a bit slurred from the alcohol, but I can still make out what she's saying. "I know you don't plan on staying, but I wish you would reconsider."

"I'm sure Rowan wouldn't object to it," Nova adds,

something unreadable passing through her expression. She sounds almost exactly like Riley does and that's when I realize how drunk the three of us actually are.

"You guys know the engagement isn't real," I remind both of them, the words tasting bitter as they roll off my tongue. I wave my hand dismissively, the movement making my head momentarily feel like it's spinning. "We've been playing house, knowing all along that this would eventually come to an end."

"But it doesn't have to," Riley interjects, just before she's cut off by the sound of an unfamiliar voice.

"I'm sorry for interrupting, ladies . . ."

The three of us whip our heads to the side, the man from the bar walking over to the circular table as he stops at the empty side that is across from me. He's between Riley and Nova and they're both looking at him with curiosity.

"Thank you for the drinks," I tell him, a smile lifting my lips as Nova lifts her drink to her mouth, shaking her head at me in disapproval. She mutters something indistinguishable, her glazed eyes finding mine.

"It's not every night an attractive man in a suit pays for our drinks," Riley chimes in. Her speech is slurred, but she tries to hold it together.

"Well, that doesn't sound right," he says as he looks at the three of us, his dark eyes twinkling beneath the lights above. "I'm Tobias. The three of you are too beautiful to not have anyone buying drinks for you."

"Aren't you sweet?" Nova says, smiling at him before she makes a movement with her hand, her ring catching the light. "Our fiancés are usually the ones buying our drinks."

His smile falters only for a second as he looks around the table. "Man, what an unlucky night for me. Are all three of you taken?"

"We are," Riley tells him before glancing at me with a devious grin. "Well, she's debatable." She raises her eyebrows at me. "Isn't that right, Hadley?"

Tobias looks at me, tilting his head to the side. "It sounds like you have a story to tell, pretty girl."

I laugh, the sound unnatural as it's laced with the alcohol we've consumed. The room tilts for a fraction of a second. "Not really. Just tied up in an engagement with a man who isn't interested in settling down."

"Well, excuse my language, but it sounds like he's a fucking idiot." Tobias stares at me, his dark brown eyes burning holes into mine. "A beautiful woman like you shouldn't be playing games with a man who clearly doesn't appreciate what is right in front of him."

"What the fuck did you just say to my fiancée?"

The sound of his voice has my heart tumbling in my chest, and my breath catches in my throat. The room spins a bit as I glance over my shoulder, but the look on Rowan's face is enough to make me feel sober enough, even if just for a fraction of a second.

"Rowan?"

"Hi, baby," he says softly, his eyes looking at me before he looks back at the man standing on the other side of the table. "You have approximately three seconds to answer me or I will put my fist through your fucking face."

Nova and Riley look at one another, sharing a knowing look as amusement encapsulates their features. They both glance at me while Lincoln and Nash appear at the table and the four of them look like they should be sharing a bucket of popcorn as they watch the scene unfold in front of them.

"Ah," Tobias drawls, a smirk pulling on his lips. He lifts his glass, taking a slow sip of his liquor before setting it back down. "Let me guess. You're her fake fiancé?"

"What's real and what's fake between us is none of your fucking business."

Tobias levels his gaze on Rowan. "I don't know your situation, nor do I want to get involved in it." He looks at me with an apologetic smile before directing his attention back to Rowan. "What I do know is that when a man fumbles a woman like her, there's always someone there to catch her."

There's a rumbling sound in Rowan's chest as I climb out of my chair and his arm locks around my waist possessively. "Listen, motherfucker," he starts, his pulse bouncing in the side of his neck. "Remove yourself from this table or I will remove you myself."

Tobias lifts his glass, smiling at all of us. "Have a good night, ladies."

I watch him for a second as he turns around and begins to move back to the bar before I'm being pulled away from the table. My feet get hung up and the alcohol rushes through my system, causing me to trip over my own shoes. "Rowan, stop," I slur, my hand reaching for his arm. "I can't walk that fast."

Without a word, he sweeps me off my feet, half throwing me over his shoulder, but still gently holding me as he carries me out of the bar. Anger and irritation radiate from him and he shifts me in his arms, cradling me against his chest. The alcohol makes my vision blur and I let my head fall heavily against his collarbone.

"You're always around to make a save, aren't you?"

I don't know where he's parked or where we're going, but it feels like an eternity until he's lowering me down into the front seat of the car. I look up at him, inhaling the scent of his cologne as he grabs the seat belt, reaching across my body to strap me in.

"Rowan," his name tumbles from my lips, my voice barely audible and partly slurred. I reach for his hand, stopping him before he pulls away. "Did I do something wrong?"

He stares at me, torment engulfing his expression, and I squint my eyes to try and focus on his face as my vision blurs further. "No, outlaw," he murmurs, his free hand reaching to brush a hair away from my face. "You could never do anything wrong."

"Okay," I say, letting out a breath as my head feels like it's about to spin again. "Thank you for coming and getting me. I know all of this is fake and we're just playing house until I have to go, but you're my safe place."

His lips part, a shallow breath slipping from him as he watches me for a beat. He closes his mouth, rolling his lips between his teeth before releasing them. "Let's get you home."

"I like that." I smile at him, lifting my hand to cradle

the side of his cheek as my eyes begin to grow heavy. "I think I might like it too much."

"Me too," he whispers, his hand leaving the side of my face, my own falling away from his cheek as he stands upright. Sadness passes through his eyes and I let out a heavy breath, unable to fight against the drunken slumber that drags me under.

I don't know how long it takes us to get home and my mind barely registers what is going on as he lifts me from his car and carries me into the house. Exhaustion and alcohol are not a good mix at all. Rowan doesn't put me down until we get to his bedroom and after he lowers me down into the bed, he climbs in with me, pulling me flush against his chest.

Instinctively, I breathe in the scent of him, feeling myself being swept back asleep. The last thing I feel is his lips pressing against my forehead, the soft caress of his warm breath as he murmurs against the crown of my head. His words are barely audible and as I drift asleep, I carry them into my slumber with me, even though I know I must have misheard him.

"I wish you were mine."

CHAPTER THIRTY

ROWAN

"Hello, Hadley," my lawyer says with a smile as he approaches Hadley who is standing in front of the room. "How are you today?"

It's just the two of us here today, because at the end of the day, we're the only two who really matter in this case. My lawyer interviewed friends and family and was able to provide their statements to show my character and ability to provide stability.

He went and met with Selena two weeks ago and she signed over her parental rights without a second thought. She didn't want to face me herself and figured the hospital was the best place to leave Lucy. Selena never intended on fighting against me for custody and for that, I was so fucking grateful.

Now, there's only one last piece to set in place to seal the deal of gaining full custody of Lucy.

Hadley and I have to sell our engagement to the judge.

I've never had to deal with an experience like this

before so I wasn't sure what to expect before we walked into this courtroom. The thought of losing Lucy, of Lucy being given to someone else or put into the system, makes my heart feel like it's going to shatter.

Hadley smiles back at the lawyer and the judge. "I'm doing well, thank you."

"As I'm sure you know, we've asked you to come today to provide a little insight on you and Mr. Taylor's relationship."

My heart stalls in my chest as her eyes find me. The softest smile lifts her lips and her head bobs before looking back at him. "Yes, of course."

"You and Mr. Taylor are engaged, correct?"

"Yes." She tips her chin, still smiling at him.

"How long have the two of you known each other?"

"Oh my," she says with a gentle laugh. "Well, we grew up in the same town and went to the same school, so it's been many years."

"So, you would say you know him very well then?"

Her eyes flash to me. "Sometimes I think I know him better than I know myself."

My breath catches in my throat and my heart skips a beat. I have to maintain my composure. This is all just for show. She doesn't mean a single word of it.

"Very well," the lawyer says with approval. "When Rowan is away for work, is Lucy with you?"

"Yes," she tells him, which is the truth. "I've taken some time off from my own job for us to get everything figured out."

"And what will the two of you do when you go back to work?"

"We have a babysitter lined up for that."

My lawyer looks pleased as he looks back at the judge. "As you can see, Your Honor, Miss Reed has known Mr. Taylor for many years and is someone who can speak to his character. With their engagement, I believe it's pretty clear that Lucy will have all her needs met and the two of them can provide the stable environment she needs to grow up in."

The judge mulls things over, looking over his notes before looking at Hadley. "Is Rowan Taylor someone you could see spending the rest of your life with, even if things were to get tough?"

Hadley doesn't falter. "Yes."

"Is he someone you would want to have future children with, presuming that was something you wanted to do?"

Again, she doesn't hesitate. "Yes."

Emotion washes over me, but I shove it back into the box inside my chest, knowing it's something I cannot entertain. Hadley is playing her part. She's doing everything I asked her to do.

And for some reason, that fucking kills me.

How badly I wish it were all true . . .

Her eyes slide back to mine. "Rowan Taylor is the best person I've ever met. He's kind and caring. He's the type of person to give you the shirt off his back. But above all of that, he's thoughtful and attentive. He loves with his entire chest and he'll do whatever he has to, to keep the ones he loves safe."

My heart is a mess inside its cage, hearing her talk

about me like this. She speaks it like it's written in stone. The truth and nothing less.

"Well, I think this is a fairly easy decision to make then," the judge says, breaking through the silence that settled in the courtroom. "Rowan Taylor, I grant you full custody of Lucille Taylor."

The next few minutes are a fucking whirlwind, like an out-of-body experience. If it weren't for Hadley, I'm not sure how any of this would have panned out. There's a chance they may have looked at me and my career and said no.

Hadley walks over in my direction and practically throws herself at me. Her arms wrap around the back of my neck as her chest melts into me. My arms instinctively go around her lower back, sweeping her off her feet. "Oh my god, Rowan," she breathes against my ear as I hold her tightly. "I'm so happy for you. You did it. You got her."

I lower her feet back down onto the floor, watching her for a moment, my eyes bouncing back and forth between hers. My hand reaches for hers, our fingers lacing together. "We did it."

A smile spawns across her face, reaching for her eyes. "I think this calls for a celebration."

"I just want to spend the night with you and Lucy," I tell her, my voice low and hoarse as emotion builds inside my chest. The only thing I want right now is to have Lucy in my lap and Hadley tucked up against my side on the couch.

Her expression softens, her hazel eyes infiltrating mine. "That sounds even better." She turns her body away from me so she's standing beside me, our linked hands between us. She looks up at me, the sun shining in her expression. "Let's go get her."

This morning we left Lucy at Nova's while everyone was at practice. I didn't tell anyone else about the court date today, except for the coaches and the general manager, and my close circle of friends. I needed to ask to skip practice this morning and they were very accommodating. The guys were going to be expecting an answer, but I would get to them later.

Right now, the only thing that matters is Lucy and Hadley.

After all the paperwork is taken care of and my copies are handed to me, Hadley and I head out of the courthouse together, one hand in Hadley's and the other holding on to all the legal documentation I need to prove that I have full custody of Lucy. In a way, I'm shocked, but most of all, I'm just relieved.

There's going to be a new wave of challenges with Hadley leaving, but I have no choice except to try and figure it out. Mia already agreed to watch Lucy for me during playoffs and then I have the off-season to figure out what will happen in the fall.

The thought of her leaving feels like a knife twisting in my chest, but I can't focus on that, not while I still have her here with me. I don't want her to leave and I know I can't ask her to stay. She loves her job and she wants to see the world. The last thing I'm going to do is try to sway her to stay with me because of my own selfish wants.

If only things could be different . . . if only she didn't have plans to leave.

———

"How long would it take for you to get ready?" I ask Hadley, feeling her warmth against my side as the movie comes to an end, the credits beginning to roll on the screen.

She moves away, my arm falling onto the couch as she turns to look at me. "I thought you just wanted to spend the night here?"

A sheepish grin pulls on my lips. "I didn't specifically say I wanted to spend it here." I glance down with a slow grin at Lucy who ended up falling asleep in Hadley's arms while we were all snuggled on the couch tonight. I glance at my phone, seeing there's a message from Mia saying she could come over for a few hours.

"I thought you didn't want to go out and celebrate, though?"

"I want to take you out, Hadley," I admit, my voice gruff as I cross my arms over my chest in defiance. "This is your last night here . . ."

She purses her lips. "I don't want you to feel obligated to do something with me because I'm leaving tomorrow," she tells me, her expression unreadable as she rises to her feet and stares. "We don't have to go out." She lets out a breath, her shoulders deflating. "Let me go put her down and we can talk about it then."

Frustration washes over me, but I don't say anything as she leaves me in the living room alone. It's her last night here and I know the quiet moments of getting Lucy settled into her crib is a top favorite of Hadley's. The thought of her not being here after tonight feels like a vise grip tightening around my chest. I can't let my mind go there.

I can't think about what it will be like without her presence here. Dread swells in my stomach and I know I'm going to miss her. She hasn't even left yet and I already feel a hollowness in my chest. There's going to be a Hadley-shaped hole inside my heart and nothing but her will ever fill that void.

And even still . . . I know I can't ask her to stay. I can never and will never ask her to give up her life or her career for Lucy and me.

As I sit on the couch, I type out a message to Mia to tell her I'll let her know what's going on and if I need her. It's Hadley's last night here, so it only seemed right to take her out . . . but now I'm not so sure. If she doesn't want to go out, then we won't.

At this point, I don't care what we do, as long as I get to do it with her.

Hadley appears back in the living room, walking over to me on the couch as she lowers herself down beside me. "I don't want to go out tonight, Rowan. I don't want to go out and be distracted by the outside world." She tilts her head to the side, her bottom lip drawing between her teeth before she lifts herself from the couch and straddles my lap. I watch her carefully, my hands finding her hips as she settles down onto me. Her hands lift, cupping my cheeks. "I just want to be distracted by you."

CHAPTER THIRTY-ONE

HADLEY

Rowan's hands slide around my backside, gripping my ass cheeks as he holds me against him. He's hard underneath me, his cock throbbing against my pussy. "I want you in my bed, outlaw."

"Then take me there," I retort, rising to my feet as he releases his grip on me. He stands up with me, his pants tenting from his erection as he moves closer to me.

His hand slides along the side of my face, snaking around the back of my head as he plunges his fingers through my locks and grabs a handful. He pulls my hair, my chin lifting up toward the ceiling as his other hand grabs under my jaw. "I want to fuck this pretty mouth, Hadley." He nips at my bottom lip. "Are you going to let me?"

Warmth instantly builds between my legs and I bob my head at him, my eyes glazing over as I stare back at him. "Yes, please."

"Good girl," he growls, his grip tightening on my hair as his mouth claims mine. He kisses me with an urgency that has me clawing at his back, like I'm trying to get inside him. My lips part the instant his tongue slides along the seam of my mouth and he pushes inside, tongues tangling in the sweetest torture.

I'm the one who slows the kiss, kissing him with a tenderness before pulling away from him. His hand is still in my hair, but he slowly releases his grip as my eyes search his. Slowly, I begin to lower myself down his body until I'm on my knees in front of him.

"What are you doing, Hadley?"

"Depends on what you do," I throw back at him, a ghost of a smirk dancing across my lips. "Are you going to let me suck your cock right here?"

He groans, his chest rising with a shallow breath. "Fuck yes."

"Then be a good boy and get your cock out for me."

Rowan doesn't waste a single second. He pushes down his sweatpants and boxer briefs, his dick immediately springing free as he shoves them down to the middle of his thighs. I lift my hand, reaching for him, wrapping it around the base of his cock as I stare up at him.

"You're so fucking sexy." He runs his hand along the underside of my jaw. "Now, let me see you swallow my cock."

A moan escapes him, the sound vibrating through his entire body as I wrap my lips around the head of his dick. I suck in the tip at first, my movements deliberately slow as I taste and tease him, watching as his head tips back from the pleasure rushing through his body.

I slide his cock into my mouth, taking as many inches as I can before it makes me gag. Rowan moans again, his hand finding my hair, fisting it against my scalp as he pulls me back enough to get my bearings straight. With my hand around the base, I use it in tandem with my mouth as I begin to move again.

My hand pumps as my head bobs up and down, sucking him into my mouth. My lips tightening around him, pulling him in and out as he begins to shift his hips, fucking my face. This has never been something I was really into, but watching him right now sends a rush of dampness between my legs. I'm wet just from sucking his cock and I'm actually enjoying this.

"Fuck me with your mouth, baby," he groans, his fist tightening on my hair. "You look so good with your pretty lips wrapped around my cock."

I smile around his length, his words making my clit tingle. My hand starts to move faster, pumping him harder as I take his dick in deeper. He hits the back of my throat and I gag again, tears instantly springing to my eyes, but I don't let it deter me. He's loving this and by default, so am I.

Rowan's hips start to buck as he holds my head in place, taking over as he starts to fuck my face instead. He thrusts against me, my hand preventing him from destroying the back of my throat and my gag reflex. Tears roll down my face, saliva spilling from the corners of my lips.

His head tips backward, a low moan tearing through his body before he looks back down at me. "I'm going to come, baby. Are you going to be a good girl and suck me dry?"

I try to nod, but my movements are restricted. Instead, I hum around his cock, bobbing my head harder, sucking him deeper inside. He pumps his hips a few more times before my name falls from his lips.

"Goddamn, Hadley," he moans, his cum spurting against the back of my throat. I taste the saltiness on my tongue and I swallow as he shoots his load. "That's it, baby," he murmurs, stroking my cheeks as he slowly fucks my mouth. "Take all of me."

My head bobs a few more times, taking every inch of him, milking him dry. He stares down at me, his eyes glazed over as I slowly begin to pull back. I release him from my mouth, lifting my hand from his cock as I wipe the edges of my mouth with the back of my hand and any residual tears from the impact of his dick against the back of my throat.

"Get up," he orders, his voice hoarse and gravelly as he reaches for me, pulling me onto my feet. "Come with me, baby. It's time for me to take care of you."

Rowan pulls his pants and boxer briefs back up, his hand finding mine before he leads me upstairs to his bedroom. He's quiet as he pulls me inside, pushing the door shut behind us. I watch him as he turns back around to face me, his hands finding my hips as he pulls my body flush against his.

His face dips down, his lips brushing against my

mouth before I pull back. He tilts his head to the side, concern washing over his eyes. "What's wrong?"

"You just came in my mouth . . ." My voice trails off before I explain. "I didn't think you'd want to kiss me."

He raises a hand to the side of my face, tipping my head back. "Nothing could ever make me not want to kiss you." His mouth crashes into me, stealing the air from my lungs as his tongue tangles with mine. He doesn't care about the cum and kisses me with a potency that has moisture pooling between my legs again.

Rowan backs me across the room to his bed, stripping me and himself of our clothing before we're both falling back onto the mattress. He moves away, slowly lowering himself down the length of my body until he's settling between my legs.

"I want to make you come now," he murmurs, lightly blowing against my flesh. "Come on my tongue and then I'll fuck you until you're coming again."

"Or you could just fuck me now instead," I tell him, attempting to give him an out.

His face begins to lower closer to me, his warm breath skating across my center as his eyes find my gaze. "And miss out on tasting your pussy?" He groans, shaking his head. "Fuck that."

My heart pounds erratically in my chest, thrumming away at a rapid pace that would have a heart monitor alarming. He stares up at me as he lowers his mouth down to my flesh, his lips warm and soft as they begin to move against me. His tongue is like silk, sliding along my pussy, licking me up to my clit.

My back arches, head tipping back, a shiver of pleasure sliding down my spine. My face contorts, my eyelids slamming shut as he begins to work his mouth against me. He's deliberately slow, licking and teasing me with every flick of his tongue. His forearms press against the insides of my thighs, holding me in place as he continues with his sweet assault.

He knows exactly what he's doing and goddamn, he's fucking good at it. Tongue flattening against my clit, he moves it around in a circular motion, damn near driving me over the edge instantly. He applies a delicious amount of pressure, his movements everything I want as the friction has warmth pooling in the pit of my stomach.

Arms lifting the pressure from my thighs, I feel his hands and fingers as they begin to trail toward my center. His mouth lifts away, his eyes finding mine as he pushes his fingers into his mouth, his tongue swirling around them before he brings them back to me. His mouth lowers once more, suctioning around my clit as I feel his fingertips against my pussy.

"Fuck, you're so sweet," he murmurs against my flesh, his tongue circling my clit as he begins to push two fingers inside me. "Mm, you're so goddamn tight."

The warmth that builds in the pit of my stomach begins to spill into my veins, spreading through my body like wildfire. He pumps his fingers, pushing them deep, before pulling them out so that just his fingertips are inside. He finds a rhythm, curling his fingers as he strokes my insides.

Looking down, I meet his gaze from where he is

between my legs. A groan rumbles in his chest as he flicks my clit over and over. My hands reach for him, sliding my fingers through his messy tousled waves. They're like soft silk between my fingers. Rowan applies more pressure to my clit, his fingers pumping harder and faster as he fucks me with his fingers and his mouth.

"Look at me, Hadley," he murmurs against my clit. "I want to watch you as you come for me."

Grabbing a fistful of his hair, I grip him tightly as my orgasm hits me out of nowhere. It erupts deep inside of me, consuming me like a fucking tidal wave. His name spills from my lips, back arching, eyes glued on his. Stars begin to dance around the edges of my vision and my body shakes, quaking and rocking against him.

He doesn't stop until I'm fully satiated, riding out the high from him. Rowan slowly pulls his fingers from me, his mouth leaving my pussy. As he lifts his head and his body, he stares at me with an intensity that hits my chest. His chin glistens from my juices and he slips his fingers into his mouth, sucking my arousal from his digits.

And then he fucking smiles.

Holy shit.

"Look at you," he murmurs, his eyes scanning over my face, down the length of my body, until his gaze zeros in on my pussy. "You're so ready for me, aren't you, outlaw? Fuck," he groans, lifting onto his knees as he pumps his already hard cock twice. "Your cunt's soaked."

"Come here," I breathe, half lifting my spine from the mattress as I reach for him. "I want you inside me."

He begins to move toward me, crawling along the length of my body until he's hovering above me. He settles between my legs, lowering himself down onto me as his cock presses against my center. I hook my ankles around the small of his back, attempting to pull him into me.

My heart stumbles inside my chest as he pauses, staring down at me with a fire burning within his irises. There's so much more than that, though. There's a ferocity that penetrates the fibers of my soul. His eyes slowly search my face and my breath catches in my throat as he slides into me.

A moan escapes Rowan and he lets out a string of curses. His girth stretches me as he fills me with his length. My pussy constricts around him, the feeling of him inside me so goddamn intense.

"You're doing so well, baby," he murmurs, shifting his weight on his arms so he can stroke my face. "Just breathe. I know you can take it all."

He begins to shift his hips, his cock stroking my insides as he begins to move with a fluid rhythm. He rocks in, filling me to the hilt before pulling out, just until the tip is the only thing in me. His eyes never leave me as he slowly works my body, coaxing my pussy to be more accepting of how big he is. He stretches me out and the pleasure it elicits is mind-blowing.

My pussy clenches around him, sucking him in, holding him deep inside me as he begins to piston his hips, shifting in and out. He falls into a steady rhythm, his lips finding me in an instant. His tongue pushes past my lips and teeth as it seeks mine. He continues to fuck me, move with every thrust, as his tongue tangles with my own.

"You're unlike anyone I've ever met before," he breathes as we break apart. Lifting his face, he cups the sides of my face with tenderness. His eyes are gentle and soft as he stares at me, directly into my soul. "Hadley fucking Reed," he murmurs, his voice trailing off as he begins to move faster.

Something about the way he's looking at me has my heart climbing into my throat. There's a sense of intimacy I've never felt with anyone else. The way he looks into my soul, the way he surrounds me, consuming every single one of my senses.

I don't know how it happened, but somewhere along the way, I fell for him . . . and that was never supposed to happen.

"I could fuck you forever, Hadley," he sighs, his forehead pressing against mine as his eyelids fall shut. I let my lids do the same, soaking in the moment with him as he rocks his hips, slowly fucking me with a tenderness that has my heart melting. "I want to come with you. I want to feel you quaking around my cock as I fill you with my cum."

His words coupled with the way he moves inside me, along with the friction against my clit from his body pressed against me, has me ready to go. I hold on to him, my nails digging into his flesh as he starts to move with more force. The bed groans under our weight and with the way he pushes into me harder. His movements become rushed, like there's an urgency to reach the peak.

I'm not objecting. I enjoy him like this with me, but I'm so close—I need that release. And I'd bet every last cent I have that he feels the same exact way. He slides one hand down to my ass, his fingertips biting my flesh as he tightens his grip on me. He thrusts harder, his hips moving in rapid succession as he holds me down against the bed.

His body presses against my clit as he fills me with his cock. Both sensations are enough to have my toes curling. A moan vibrates in his chest and his hand grips my ass tighter. Moving faster, his balls slap against my flesh and he looks down at me. "Come with me, Hadley. Come all over my cock for me."

That's all it takes for him to send me falling into an endless abyss of pleasure. My orgasm tears through my body and I lose myself around him the same time he loses himself inside me. He pumps his cock in my pussy, spilling his warmth deep inside me until I'm filled with every last drop of his cum.

His thrusts begin to slow and he murmurs my name against the side of my neck. As he slides his hand away from my ass, I can feel the imprint he left in my flesh and I'm sure it will bruise tomorrow. Rowan drags his hands all over my body, stroking me with featherlight touches.

Moving above me, he repositions himself so he can see me, watching me as he pulls out. I immediately notice his absence, lifting my head as I see him getting off the bed. He moves over to the side, immediately finding me as he bends forward. I let out a gasp as he slides his arm beneath me, lifting me into the air.

"What are you doing?"

He smiles at me, his lips finding mine before he starts to walk toward the bathroom door. "Taking you to the bath," he says softly, his eyes slowly searching my expression. "I want to wash you and clean you up and then bring you back here so I can hold you while you fall asleep beside me one last time." He pauses, his throat bobbing as he swallows, and my chest constricts. "Is that okay?"

I don't dare trust myself to speak. I swallow back my emotions, pulling my bottom lip between my teeth as I incline my head forward. "I can't think of a better way to spend my last night in Aston."

Sadness passes through his expression. "Good."

He carries me into the bathroom, kind and gentle as he sets me down and draws a bath. After the tub is filled, he helps me in, before easing in behind me. There's nothing sexual about it, but the intimacy is unlike anything I've experienced before. He washes my body, cleaning every inch before washing and conditioning my hair for me.

He makes good on his promise and carries me back to his room afterward, tossing me one of his t-shirts to sleep in before pulling me into his arms. My back is pressed against his chest and his face is in my hair, breathing me in.

Rowan may not think he's relationship material, but I've never met a man as kind and as doting as him. He's a safe place to lay your head at night, a comforting shoulder when the world feels heavy. He's everything someone would want in a potential partner.

And whoever ends up capturing his heart will be the luckiest woman in the world.

CHAPTER THIRTY-TWO

HADLEY

Standing at the threshold, I stare into Rowan's living room, my eyes scanning over all of the things Lucy has acquired the past few months. Past that, I can see into the dining room and kitchen where I've spent so much of my time since moving in to help Rowan.

Absent-mindedly, I slide my right thumb and fore-finger over the ring on my left hand, spinning it around as emotion washes over me. I forgot to take it back off last night after Rowan told me to put it on. It's not mine . . . not to keep, at least.

Just like he was never mine to keep.

At the end of the day, it was all a means to an end. Every moment was fake and simply to ensure Lucy got to live with her father.

Walking over to the sink, I find a few dirty dishes and rinse them off before setting them in the dish-washer. Rowan is going to be busy the next few weeks with juggling a baby and the playoffs.

I already feel guilty enough for leaving him to figure out what he's going to do without me. The least I can do is put a few dishes into the dishwasher.

"You didn't have to do that."

The sound of his voice slides across my eardrums like silk and I suck in a deep breath, pushing my emotions back down as I slowly turn around to face him. "I know, but it needs to be done."

Rowan's eyes slowly search my face, his expression unreadable as he adjusts Lucy in his arms. "Thank you, Hadley," he says softly, his throat bobbing as he swallows roughly.

I force a smile onto my lips and it feels unnatural. It feels wrong in a moment like this. "It was just a few dishes. No big deal at all."

He tips his chin, the movement drawn out before his eyes survey the kitchen, coming to a stop on the clock on the stove. "Are you ready to go? If we want to get you to the airport on time, we should probably go now." His gaze slides back to mine. "Do you have all of your things?"

Everything except for my heart . . .

"I think so," I tell him, my voice quieter than I mean for it to be. "I left both of my suitcases by the door to the garage."

"Can you take Luce and I'll get them into the trunk?" he asks me, closing the space between us with his long strides before stopping in front of me. "If you want to meet me out there, we can hit the road then."

My hands brush against his and a shock of electricity

travels along the nerve endings in my skin. I ignore the shiver it sends down my spine and pull Lucy against my chest as I tilt my head to look at him. "Don't worry, I'll be out of your hair soon enough." I half laugh, winking at him as I feel a twinge of pain deep inside my chest.

He blows out a breath as he stares down at me for a beat. "You were never in my hair, Hadley."

"Yeah, well, you know what I mean," I retort, forcing that plastic smile across my lips again. "Are you sure it's okay if some of my things are still here?"

I told Rowan I could get a storage unit to keep the things I'm not taking with me to California, but he insisted it was senseless. No one else is going to be using the guest room that I've been occupying, so he was adamant that my belongings stay here until I figure out what I'm doing when my next travel assignment is up.

"Yes."

He's been quiet all morning and I hate it. None of this is easy for me and I know he's not particularly happy about me leaving right before playoffs start. We both knew it was going to end up working out this way timewise, but now he's stuck having to make other arrangements and I'm sure that's where his frustration is stemming from.

Rowan disappears from the kitchen, leaving Lucy and me as he heads out into the garage, taking my suit-cases with him. A few minutes later, I finally pull myself from the comfort of his home and walk out to the car. I get Lucy secured in her car seat and tears form along my lower lids as I know this is probably the last time I'll get the chance to do this.

I climb into the passenger seat, glancing at Rowan as he rests his hand on the gear shifter, his eyes slowly searching mine after I secure my seat belt.

"Are you ready?"

No.

"Yes."

———

The car ride to the airport is painfully silent outside of the music Rowan has playing. I don't pay attention to the lyrics, but I notice that he continues to turn it up, almost as if he's trying to block out the silence that stretches between us.

I want to say something, but I know I can't. What could I possibly say? There's no place for my feelings in a situation like this. I fell in love with a man I was never supposed to love. He needed me here to help him settle into life with his daughter.

And now he doesn't need my help.

There's no reason for me to stay.

Rowan follows the signs that point to departures, slowing to a stop outside of the doors that lead into the airport. Just beyond the sliding glass is the check-in for the airline I'm flying on and reality is hitting me directly in the center of my sternum.

Emotion wells in my throat and I struggle to swallow it back as Rowan puts the car in park. His knuckles are white as he holds on to the steering wheel, staring straight ahead. I watch him for a moment, unsure of what I'm supposed to do. He slowly uncurls his fingers, his chest deflating as he lets out a deep breath.

He doesn't look at me, instead letting himself out of the car before walking back to his trunk. I can't stop the tears that fall from my eyes in rapid succession, although I brush them away in a haste before sucking in a breath. I can do this.

Traveling was something I always wanted to do and this is a great opportunity for me. It's a job at one of my dream hospitals, working in a field I wanted more experience in.

It just sucks leaving like this.

I've grown too attached to Lucy . . . and too attached to Rowan.

I force myself out of the car and meet Rowan along the side where he's standing with both of my suitcases. His face lacks color and his eyes are distant as he watches me in silence. My feet don't want to move, but I force them to anyway and I stop in front of him as I adjust my purse on my shoulder.

"I brought this for you to take with you." He pauses, holding out the vase to me that we made together. "If you want it."

I stare down at the blue vase, emotion engulfing me as I struggle to dissect what the hell I'm feeling. "Of course I want it," I whisper, my words barely audible. "I thought maybe you would keep it."

He shakes his head as I lift my gaze to meet his. "It's yours."

It's not the only thing I want to be mine . . .

"Can I say bye to Lucy?" I ask him, my voice cracking around the words as my eyes search his. I can't help but wonder if I'm that delusional, that I'm the only one who's been feeling things between us. I wish he would tell me to stay, I wish he would try to change my mind about leaving.

Anything to show me that he feels this too . . .

"Of course," he says, his voice hoarse as he lets out a ragged breath. His lips part as if he's going to say something else, yet he doesn't. He clamps them shut, rolling them between his teeth before he opens the door to the back seat for me.

Stepping past him, the smell of oakmoss and cedar invades my senses, a cruel assault on my heart. It takes everything in me to ignore it as I step closer to the car, bending down to Lucy. She's strapped in her car seat, her blue eyes resting on me as I press my hand against her soft cheek.

"Hey, little Lu," I murmur, my voice catching in my throat as I blink back the tears that well in my eyes. "I know your daddy can be a bit of a pest, but I'm going to need you to be good for him, okay? He's going to be a little stressed for the next month or two, so try not to give him too much trouble . . . but don't make it too easy for him either."

I smile at her, even though she has no idea what I'm saying. Her little hands reach for me, her mouth opening as she smiles wide at me.

"I love you, sweet girl, and I hope I get to see you soon."

Lucy smiles at me, a soft cooing sound escaping her, followed by a babbling. I stroke the side of her face once more, knowing I have to tear myself from this moment. Tears blur my vision and I wipe them away before pressing a kiss to her forehead.

I can't look at her and I can't look at him.

Ducking my head, I wipe the tears from my face, avoiding eye contact with Rowan like a fucking coward as I grab the handles of my suitcase. "Thank you for driving me here," I tell him, my voice hushed as I look through the glass doors into the airport.

"I'm the one who should be thanking you."

I slowly turn my head, knowing I can't leave like this. None of this is Rowan's fault. I can't expect him to get down on his knees and beg me to stay. He has a life to live, one that doesn't involve me living in his house with him.

He has a village. He has the people he needs. I served my purpose here and now it's time for me to get back to my own life.

I was never supposed to fall in love with Rowan Taylor, and I failed miserably.

Glancing down at my hand, I see the ring still on my finger. The ring that was never truly mine. "Here," I whisper, pulling it free from my finger before handing it to Rowan. "I meant to take it off last night."

Rowan stares down at the ring in his palm, not speaking a single word as he lifts his gaze to me. It's unreadable and his eyes are bloodshot as they burn holes directly into my soul. "I don't want this."

I shake my head at him, refusing to accept it. The

ring was never for me to keep and, honestly . . . I don't want any of this. "Neither do I."

His eyebrows pull downward, creating a crease between them as a wave of pain passes through his eyes. His lips part, but I speak before he gets a chance to say anything.

"Bye, Rowan."

I don't wait for him to respond as I force myself to turn my back to him and walk directly toward the sliding glass doors. They part and I step through them, entering the airport with the ever-present urge to chance a glance in his direction.

My footsteps falter and I half expect him to be behind me. No, I never expected it, but goddamn, I fucking hoped he would have followed after me. Anything to stop me from leaving.

But he doesn't . . .

My vision blurs and the tears begin to fall as I start to move forward.

And I don't look back.

CHAPTER THIRTY-THREE

CARSON

Cocking my head to the side, my eyebrows lower in suspicion as I stare at the instant mac and cheese and mashed potatoes on the shelves at the grocery store. I'm supposed to be going to Lincoln and Nova's for our first friends' dinner. It's something Riley and Nova decided they want us all to do once a month together.

The only kicker is, it's supposed to be a potluck situation . . . and I can't make ramen noodles without turning them to mush.

Pulling out my phone, I open up my messages and do a quick glance at the group text, realizing none of the guys were in charge of food. I see Rowan's name and tap on it. I trap it between my ear and my shoulder as I pull off a box of instant mashed potatoes to read the instructions. I hear my call being picked up, but I'm greeted with silence.

"Did you talk to anyone about food tonight? No one said anything about what they were bringing and I was going to just bring mashed potatoes. Can I bring instant ones or will that be weird?" I ask, pursing my lips in contemplation. "I don't think anyone would be able to tell that they're not real."

There's still silence and I'm wondering if Rowan even actually answered my call. I set down the box, releasing my phone from my shoulder, and pull it away as I look down at my phone. It's connected.

"Hello? Did you fucking hang up on me?"

"No, Ford," he mutters in response, his voice seemingly disinterested.

"What are you and Hadley bringing? Did she talk to Nova or Riley at all about food?"

Silence again.

"Rowan?"

"Hadley isn't coming tonight." Rowan sighs, his voice trailing off into silence.

"Oh, is she sick or something?" I corkscrew my lips, shuffling down the aisle as I lean forward to look at the boxes of pasta. I'm not so sure I should show up with mac and cheese, but maybe something similar would suffice.

"No." The word is vacant and flat as it comes through the speaker.

"Then why won't she be there?" I question him as I stand upright again, glancing around the aisle, not sure why the hell they put any expectation on someone like me.

"Ford."

My brain is still hung up on the food situation and I don't even register what he said. "Can I just get a pasta salad from the deli counter or something?"

"Carson Ford."

"What?" I respond, holding my phone against my ear as I pause in the aisle, standing in front of the mac and cheese section.

"I don't give a flying fuck what you bring to Lincoln and Nova's tonight. I don't plan on going."

My eyebrows pull together. "What? The girls are insistent on making this a thing." I let out a deep sigh, rolling my eyes in frustration. "You don't get to get out of this. You have to go tonight and if Hadley isn't sick, she should probably come too."

"Hadley can't come because she fucking left." He mutters a curse under his breath. "I just dropped her off at the airport and she'll be on a flight to California in an hour."

My entire body falls rigid. "You let her leave?"

"What the fuck was I supposed to do, Ford? Beg her to stay?"

"Umm, yes, you idiot." This time when I roll my eyes, it's because I can't reach through my phone and smack him. "If you love her, you can't let her go."

"I can't ask her to stay, Carson. She has plans, she has a life to live. I can't ask her to stay here when I can't give her the relationship she deserves."

I'm silent for a second as I chew on his words. "I'm confused why you think you can't give her what she deserves . . ."

He lets out a harsh breath. "My schedule is far too demanding and we're gone so often. I don't want her to be with me and feel like I just want her around to take care of Lucy."

Man, he really is dumber than I thought.

"Rowan, she already knows and understands your schedule." I pause, trying to figure out how to go over this without telling him he's stupid. "If you don't want her to feel that way, then don't make her feel that way. Tell her how you feel, tell her you want her here because you want *her*."

"It's too late," he mumbles after a beat or two of silence. "She's already in the airport and probably heading to her gate."

"Where are you?" I ask him, shifting my weight on my feet as I absentmindedly survey the boxes of mac and cheese again.

"Sitting in a drop-off area outside of the airport."

I thought he had more than two brain cells, but now I feel like I'm talking to a replica of my own brain.

"Rowan . . . bro. Seriously, what the fuck are you doing?"

"I was getting ready to come home but Lucy started crying, so I pulled over and then you called—" He rambles, his explanation a string of words, but I abruptly cut him off.

"Turn the hell around and go get her. You cannot let her get on that plane," I tell him, my voice urgent. "You need to find her and tell her how you feel, and then it's up to her whether she decides to go or not."

"I don't want to sway her decision."

Good Lord. How the hell can he not see what's right in front of his face? It's as clear as day that

Hadley is in love with him. I sigh again. "Do you love her?"

"Yes."

"Have you told her that?" I question him again.

"No."

"Well, then, she's not making a well-informed decision, is she?" I say, shaking my head at how ridiculous this is. If he would have just communicated with her, this could all have potentially been avoided.

I also know how important Hadley has become to my best friend, and the last thing I'm going to do is let him fuck this up.

"Here is what you're going to do—you're going to go into the airport, buy a fucking bullshit ticket to wherever the hell the next plane is going, get through security, and find her. You're going to find her and you're not going to let her be the one who got away, do you understand me?"

Something pulls on my pocket and I glance down at a small child tugging on my shorts. I tilt my head to the side, his gray eyes meeting mine as he gives me a sheepish grin. "Excuse me, mister."

"Oh, shit, hold on, Ro," I say into the speaker, smiling down at the little boy who doesn't look to be older than five. "What's up, little man?"

"Does this have milk in it?" He holds up a box of instant mac and cheese, trying to show it to me. "Milk makes my belly hurt but I wanted to show Mommy I can pick out my own without needing any of her help."

I take the box from his small hand, my eyes scanning the list of ingredients, frowning when I realize it's a gluten-free type, but not a vegan one. "Yeah, bud, this one has milk. Let's see if we can find one without it."

"You're right, Ford," Rowan's voice comes through the speaker. "I'm being a fucking idiot and I'm turning around right now. I'm going back to the airport and I'm not letting her go without telling her the truth."

"Wait, say that again." I drop one of the boxes I find on the shelf that says it's vegan. "Shit," I mumble, crouching down to pick it up. "Here, buddy. This one says it's vegan, so it means it doesn't have any milk in it." He reaches out with his left hand to take it from mine.

"That I'm going back to the airport?" Rowan asks, the confusion evident in his voice.

"No, the part where you said I was right," I chuckle, watching the kid as he tries to read the back of the box.

"Oh my god, there you are, *bambino*."

My entire body falls rigid, my heart stalling in my chest. That voice—my god, I know that voice . . .

Lifting my gaze from the little boy, I'm momentarily transported back in time when my eyes collide with hers. Those gold-and-green eyes that have been swirling around in my mind since that one night almost six years ago. "Andi?"

"Carson." Her eyes widen with recognition, her cheeks flushed as she tucks a lock of chocolate-colored hair behind her ear. "Hi."

My throat constricts as I look between her and the little boy, him smiling up at me with eerily familiar gray eyes. Panic passes through her expression, her hazel eyes watching me as I connect the dots in real time. His hair isn't black like hers, but instead it's a dark brown, a few shades lighter.

There's no fucking way . . .

"Rowan, I'm going to have to call you back," I tell him, my voice sounding foreign and distant as my gaze slowly settles on Andi's.

Her slender throat bobs as she swallows hard, her hand protectively finding her son's opposite shoulder as she pulls him flush against her body. He holds on to the box of mac and cheese, lifting it with his left hand for her to see.

None of this is making sense in my brain right now.

"Yeah, sure. Thank you for your help, bro," he says, the words not even registering in my mind as I pull the phone away from my ear with my left hand without ending the call.

I tilt my head to the side, looking back at the boy again, my stomach feeling like it's going to fall onto the fucking floor. "What's your name, little man?"

"Matteo," he says with his eyes bright and a grin spreading across his face. "What's your name?"

"Matteo, *caro mio*," Andi starts to speak to him, her voice soft and gentle as she directs her gaze to her son. "We should stop bothering Mr. Ford and let him get back to his shopping."

Mr. Ford.

I resist the urge to scoff at her formality. She says my name like she wasn't screaming it the last time I saw her.

"I'm Carson," I answer, ignoring Andi's interjection. It's been almost six years since we last saw each other.

My heart is unsteady in my chest as I slowly ask him the next question. "How old are you, Matteo?"

His smile grows as he lifts his hand to show me his fingers, all spread apart. "Five!"

My eyes flash to Andi's and she looks at me, inhaling sharply as her eyes widen with apprehension.

What. The. Actual. Fuck.

CHAPTER THIRTY-FOUR

ROWAN

"I need to purchase a plane ticket."

The woman stares back at me, her expression unenthused. "To where and when?"

My eyes scan the list of flights behind her and I see one that's leaving a little after Hadley's. The timing is perfect, so long as there are tickets available. I read off the flight information from the board before looking back at her.

She gives me a strange look, popping a bubble of gum before she pulls it into her mouth with an obnoxious chew. Her attention is directed back to her computer screen and she moves the mouse around, clicking a few different times.

I adjust Lucy in the baby carrier strapped to my chest, rolling my wrist toward my body as I check the time again. Hadley's flight leaves very soon and they'll most likely begin boarding soon.

"One ticket, correct?"

"Yes, please," I tell her, reaching into my back

pocket to pull out my wallet. I flip it open, taking out my credit card and ID, before setting them down on the counter.

"Do you have any bags you're checking?"

"No."

She purses her lips, cocking her head to the side as she looks at me and Lucy. I know the policies. I don't need a ticket for Lucy and if we were actually flying, she could sit on my lap. The woman doesn't make any comments and turns her attention back to the computer in front of her. It feels like an eternity stretches as she enters in my information, making sure everything is correct before finally printing out the boarding pass.

She slides my cards back to me and I don't bother putting them in my wallet. Instead, I shove them into my front pocket since I'm going to need my ID to get through security anyway. I adjust Lucy in my arms as the woman finally hands me the stub.

"Thank you and I hope you have a nice trip," she says, raising a questioning eyebrow as I grab it from her in a haste.

"Thanks." I mumble out the word as I'm already spinning on my heel, my eyes scanning the space as my mind draws a blank on what I'm doing or where I'm going. I know I need to find Hadley and that's the only thing that fucking matters.

Naturally, when I make my way over to security, there's a line, and I quickly find my place in it, rocking back and forth in an effort to keep Lucy content. I have everything I need to make her a bottle in the diaper bag I brought, but I just need to get through security first.

I can't stop from looking at my watch every step we take that gets us closer to the end of the line. I can't help but feel like I'm running out of time at this point. There's twenty minutes left until they start boarding for her flight and—holy shit—what if I don't make it?

Anxiety builds in the pit of my stomach, but I can't let it consume me. Not now. Not when I'm so close to reaching her. If I don't get there in time, they won't let me on the plane to get her. I don't want to text her to let her know I'm coming for her, but if she ends up getting on the plane, I might have to do that because the last thing I'm going to do is let her get on a plane to the other side of the country without hearing what I have to say.

Lucy and I get through the first step of security. My boarding pass and ID are scanned and we're on our way to the final part. I kick my shoes off, shoving them into one of the plastic bins before putting the diaper bag in the one after mine. Because I have Lucy in my arms, I'm waved through one of the metal detectors instead of the one that does a full-body scan, and I keep on moving. When I get over to the belt, I find my shoes and drop them onto the floor, slipping them on as I wait for the diaper bag.

I see it coming out from the scanning machine and it's inching closer. At the last minute, it juts into a different lane and slides down to one of the TSA agents. What. The. Fuck.

I cannot afford a hang-up like this right now.

"Sir, is this your bag?" one of the agents at the end

of the line questions me as he sees me eyeing it from where I'm standing.

"Yes," I tell him, jerking my chin as I try to give Lucy a pacifier. She pushes it away and instead shoves her fist into her mouth, sucking on her fingers vigorously. I need that damn bag so I can make her the quickest bottle of my life. "Is there something wrong?"

"It appears it was flagged for an item that doesn't pass security." He stares at the screen for a moment and I swear I can hear the ticking of the clock inside my brain. "Do I have your permission to search the bag and find the item?"

"Absolutely." I dip my head again without any hesitation. He could throw out the entire fucking bag at this point and I wouldn't care.

Okay, that's a lie. I need to be able to make Luce a bottle as soon as humanly possible.

The man unzips the pockets, going through each one, before he pulls out a filled water bottle from inside the biggest compartment. "Here's the culprit." He chuckles, shaking his head as he holds it up to me. "Liquids more than three ounces are not allowed."

Dear God, I'm an idiot.

"I must have forgotten that it was in there."

He smiles, setting the bottle to the side. "It happens more often than you would think. I'm going to have to dispose of the bottle."

"Yeah, sure. Do whatever you have to with it."

I don't want to draw more attention to myself by asking him to hurry up, but this man needs to hurry the fuck up. Rolling my wrist, I glance at my watch again. Ten minutes. Ten minutes until they start boarding and I'm still waiting for this stupid diaper bag.

He finally finishes zipping it up, making whatever notes he has to make in his system before handing the diaper bag back to me. "Here you are, sir. I hope you have a safe flight and a nice trip."

"Thanks," I mumble, barely paying attention to him as I sling the bag over my shoulder and quickly rush over to one of the benches. I drop down onto it, checking the time. I need to move quickly and now I don't have a water bottle.

Goddammit.

I dump the formula into the bottle, shoving everything back into the bag before rising to my feet again. The diaper bag hangs on my shoulder and I hold Lucy against my chest as I stride over to the closest convenience store. I luck out and find a bottle of room temperature water and promptly buy it. I pour the amount needed into the baby bottle and shake it vigorously.

Shoving the bottle of water into the bag, I take Lucy from the carrier, cradling her in one arm as I take the bottle in my other hand and slide it into her mouth. She looks up at me, her gaze soft as she begins to suckle on it. "I know, Luce. We have to hurry or we're not going to get to her in time."

I don't even know where to find her.

Moving over to one of the boards, it takes me a few seconds to find her flight and which gate she's at. Looking at my watch again, my stomach sinks. There's two minutes left and the gate is down a separate corridor.

"I don't know if we're going to make it, Luce."

She stares at me, blinking as she continues to drink her bottle. Holding her close against me, my footsteps are rushed, my strides long, as I try to get to the gate as quickly as I can without jostling Lucy around too much. It's such a precarious balance because the last thing I want to do is upset her or make her sick from moving her around like this while she's trying to eat.

There's a part of me that feels like a terrible father right now, but then there's my heart . . . and I know deep down I have to find Hadley.

As I round the corner and step into the corridor where her gate is, I see the sign for the one she's at and it's three gates away. Just as I start to move down the hall, I hear the sound of a voice coming across the speaker from her gate.

"We're now going to begin boarding for zone 2. Please line up by the desk and have your boarding pass ready to go."

My stomach falls onto the floor.

Fuck.

I'm so goddamn close. I don't know which group she's boarding with but I can only hope she didn't board with the first zone. My footsteps are even more rushed and I hold Lucy closer, her little hands lifting to hold on to the bottle. The movement from her isn't intentional but my heart still constricts because it feels like she's doing it to try and help me.

We make our way to the gate and I stop short, my

eyes surveying the entire area, looking for any sight of her. My heart pounds erratically against my rib cage, threatening to break free as I try to find her. My eyes slide along the people in line, dread washing over me when I don't see her.

I don't see her anywhere, which means she's already on the plane.

If I call her and she gets off the plane, she won't be able to get back on. I'm going to completely derail her plans and I just hope she feels the same way about me, or else I'm about to fuck everything up for her.

"Rowan?"

My heart immediately stops in my chest, my breath catching in my throat. I spin around on my heel, my head whipping around as I find her standing right there. My eyes widen as shock and relief flood me. "Hadley."

She tilts her head to the side, her eyebrows pulling together as she assesses me and Lucy with a perplexed look on her face. "What . . . what are you doing here?"

My nostrils expand, my heart skipping a beat in my chest. "I can't let you get on that plane, outlaw."

She swallows roughly, her lips parting as she lets out a soft breath. "Why?"

"Because I can't let you go." I pause, rolling my lips between my teeth, my tongue darting out to wet them. "I'm in love with you, Hadley, and if I let you get on that plane without telling you the truth, I don't know that I'd ever be able to live with myself."

Her eyes widen and she stares back at me with an unreadable expression. "You're in love with me?"

"Yes." I pull the bottle from Lucy's mouth as she finishes and I notice she's in a milk coma in my arms. I tuck the bottle in my back pocket. "I don't know when it started, but I only realized when it was far too late. When I had already begun to fall, and now I just can't get you out of my fucking head. You're everywhere I turn, everywhere I look." I pause, letting out a ragged breath. "I love you, Hadley Reed. And I don't want you to go."

"But you don't need me anymore . . ." she says softly, her voice trailing off as tears fill her eyes.

Closing the distance between us, I reach for the side of her face with my free hand, sliding my palm against her cheek as I push my fingers through her auburn hair. "But we do," I admit, my voice soft as my eyes probe hers. "Just not in the way we once did. We don't need your help, but we need *you*."

Tears fall down her cheeks and I catch some with the pad of my thumb. "Please don't get on that plane, baby. Come home with us, where you belong." I let out a breath, emotion welling in my throat. "I want to wake up every morning with you in my bed. I want to find you curled up on the couch with Lucy tucked in your arms. I want to find you creeping in my pottery shed late at night."

"I do not creep," she says, laughter falling from her lips as her eyes shimmer.

"You totally do." I chuckle, shaking my head as a smirk lifts the corner of my lips. "But I want it to be you. You're the one who is supposed to be with me."

"What about my job? They're expecting me."

My heart clenches and I tilt my head to the side, my thumb drifting across her skin. "Do you want to go?"

"No, not really." She pulls her bottom lip between her teeth as she shakes her head. "I never wanted to go."

"Tell them you can't make it." I let out a ragged breath, my heart crawling into my throat. "Plans can change, outlaw."

"Isn't that the truth, because falling in love with you was never a part of mine, but you made it inevitable. There was no way to stop this from happening and I wouldn't have wanted to even if I could," she says softly, her hands reaching up to drag my face down to hers. "I love you, Rowan. I've loved you for a long time," she breathes against my lips, her mouth capturing me in the softest kiss. "You made your save, now take me home."

I pull back from her, my eyes getting lost in the brown and green hues. I can't believe I almost let her get away. She stares back at me with a ferocity that rocks me to my core. She's nestled in my heart, seeping into my soul, and I know that's exactly where she belongs.

Hadley Reed everywhere and everything . . .

And I know I'll never let her go.

EPILOGUE
ROWAN

EIGHT MONTHS LATER

"Happy birthday, dear Lucy. Happy birthday to you!"

Everyone starts to clap their hands and Lucy claps along, a high-pitched squeal coming from her before she lets out a string of laughter. Hadley stands beside me, sliding closer as she slips an arm around my back. She presses her side into me and I dip my head down, pressing a kiss against the top of her head.

"Are you ready for cake, Luce?" Hadley asks my daughter as she pulls away from me and takes a step toward her. "Aunt Rae has the pretty princess one and then we have a special one just for you."

We decided to have a small party for her at home with our friends, my parents, and Raven. Beau recently got a new job that he's been traveling for, so he wasn't able to stop by. He's been doing really well in life and we've all just been watching in amazement, offering our support from the sidelines as he finally gets his life on track.

Hadley passes my sister Raven just as she comes into the dining room with my mother hot on her heels. One of the nurses Hadley works with has a bakery business on the side and she offered to make the cakes for us. After deciding to stay in Aston, Hadley's been working her dream job at a neighboring maternity center.

She's been talking about wanting to eventually cut back her hours for more time with Lucy, but I just want her to do what she wants to do. Mia has stepped in more as our regular babysitter, so we have a plan in place, regardless of what Hadley decides she wants to do.

Her co-worker made two cakes, one for everyone to eat and one for Lucy to smash, since that is apparently a tradition or something. The bigger cake immediately catches Posey's attention. It's shaped like a castle, looking more like a model than something you can eat, with a princess standing outside of the front door.

"A pretty princess!" Posey calls out as she comes jogging over to the high chair. She reaches for the tray, lifting herself on her tiptoes as she tries to get a better look. Lucy plants her palm against the side of Posey's face, her eyebrows pulling together in annoyance as she tries to push her away from her cake.

"Lucy, that's not very nice," I tell her, half scolding

her as I try to bite back my grin. Posey sticks her tongue out at Lucy as she drops back down onto her feet. She tucks her stuffed hockey player under her arm, before crossing them over her chest. Crouching down, I get to Poe's level. "I'm sorry, Poe. Lucy needs to take her nap and she doesn't understand what's going on today."

Posey pouts. "I just wanted to see the cake."

"Look," Raven says, lifting the cake from the tray on the high chair, and lowers it so Posey can see it. "Isn't it super pretty? Look at all the pinks!"

"Pink is my favorite color," Posey tells her with a grin spreading across her little face.

"Well, then I'll make sure you get a piece with all the pink icing!"

Posey claps her hands in excitement, bouncing up and down as she stays in place and watches Raven take it over to the table. Hadley appears back beside Lucy, lowering a circular cake down onto the high chair for her to inspect herself.

Lucy wastes no time, digging her hands into the cake and icing immediately as everyone snaps pictures and takes videos of her. She fucking loves the spotlight and she literally has everyone eating out the palm of her hand.

No, seriously . . . She holds out handfuls of cake to Hadley and me before offering them to anyone who makes eye contact with her. No one has the heart to tell her no and it becomes quite a messy ordeal.

My mother and Raven fawn over Lucy as everyone falls into a cake coma, settling into the living room.

Raven pulls Lucy from her high chair, cleaning her up before my mother takes her out toward the couch where my father's sitting.

Hadley picks up the cake, taking it into the kitchen, and I follow after her, dragging the high chair on its wheels across the wood floor. Wiping down the surface, I clean what I can as Hadley gets the cake and everything else sorted.

I strip the cloth material from the high chair, setting it with the bib she was wearing, but Hadley picks it up immediately. She gives me a grin and a soft laugh. "I'll throw it in the wash now. I don't know if the pink icing is going to end up staining anything."

"Good thinking," I tell her as I go to slide the high chair back to the dining room table. As I enter the space, I glance around the rest of the house, seeing that everyone else seems to be occupied and not noticing my absence, or Hadley's.

She's still in the laundry room, waiting for the washer to fill with water as I step into the room with her. Pushing the door closed behind me, I make sure that it's actually shut and lock it for good measure. Hadley looks over at me, raising an eyebrow as she begins to spin around to face me.

I stalk toward her, immediately entering her space as I slide my hand along the side of her face. My thumb slides beneath her jaw, tilting her head back before my mouth crashes into hers. She tastes like sugar and she lifts her hands to grip the front of my sweatshirt, pulling me closer as my tongue tangles with hers.

I swear, I can't get enough of her and I don't think I ever will.

"Fuck, I've been waiting all day to get you alone," I murmur against her lips, nipping at her flesh with my teeth. My cock is already hard in my pants and I press against her, so she can feel me. "This is what you do to me, Hadley."

"Mm," she moans against my mouth, one of her hands dropping down to fist my cock through my pants. She slides her other hand along my chest, over my collarbone, before reaching my shoulder. Her nails bite my skin through the fabric of my shirt.

"You know everyone's out in the other room, right?"

"Ask me if I care, outlaw," I growl, my cock throbbing in my pants as I pin her against the dryer.

She stares up at me, lust building deep within the depths of her eyes. "I want you inside me, Rowan." She drops her other hand down to the waistband of my pants, shoving them down far enough to pull out my cock. "You have to be quick and quiet, though."

"Done."

Hadley watches me, her lips parted, chest heaving, as I slide her pants and panties down. She steps out of them, leaving them on the floor. A gasp escapes her as I lift her up into the air, gently setting her down on top of the dryer.

She spreads her legs, her knees bent as she plants her hands on top of the machine, leaning back slightly as she stares at me with a sultry look. "Spit on it."

Holy fuck. If I wasn't going to be inside her within

the next few seconds, I would undoubtedly come in my pants.

"Yes, ma'am."

Gripping her knees, I spread them farther, her body shifting so her pussy is tilted toward me. I stare at her, my eyes not leaving hers as my cheeks pull in, drawing spit onto my tongue. Her eyes are glazed over, her chest rising and falling with ragged breaths.

Parting my lips, I roll my tongue, before spitting onto her cunt. Hadley's eyes fall shut, a moan slipping from her before she looks at me once more. "Good boy."

"Good boy, bad girl, huh?" I smirk as I wrap my arms around her thighs, pulling her toward me as I slide the tip of my cock against her pussy. Her head falls backward, her eyes rolling back in her skull as I push inside her.

"Fuck me, Rowan," she breathes, lifting her face as her lust-filled gaze collides with mine. "Fuck me before someone comes looking for us."

"Your wish is my command."

Holding on to her, I begin to piston my hips, drilling my cock into her in rapid succession. She lifts her arms, gripping my shoulders as she clings onto me, taking every thrust I deliver. She takes every inch of my length, her teeth biting into her bottom lip as she swallows back her own moans and sounds.

The thought of someone knocking on the door makes my heart pound harder and faster. The possibility of getting caught has a way of making the fire grow at a rapid pace. Her nails bite into my skin and my fingers dig into her flesh. I slam into her, unable to help myself. The dryer shifts under our weight and her eyes widen as she stares at me.

"We have to be quiet."

Rolling my lips between my teeth, I jerk my chin at her before I pull out. Her eyebrows pull together in protest, but I quickly sweep her off the dryer, lowering her feet onto the ground. She looks up at me as my hands find her hips. Without any protest, she spins of her own accord, leaning forward with her hands planted on the wall as I grab her ass cheeks.

My cock presses against her center and I slide back into her tight cunt, feeling how soaked she is around my length. She accidentally lets out a moan and glances at me from the corner of her eye as she turns her head.

"Bad girl," I murmur, removing one of my hands from her ass. I slide it up along her body before placing it over her mouth. "If I have to be good and keep quiet, so do you." I tilt my head to the side, fucking her slowly. "Are you going to be a good girl for me?"

She bobs her head with my hand still planted over her mouth.

"Okay," I breathe, my heart pounding erratically in my chest as warmth spreads across the pit of my stomach. "I'm still going to fuck you like you're a bad girl, though."

Hadley's eyes lock on me with her head turned to the side as I begin to move my hips again, pistoling them as I drive myself into her over and over again. She presses back against me and I fuck her harder. She begins to constrict around me, her pussy sucking my cock deep inside her before I'm falling over the edge with her, pumping my hips until she's filled with my cum.

I release her mouth and we're both breathless as I slowly slide out of her. Grabbing her hips, I spin her around to face me. My hand slides beneath her chin, gripping her face as my lips claim hers again. The movement is urgent and hard, but the way I kiss her is so fucking tender, it feels like my own heart is melting in my chest.

"Marry me," I breathe against her lips.

She stills against me. "What?"

"Marry me," I repeat, not giving a shit that this isn't the way I had originally planned to do it. I planned on proposing to her while we are in Brazil next month, but I'm tired of waiting. I've waited long enough. I run my finger over the ring she wears on her middle finger now. It's the ring that was her first engagement ring, but it wasn't real. "I want to replace this with a real one and for you to wear it on the proper finger."

She stares at me for a moment, her eyes wide. "You're serious."

"Yes, Hadley. I wanted to do it differently than this, but fuck it."

A slow smile pulls across her lips, her eyes filling with tears. "Yes, Rowan. Yes, I'll marry you." She lets out a soft laugh as she lifts her hands to cup the sides of my face. "I will say, you're slightly ridiculous." She smiles at me, shaking her head. "I don't even have pants on and your cum is currently running down my thighs."

"Just how I like you," I murmur, a smirk lifting my

lips before I capture her mouth once more. Our lips melt together, the strands of our souls intertwining, and I'm home.

There was a point in my life where Hadley Reed felt like an unattainable dream, like she was a mirage that would never be mine.

But now I have her.

And I swear I'll never let her go . . .

WANT MORE?

Scan the QR code below for a Rowan & Hadley bonus scene!

A LOOK INSIDE THE
NEXT BOOK

Flip the page for a look inside the next book in the Aston Archers series coming Summer 2025

PROLOGUE
CARSON

SIX YEARS AGO

A soft body collides into the back of mine and liquid splashes, soaking the material of the back of my t-shirt. It's cold against my skin and my spine straightens, my body tensing from the sensation. Music bumps from the speakers throughout the club, the strobe lights above flashing in tandem to the beat, yet somehow, over all the commotion, I can hear the sound of her velvety voice when she speaks.

"Oh, fuck." She lets out a breath, her tone flustered and annoyed. "I'm so sorry."

My movements are slow as I spin around to look at the stranger and I'm delighted in what I find. My 6'4" frame towers over hers and I have to tip my chin to look at her, even with her feet shoved into a pair of white heels. Her cheeks are tinted pink, her high cheekbones sparkling beneath the strobe lights overhead. Her long dark hair is pulled back in a sleek high ponytail, without a single hair out of place. Her long lashes flutter, revealing the most beautiful hues of gold and green shimmering in her irises.

The best part of all?

The annoyance written in her expression. The way her dainty nose is scrunched, her dark eyebrows tugging together. She looks like someone spilled their drink on *her*. The black dress she's wearing hugs her curves in all the right places, stopping just along the middles of her tanned thighs.

Amusement washes over me and I cock my head to the side as she stares up at me. "Did you spill your drink on me?"

"Yes. Some asshole bumped into me and knocked me into you." She closes her eyes, her nostrils spreading as her chest rises from the deep breath she sucks in. She takes a second, blows it out and looks back at me once more. "This place is packed tonight, there's barely any room to move." She shakes her head, like she's trying to shake away her irritation. "Can I buy you an apology drink or something?"

"There's no apology needed," I tell her, a smile lifting my lips. "But I'll buy you one instead."

Her red lips spread, revealing her bright white teeth as she ducks her head and lets out a soft laugh. " I appreciate the offer, but I don't really drink except for the occasional glass of wine." She lifts her glass, shrugging as a sheepish look dances across her expression. "This is just water."

"Aren't you refreshing?" I let out a low chuckle, resisting the urge to trail my fingers across her exposed collarbones. I didn't come here with the plan of taking someone home, but I'm not opposed to entertaining that idea with her. "What brings you out to a place like this if you aren't drinking?"

She pulls her bottom lip between her teeth, dragging the top ones of her flesh before releasing it. "I came here to dance and forget about my ex's engagement announcement." Her eyes scan my face. "What about you? Are you just here to drink?"

There's my confirmation that she's single.

"Maybe I came here to dance too."

Her face cracks and her laughter teases my eardrums. "I highly doubt that."

"Want to find out?"

She tips her head to the side, watching me with a decisive look in her gold and green orbs as she raises a manicured eyebrow. "You're rather brazen, aren't you?"

"I wouldn't say that," I tell her, my voice dropping lower as I inch closer to her. I enter her space, standing close enough that I can smell the floral notes of her perfume. Warmth radiates from her body, but I don't dare to touch her. Not without her consent. "Something caught my interest and I'm not in the habit of letting opportunities slip away."

Her plump lips part, demanding my attention as she lets out a ragged breath. "And what opportunity do you think presented itself?"

It's getting late and I might as well lay the bait now and see if she takes it. I'm not interested in anything other than a good time and considering the fact that she's a bit jaded, maybe she's looking for the same.

"One that offers a few hours of distraction without any promise of attachment." My tongue darts out to wet my lips as I drag my gaze back to hers. "The kind that will remind you that your ex isn't shit."

Her eyes slowly scan mine, slow and seductive as the corners of her mouth lift just a fraction of a centimeter. "You are absolutely brazen."

"Maybe," I chuckle, shaking my head at her. "Or maybe I just know what I want and find it easier to be straightforward about it."

She stares at me for a moment like she's contemplating what I said before she takes my drink from me and sets it on the high top table beside me. She sets hers down, moving closer. Her hand slides into mine, her fingers threading through the spaces between mine as she smiles at me. "Come dance with me and we'll see where the night goes."

"Lead the way."

I let her lead me back into the crowd of people, pulling me deeper into the center before she turns around to face me. Her eyes find mine as she begins to move her hips, swaying them back and forth as she finds harmony with the beat that pumps through the speakers. I stand back for a moment, watching her, completely mesmerized by the way she begins to weave her body to the music.

Her head tips back, her eyes falling shut as she lifts her arms above her head, winding and twisting to the melody. My eyes don't dare to leave her and as the crowd around us grows tighter, I immediately step closer in an effort to keep anyone else away.

She straightens her spine, her eyelids lifting as she finds my eyes with a dazed look in hers. It's absolutely intoxicating and my god, I want to drink from her. I want to be intoxicated too. She's drunk on endorphins and a smile dances across her lips as she reaches for me. Her hands find mine and she tugs on me, pulling me closer.

My feet move without instruction and I close the distance until my body is almost flush with hers. My hands abandon hers, reaching for her hips as I shift her closer. Her body moves, still shifting with the music and I start to move with her, letting myself get lost in her as our surroundings begin to fade away. The blood rushes to my cock and it throbs as it grows, pressing against the zipper of my pants.

Leaning forward, my cheek brushing against hers, my mouth dipping closer to her ear. "What's your name?" I murmur, my lips grazing the outer shell. Her body reacts, a shiver rippling through her as she inhales sharply and rolls her shoulders.

Shifting away from me, she lifts her arms, hooking her wrists around the back of my neck. Her hands slide along my nape, her fingertips plunging through my hair. "Andi," she breathes, her eyes hooded as she gazes up at me. "What's yours?"

"Carson."

She stares up at me for a few seconds before dropping her arms away from the back of my neck. My hands are still on her hips and as she shifts her weight, she spins around in front of me, my palms sliding over the silky material of her dress until I'm gripping her again. She shimmies back towards me, her ass pressing against my cock as she begins to grind against me.

My cock pulsates as she moves against my length, only making it harder. I can't help myself as I shift my hips forward, grinding myself into her in tandem with her movements. My heart pounds in my chest at the thought of getting her out of here and out of this dress.

Taking someone home is always like rolling the dice, but our chemistry is off the charts. We've barely even spoken, yet I'm drawn to her like a moth to a flame. Perhaps it's the mysteriousness to her or her being a stranger.

Fingers spread, I begin to move my palms around the fronts of her thighs, my fingertips drifting across her skin beneath the bottom hem of her dress. She presses back into me harder as I move my hands beneath the material, slowly dragging it up her thighs. We're in the middle of a room full of people, but it's too dark for anyone to see what's happening.

I could probably slide my cock into her right now and no one would even notice.

Andi's head falls back against my shoulder as my fingertips move to her inner thighs, just nearly brushing against her cunt. Heat radiates from her and a groan rumbles in my chest as she lets out the softest moan. Just as I skim along the outside of her panties, she abruptly spins in my arms, my hands now falling onto her ass.

She slides her hands around the back of my neck once more, pulling my face closer to hers. I stare down at her, watching her eyes as they bounce between my eyes and move to my lips before completing the same triangular pattern.

I can't control my gaze as it hones in on her perfect mouth. My tongue darts out to wet my lips and I wait for her move. She lifts herself onto her toes, her lips nearing closer to mine before I meet her in the middle, my mouth immediately capturing hers.

The tension swirls in the air around us, growing thicker by the moment. Her lips move against mine and when I slide my tongue along the seam of her mouth, she doesn't hesitate to let me in. Her lips part and my tongue finds hers, soft like velvet as she kisses me with an intensity that rocks me to my core. Goddamn, who the fuck is this woman?

Her fingers dig into my skin, her nails cutting into my flesh. Intentionally slowing down the kiss, I move my lips slowly, nipping, tasting, touching and teasing her with every sweeping movement of my tongue. She matches my energy, equally torturing me until it feels like I could potentially come apart at the seams.

Abruptly, I pull away from her, both of us breathless as my eyes search the depths of hers. She's giving me all the signs that point in the right direction, but I need to hear her words. I need her to give me that verification that she wants the same thing I want.

Neither of us are looking for anything more than a good time.

Andi moves closer to me, lifting back up onto her toes as she peppers kisses along the underside of my jaw. Her tongue is soft as it slides along the side of my neck, her teeth sinking into the lobe of my ear before her voice penetrates my eardrum. "I want you."

Goddamn, I love a woman who doesn't fuck around.

"Do you want to come back to my place?"

"No." She shakes her head, her cheek moving against mine. "I want to do something spontaneous that I've never done before." She pauses, her hands sliding along my biceps. "How do you feel about finding somewhere to fuck me here instead?"

Holy fucking shit.

"You want me to fuck you here, where everyone can see?" I murmur, my face dipping closer to her ear. "Does the thought of that excite you?"

"It does," she admits, her voice filled with lust as she presses her body against mine. "But I'd rather go somewhere a little private so people don't see us."

"Come with me," I tell her, my tongue tracing the outer shell of her ear before I pull away from her. "I'm sure there's somewhere we can go."

Andi follows behind me, her hand in mine as I pull her through the thick crowded room. We reach a break in the sea of bodies where it opens into a hallway. It's dark and the music is still loud, but it's a bit quiet. A little more private. I lead her deeper into the hall and farther away from the rest of the people. We pass the bathrooms and there are a few other doors. My hand finds the handles and I test each one until finally finding one that's unlocked.

It must have accidentally been left that way, because when we slip into the room, it looks like it's someone's office. I hit the light switch, letting it flicker on as Andi surveys the space. She spins around, her eyes finding mine. "I don't know if we should be in here."

"Maybe we should be in here then," I tell her, a smirk lifting my lips as I stalk closer. "We're somewhere private, but the risk of getting caught still exists."

Lust burns deeply in the green and gold hues of her eyes. "If that's the case, we're only wasting time with meaningless words."

"Tell me what you want, baby. You want me to bend you over that desk and fuck you?" My hands find her hips as I abruptly pull her flush against me. She inhales sharply, her nails digging into my shoulders. "Or perhaps you'd rather I sit in that chair and you climb on top of me and ride me."

She stares at me for a moment. "We're not going to exchange numbers or anything after this, right? I want to walk out of that door with not a single string attached."

A chuckle rumbles in my chest as I lift my hand to the base of her neck. "I don't do strings, darling." My face dips down to hers, my teeth nipping at her lips. "I think we're both here for the same thing."

"I've never had a one night stand before."

Her words catch me by surprise. I wouldn't have pegged her as this being her first time with how forward she's been with me. I pull away, just far enough to peer down into her eyes. "You've come to the right place then." My hand grips her neck, the other sliding along her collar bone before shoving the thing strap of her dress past her shoulder. "Let me show you how it's done."

My mouth finds hers once more, my hand plunging beneath the neckline of her silk dress as her tongue slides between my lips. Tongues tangling, she moans into my mouth and I swallow the sounds as my fingers drift over her nipples. Her soft flesh pebbles beneath my touch and I take my time, touching and teasing each of her breasts while my other hand grips her neck.

Her hands drop down to the waistband of my pants, sliding the button through the hole before she begins to pull down my zipper. Cool air grazes the bottom of my abdomen and her soft fingers shove down my boxer briefs, freeing my throbbing cock. She moans into my mouth again, the sound vibrating directly to my balls as she wraps her hand around my length, slowly pumping her fist around me.

If she keeps doing that, I'm going to fucking ruin this and come all over both of us.

Breaking away from her, my hand abandons her throat and I drop the both to her hips as I spin her around to face the opposite direction. My legs press against hers, the precum on the tip of my cock undoubtedly leaving a mark on the back of her dress as I urge her forward. We don't stop until we reach the desk.

Leaning forward, I sweep everything off the surface, not giving a fuck about what tumbles unto the ground. Andi lets out a soft breath, raising an eyebrow at me as she glances at me over her shoulder. Silently, I tear my gaze from her, my hands sliding beneath her dress before I find the waistband of her g-string. I hook my fingers under the material, lowering myself to the floor to remove them before standing back upright, setting her panties on the desk near us.

"Lift your dress and bend over the desk for me," I command, my hand pressing against the nape of her neck as I trail my lips over the tops of her shoulders. "Show me where you want me to fuck you."

Andi does as she's told, lifting her dress until it's bunched around her waist. She leans forward, pressing the front of her body against the desk as I step up behind her. My hand rubs her ass cheek, drifting across her crack before palming the other. Her body is taut and it's clear she works out and takes care of herself. I'm fucking obsessed.

Are you sure you want to do this?" I question her as I reach into my back pocket for my wallet. I keep an emergency condom in there in case a situation ever arises. I need to make sure this is what she wants before I proceed.

She doesn't hesitate and the word comes out breathlessly. "Yes."

My cock pulsates as the tip brushes against the center of her cunt. Warm and wet, ready and accepting. I flip open my wallet and begin to move the cards around, digging for the condom I could have sworn I put in there. I practically empty the entire fucking thing and come up empty handed.

"Fuck."

She lifts her chest, propping herself on her arms as she looks back at me. "What's wrong?"

My eyes fall shut and I let out a breath as I run a

frustrated hand through my hair. "I don't have a condom."

"That's okay," she says in a rush, her voice breathless. My eyelids flutter open, immediately meeting her gaze. "I have an IUD."

Oh thank fuck.

Although it pulled us from the moment, as soon as she presses her ass back against me again, we're both thrown back into the rush, into the lust. And fuck me, I need to be inside of her. Lifting my hand, I spit into my palm and lower it to my cock. Wrapping my fingers around my girth, I pump it a few times, getting myself wet before pressing against her again.

Andi lowers herself back onto the desk, her hands gripping the edges of it as she lifts herself up, granting me better access to her pussy as she pushes against me. The tip of my cock presses into her, pushing into her warmth. She inhales sharply, her head turning to the side as her eyes widen.

"Goddamn, you feel so fucking good," I groan, sinking deep into her with one fluid thrust of my hips. Andi moans, her eyes rolling back in her head as I fill her to the hilt, my balls pressing against her.

"Jesus Christ," she breathes, half moaning as she white knuckles the edge of the desk.

"You can take it, baby," I moan, my hands sliding over her body. I shift my hips and slowly begin to move, thrusting in and out of her. Andi's face is pressed against the desk, her eyelids fluttering shut as she lets out a soft cry. "You're doing so good, taking every inch of me."

She's soaked, her pussy gripping me as I slide in and out, stroking her insides. Her body lurches forward and my hands slide down to her hips, gripping her as the desk groans beneath the force of my thrusts. What starts out as slow and teasing, quickly becomes something rushed and driven by urgency. My fingertips dig into her flesh as I fuck her harder, earning moans and soft cries from her as I fill her to the brim with every hard thrust.

Abandoning her right hip, I drag my fingertips along her spine, making my way up to the back of her neck as I continue to pound into her. Her cunt stretches around me, sucking my cock in every time I press back into her. My hand grips the back of her neck, holding her down against the desk as I move my left hand around the front of her body, pushing my fingers between her legs.

"Open wider for me, baby. I want to play with your pussy while I fuck you."

Andi's knuckles are white and she does as she's told, parting her legs as she remains bent over the side of the desk. My fingers brush against her clit and she immediately tenses, her cunt clenching around my length. My movements become a bit slower as I pump my hips while finding a rhythm with my fingertips rubbing her clit.

"Don't stop, Carson," Andi moans, her ass pressing harder into me as she takes every thrust. "I'm so close."

Fuck, she's hot.

Applying more pressure, I roll my fingers, circling her clit as I feel her getting even closer. "That's it," I moan, my head tipping back as my face screws up. My eyelids slam shut, the muscles in my shoulders tightening as the warmth in my stomach begins to overflow. "Come for me."

I groan, my hand gripping the back of her neck tighter as I pound into her harder. She cries out, the walls of her cunt pulsating around my cock as she loses herself around me. Her orgasm sends shockwaves through her body, her pussy gripping me so fucking tight, it sends me over the edge. My cock fills her completely as I start to come, pumping her full as I slowly thrust in and out.

She's a mess of breathless moans by the time we're both done. I slide my hand away from the front of her body, withdrawing as I slowly pull out of her. My hands find her hips and I pull her away from the desk, helping her to stand upright as she gets her bearings straight.

Her chest rises and falls in rapid succession, shallow breaths escape her as she stares back at me. Her hair is disheveled, her cheeks tinted pink, eyes glazed over and lips swollen. Reaching down, she pulls her dress back down her thighs, covering herself.

"That was the best distraction I've ever had."

Bending down, I grab a box of tissues I knocked off the desk and hand them to her as she cleans herself. "You know, I could give you my number and be of service any time you want."

What the fuck am I saying?

Her eyes slide to mine as she pushes away from the desk. She clicks her tongue as she walks past me, stopping by the trashcan by the door as she disposes of the tissues. I wipe off my dick and shove it back into my pants as I get myself straightened.

Turning back to look at me, she shakes her head, amusement lighting up her expression. "That wasn't what we agreed to," she says with a wink and a lazy grin. "But if we ever happen to run into each other again, I'm sure I can use another distraction."

"Consider it a deal."

"Thanks, Carson. You made my first one night stand an enjoyable experience," she says, smiling at me once more as she reaches for the door handle. She gives me one last lingering stare before pulling the door open. "Enjoy the rest of your night."

I watch her as she disappears through the doorway, leaving me alone in the office without another word. I'd enjoy the rest of my night a little more if I got to spend it still buried inside of her, but goddamn, I cannot complain one bit about what just happened. I know virtually nothing about her, except that she takes my cock like no one else does.

What a shame this was limited to a one night thing. We could have had a lot of fun.

Leaning back, my hands land on the desk and I feel the soft material beneath my palm. Wrapping my fingers around it, a smile dances across my lips as I lift it into the air and realize what I'm holding.

Her underwear.

A soft chuckle escapes me as I tuck them into the front pocket of my pants. At some point tonight, she's going to notice they're missing and they'll be long gone by then.

I exit through the same door and I push my way through the club until I finally make my way to the front of the building. The front door is guarded by bouncers and they nod as I slip outside, walking to the curb as I pull out my phone to get an Uber. I secure a car and lift my gaze from my phone just as another vehicle pulls up a few feet away.

My heart pounds in my chest as I see Andi striding towards it. She pulls it open, moving around to the car to lower herself in when her gaze meets mine. Eyes locked, her lips lift and we share a moment, the particles crackling between us through the cool night air.

I could walk over and try to get in the car with her, but I don't. Tipping my chin, I nod at her once more, bidding her goodbye with her thong tucked away in the front pocket of my pants. Andi's gaze lingers once more before she lifts her hand to give me a small wave.

I watch her get into the car, the door closing behind her and there's a pause before the vehicle begins to pull away from the curb, easing onto the street. She was only looking for a distraction and I was more than happy to give her exactly what she wanted. I've never been one to look for anything more than a hookup.

She was just a passing moment in time, but I know she's not one I'm likely to forget.

ABOUT THE AUTHOR

Cali Melle is a USA Today Bestselling Author who writes sports romance that will pull at your heartstrings. You can always expect her stories to come fully equipped with heartthrobs and a happy ending, along with some steamy scenes.
In her free time, Cali can usually be found living in a magical, fantasy world with the newest book or fanfic she's reading or freezing at the ice rink while she watches her kids play hockey.

ALSO BY CALI MELLE

ASTON ARCHERS SERIES

Make Your Move

Make Your Play

Make Your Save

ORCHID CITY SERIES

Meet Me in the Penalty Box

The Tides Between Us

Written In Ice

Dirty Pucking Play

The Lie of Us

WYNCOTE WOLVES SERIES

Cross Checked Hearts

Deflected Hearts

Playing Offsides

The Faceoff

The Goalie Who Stole Christmas

Splintered Ice

Coast to Coast

Off-Ice Collision

STANDALONES

The Christmas Exchange

The Christmas Rebound

Tell Me How You Hate Me

The Art of Breathing